T0380296

TOWARD
Light

ROSE WILSON

WESTBOW
PRESS®
A DIVISION OF THOMAS NELSON
& ZONDERVAN

Copyright © 2024 Rose Wilson.

All rights reserved. No part of this book may be used or reproduced by
any means, graphic, electronic, or mechanical, including photocopying,
recording, taping or by any information storage retrieval system
without the written permission of the author except in the case of
brief quotations embodied in critical articles and reviews.

This is a work of fiction. All of the characters, names, incidents,
organizations, and dialogue in this novel are either the products
of the author's imagination or are used fictitiously.

WestBow Press books may be ordered through booksellers or by contacting:

WestBow Press
A Division of Thomas Nelson & Zondervan
1663 Liberty Drive
Bloomington, IN 47403
www.westbowpress.com
844-714-3454

Because of the dynamic nature of the Internet, any web addresses or
links contained in this book may have changed since publication and
may no longer be valid. The views expressed in this work are solely those
of the author and do not necessarily reflect the views of the publisher,
and the publisher hereby disclaims any responsibility for them.

Any people depicted in stock imagery provided by Getty Images are
models, and such images are being used for illustrative purposes only.
Certain stock imagery © Getty Images.

All Scripture quotations are taken from the Holy Bible, NEW
INTERNATIONAL VERSION®, NIV® Copyright © 1973, 1978, 1984,
2011 by Biblica, Inc.® Used by permission. All rights reserved worldwide.

ISBN: 979-8-3850-2269-4 (sc)
ISBN: 979-8-3850-2270-0 (e)

Library of Congress Control Number: 2024907159

Print information available on the last page.

WestBow Press rev. date: 04/09/2024

This book is dedicated to KFB and her mother, SSF. I wouldn't know how to write about a friendship or even a best friend if God hadn't put us together more than thirty-five years ago. As we launch into our fifth decade of life, full of aging parents and adulting children, I am so very grateful to be doing it with you. Your mom was so good to me as a teenager, and I will always have living, colorful memories of her generosity and kindness.

Prologue

I HAD WOKEN UP AT 4:00 a.m., and I was unable to get back to sleep. I walked into my quiet kitchen, which was still a mess from the late afternoon New Year's party the day before. I grabbed my Bible, journal, and pile of books and sat on the couch while my coffee was brewing. I began to write, reflecting on the period of mourning that I had been living in. I looked down at all those books that were trying to help me navigate the loss and the new life I was leading.

I sighed. *When does it end?* I would begin to think I was stepping out of it, and then a letter or bill sent me right back into grief. *Is there an end? Or does one never stop mourning the person who used to be such a big piece of one's life?* I finally concluded that you stop consciously thinking about it, but it was always there. The more days we had lived without Tommy, the easier it became and truthfully, the closer we were to seeing him again. Each day lived was one day closer to heaven. I found solace in that. But still, there I was trying to navigate the daily potholes of raising kids and being a widow at forty.

I wanted the new year to be more about life and light than about grief and darkness—more clarity than fog. *Lord,* I prayed, *just keep moving me toward the light. Continue to walk me out of this tunnel of sadness and into your light of laughter and love.*

I reminded myself of 1 Peter 2:9, which says, "But you are a chosen people, a royal priesthood, a holy nation, God's special possession, that you may declare the praises of him who called you out of darkness into his wonderful light."

Chapter 1

M Y STOMACH WAS DOING FLIP-FLOPS. I tried to walk around the room backstage, but my legs felt unsteady. So I sat down on an amplifier that had been left out. *Breathe, Ellie. In and out. Just breathe*, I told myself.

I went to twist my wedding band—an old nervous habit—but it wasn't there. Even after I put it on my right hand, it startled me to not have it where it had been for twenty years. I slid it back onto my left hand. Immediately, the conflicting emotions of betrayal and a desire to move forward clouded my thoughts. I slid it back on my right hand.

"Fifteen minutes, Ellie." Adam, the worship pastor, stuck his head in the door. A look of concern filled his face. "You OK?"

I took a breath and smiled my big smile. "Yes. Just some jitters. I will be fine."

"You sounded great at practice. I am not worried." Adam smiled and shut the door.

I can't believe it has been over a year. It's been a year and a half since Tommy died. Each month since then, I have been amazed at how life moves on. I have even yelled at the sun to stop setting and rising. People and the world have moved on, whether any of us are ready or not.

The last time I sang was at Tommy's celebration of life service. Luke, my oldest son, sang with me. I smiled. Luke had been such a gift to me. In their own ways, all my kids had kept me going that past year. Tea, at eleven, was my super-social, nonstop talker, who did all the things. She kept my hands and mind busy. Whit, at fourteen, who had such a kind heart, helped me so much around the house, probably more than was healthy for a young teenager. He developed a knack for fixing things, cleaning up the kitchen, and taking out the trash. He was Tommy's shadow for so many years. Finally, sweet Brooke was my calm and quiet presence. She would just sit next to me and hold my hand. I would miss her terribly when she was away at college.

Luke wanted to sing with me at Tommy's service. I wasn't so sure I could do it, but Luke persisted. Since he was little, he had always been pushing boundaries and insisting he could do everything well—and he had. He was twenty-one and about to graduate college. He had a teaching and coaching job lined up for the fall, which was only forty minutes away from our house, thank God.

At the service, Luke and I stood up onstage together—it was more like he held me up—while we sang "Rise" by Shawn McDonald.[1] The line, "I will rise, out of the ashes, rise, from this trouble I have found and this rubble on the ground, I will rise," almost did me in. However, the words from the song were prophetic because we did rise. All five of us rose out of the ashes. We were making it.

I remembered each word I spoke at Tommy's service. I had agonized over them the night before. I had prayed for the words to say that would honor Tommy and bring hope to everyone in the room. It was mid-August, and it was Texas hot—oppressive. The air-conditioning units at our church were running full out. I looked over the first few rows and saw all my people: my best friend since sixth grade, Katie, and her family, Katie's parents, my dad and kids, and Tommy's best friends from high school and college.

I had taken a deep breath and begun. "Tommy and I used to joke that whoever makes it to heaven first wins. He won. I am not angry he won. I am jealous. He gets to be whole, complete, and perfect before the rest of us. I am jealous he gets to live in the middle of a worship song right now while we are still here, trying to figure out how to get through the next minute, the next hour, and the next day.

"One of my favorite authors, Nancy Guthrie, said in one of her books, 'Yearning for Heaven is one of the purposes and one of the privileges of suffering and of losing someone you love.'[2]

"I know that the brokenness and loneliness and sorrow that rules here on Earth is only for a brief time. I have hope. We have hope. By the unending grace of God, we have hope. Hope that each day, God will sustain us, as He always has. Hope that our suffering will be used to glorify God."

Then my four children joined me on stage, and we led the service in singing "Great Are You Lord."[3] The kids wanted to do something together. Whit played the keyboard. Luke, Brooke, Tea, and I sang. As we sang, my close friends came up on stage to sing with us. It was truly one of the most agonizing and gorgeous moments of my life.

That had been the last time I sang. And now, after several tentative asks by Adam, I had finally agreed to sing with the worship team again for both services. Luke had come in for the weekend to be supportive. He was more excited than I was.

Lord, move in this house of worship today, I prayed. *Please calm my heart, mind, and soul. Let me not think of who is watching me. Don't let me be self-conscious. Lord, may your Spirit fill me right now to where all I can do is lift my hands and worship You.*

I swallowed. I remembered to breathe. I walked onto the stage. I was shaking on the inside. That moment felt more significant than maybe it should have. It felt like I was walking into a new life. It was time to move forward while preserving a place for Tommy in our hearts and conversations. I was stepping into my future, and God was reassuring me that it was good. He still had good things for me in this life. I felt His presence and voice saying that it was time to turn the mourning into dancing.

Chapter 2

THE FIRST FEW BEATS OF "House of the Lord"[4] by Phil Wickham played, and everyone was clapping. The stage lights were bright, and I could hardly see out into the sanctuary of a thousand people. All my nerves settled, and I smiled. I held my microphone up and joined the worship team in singing about joy. It felt so good to be back. I couldn't stop smiling.

Adam said a few words of welcome. I sang backup in the next song. Then I was up. I walked to the front of the stage and kept my eyes up toward the balcony. I placed the microphone in its stand. I was shaking too much to hold it. My heart was beating fast. I breathed. I started the first verse without music and just my voice.

"I feel it in my bones, you're about to move. I feel it in the wind, you're about to ride in. You said that you would pour your spirit out. You said that you would fall on sons and daughters, so come." Then, the music to "Spirit Move"[5] started. I felt the power of the song running throughout the church. I picked up the microphone and repeated the first verse. Then I closed my eyes and lifted my free hand.

When I had gotten to the part Tea called the "yell singing," I put the microphone up, took a big breath, and stood center stage with both arms up, eyes up, and all my power behind my voice. Once I got through that, the rest was easy. I could squint out into the congregation and see my four kids in the front row, singing their hearts out with me. The song ended. I couldn't stop looking at my kids, and that's when tears started to flow. They were such amazing humans and beautiful gifts from God. Luke was a perfect mixture of me and Tommy: tall, big shoulders, my eyes, Tommy's nose, my smile, and Tommy's darker hair. Brooke had my face shape but blue eyes like Tommy's and thick blond hair. She was built long and tall, which was so much like Tommy's mom. Whit had his red hair and blue eyes, but he was built more like me—slender and athletic. Little Tea was all Tommy: dark thick hair, blue eyes, and even his gregarious personality.

And we did it. We had made it through the most devastating loss of their young lives. We were going to be OK—not perfect or without difficult days but OK.

Chapter 3

I WALKED OFFSTAGE TOWARD THE DOORS that led to the ladies' room, but on the way, Katie grabbed me and hugged me hard. She had known how difficult it was for me to get back onstage and sing. I pulled back and saw her big light-blue eyes filled with tears. Her auburn hair, straight and long past her shoulders, was such a contrast to my wild, dirty-blond curls. Those shoulders were where I had cried the past year and a half. My Katie was so sturdy and strong.

"I am so proud of you. I know it wasn't easy," Katie told me.

Her three girls wrapped their arms around me. "I love it when you sing, Auntie Ellie," Landry, her youngest, said.

I gave her an extra squeeze and walked toward the doors. Different people were stopping, hugging, and telling me how good it was to see me singing again. My heart felt light.

My church was imperfect and full of messy people, but these people had seen me through a rough eighteen months and had picked up the pieces of my life right beside me. It made me so very sad to think of people who didn't have a church family to walk with them in dark days and joyful moments.

I finally made it to the bathroom. I was alone. I looked in the mirror. My curls were somewhat tame and tied back in a low ponytail. My hair had darkened in the winter, especially underneath. As soon as I spent a minute outside, the summer sun always gave me natural highlights. I had spent so much time on my kids' well-being.

I had definitely neglected my own self-care. At this length, my hair looked more like a jumble of tangles than the ringlets I had when it was shorter. My mascara and eyeliner were still intact around my green eyes. I had so many freckles—ugh. Katie said they made me look at least ten years younger, so I should be grateful. The hundred or so that ran across my slightly turned up nose were less noticeable in winter. Small crow's feet had begun to settle in around my eyes since I had turned forty-one last year.

I was thin for my five-feet-five-inch frame. I was more than five feet seven inches that day with my black-heeled boots on. But who could blame me for not feeling like eating the past year? My skin was in good shape thanks to Katie, my best friend and dermatologist. I was flushed from the singing. Overall, I looked better than I had in a while. The dark circles under my eyes were slowly fading. I reapplied my ever-handy lip gloss and made sure my hoop earrings were still on. I smoothed out my light-gold-colored sweater and black pants. Then I walked out into the church foyer.

Chapter 4

As I walked out of the ladies' room, my good friend and neighbor Shay walked up to me. "Ellie," she called as she hugged me, "that was absolutely beautiful! God has gifted you with such an amazing voice. I am so happy to see you using it!" Shay's son and Luke had been friends since fourth grade. She had been through some tough years with her husband, yet she was always pure joy to be around.

As we talked, my eyes caught a familiar face on someone standing a few feet away. For a minute, I couldn't register who it was. He was looking right at me. It clicked. *Holy moly. It's Bo Channing. Unbelievable.* I had inadvertently sucked in my breath with surprise. I wasn't sure my legs were going to hold me up. Shay must have seen my expression and turned around.

Bo started walking toward us. He was smiling warmly at me. My entire being started to react to his presence. I wanted to run away and run toward him all at the same time. Like a good southern girl, a smile came to my face as he got closer. My heart beat incredibly fast. I knew my cheeks were getting rosy. Luckily, Shay got to him first, shook his hand, and started talking. I was trying to not overthink how to greet him. *How do I say hello to someone I haven't spoken to or seen in three years?*

I found myself in a side hug with him. It felt safe but a little awkward. We separated and looked at each other. I was trying to remind myself to be calm. Inside, I was full of questions. *Why is he here at my church? How has he been doing the last three years? Does he ever think about me?*

It felt like his brown eyes were looking straight through me. "It looks like I came on the perfect Sunday to hear you sing," he said with that East Texas drawl that was more charming than it should be. We were smiling at each other, and I didn't know how to respond. I shrugged a little, unsure of what to say or how to say it. "It felt really good to get back onstage."

"Your voice is amazing. It is mind-blowing that such a small person can have such a big voice." He smiled at me.

"Well," I said playfully, "if you stick around, you can hear it again at the 11:00 a.m. service." That was a silly thing to say. I was not good at playing it cool. I never had been.

"I might do that!" he said.

I looked at Shay, and she was looking a little confused at our banter. I felt more confused than she looked. Shay knew Bo because he had renovated an old downtown icehouse into a beautiful law office for her husband—the same law office where her husband had an affair with his secretary. It made me nauseous for Shay just thinking about it. But I was in no position to judge her husband or the secretary.

Having Bo in my life had started so innocently. I was outside in my front yard playing with my kids and our new puppy. And Bo was across the street, helping my neighbors—his great aunt and uncle—redo their kitchen and bathrooms. My mind was reeling from seeing and talking to him and remembering how he left. I just stared at him without being able to think of anything to say.

Just then Tea ran up to me. "Mom, come sit with us. Oh, hi, Ms. Shay.

"Hi sweetheart," I said. "I was on my way. Do you remember Bo? He used to work on our street. You were eight years old, so you may not."

Tea looked at Bo and smiled. "Hi, Bo. I do remember you. Didn't you move to Florida?"

Bo laughed and commented on her excellent memory. "Thank you for making an old guy feel memorable."

Old? Ha. I'm older than him by a few years if I remember correctly. I didn't see a wedding band, so I guessed he was still single. I never could understand why. He was five feet ten inches and definitely worked out. I was pretty certain that he was a self-made millionaire and super smart. He loved God. He had kind brown eyes, short blond hair, and a tan. I needed to stop taking inventory.

Tea grabbed my hand and smiled at me. "Come on, Mom. Bye, Ms. Shay and Mr. Bo."

My head was swimming, and my heart still wanted to be standing next to him. I looked back as Tea dragged me away. I caught his eye, and he smiled.

As I sat in between Luke and Tea, I could barely pay attention to the sermon. I had gotten out my journal where I write down notes for the sermon and just stared at it. My stomach was in knots. *What in the world just happened?*

Chapter 5

I STARTED THINKING ABOUT THE LAST day I saw Bo. It was three years ago. I was downtown at the library returning books. The city hall was located next door. As I walked out of the library, I looked up, and there was Bo, sitting on a bench by the doors with his head in his hands.

"Bo!" I said happily. I was always happy to see him. He always made my heart smile.

When he looked up, he didn't look well. *Maybe he's sad?* I couldn't exactly tell. "Are you OK? Is everything OK?" I asked and sat next to him, placing my pile of books on the bench between us.

His demeanor was forcibly changed as he smiled and said in a jovial way, "Hey, I was hoping I would catch you coming out. I saw you go in from city hall. I was submitting final plans for a project." He probably said this to make sure I knew he wasn't stalking me. And of course, he wasn't. We lived in a smallish town where you saw people you knew constantly. It used to be smaller until the city to the north of us grew bigger. Our town became a country suburb to those who wanted land and crowded two-lane roads.

"It's good to see you." I smiled at him. Hunting season had started, and he was out of town often. I had been on my way home from work, so I was dressed in navy-blue slacks and a white button-down shirt, and I had a sweater over my arm. Texas fall weather was cool in the mornings but warm in the afternoons. My hair was up in a bun; bobby pins held my curls in place. The clarity of that memory shocked me. I had purposely not thought about it for a long time.

Bo had leaned in and looked at me with his brown eyes. He had always been able to make me feel that I was the only human on the planet. He said, "El, I wanted to let you know that I have decided to sell my business and move to Florida to start a deep-sea-fishing excursion business with an old friend of mine. You know that fishing and boats are my first love, and I am not getting any younger. I want to try something new. I leave in a few weeks. I am handing off all my projects to other construction managers."

I remembered smiling and telling him how amazing it sounded and how excited I was for him on this new adventure. Yet it felt like a gut punch—one that I knew was coming.

We needed to not see each other. Small-town life had a way of keeping us connected. We knew the same people, shopped at the same stores, and ate at the same restaurants. He needed to move away. He needed to move away because of me.

The lines had become blurred at some point. There was an underlying attraction like electricity between us. Though we had never said a word, I was certain we both felt it. His leaving confirmed it, which made it so much harder. In every interaction we had had in the last few years, I had felt that he saw me—really saw me. He saw me in a way that after eighteen years of marriage, Tommy just didn't see me anymore.

We stood up together, and I gathered my books and sweater. He walked me to my car and watched me throw the books and my bag into the front passenger side of the car. I turned around, and we looked at each other for a few seconds without saying anything. I reached out and gave him a quick hug.

"Goodbye, Bo. Please keep Facebook updated with how you and the business are doing."

He smiled and said that he would. And that was it.

Chapter 6

TOMMY AND I HAD MET in college. I was a young nineteen-year-old and an only child. I had been raised by my dad on a ranch in the middle of West Texas. Tommy was older and about to graduate. He was tall, dark, and handsome. He was stable, was goal-oriented, and loved Jesus. I thought he was the answer to my loneliness—the loneliness that had been with me as I grew up without a mother.

My mother had died of breast cancer when I was five. My dad raised me on a thousand-acre working ranch. I spent a lot of time playing by myself. It was me and all the farm animals, barn cats, hunting dogs, baby chicks, sheep, goats, horses, and donkeys. I sat in my tree house for hours on the weekends, just reading or pretending I was on a deserted island, abandoned pirate ship, or lone log cabin in woods that no one traveled.

Tommy was an only child like me, which was why we initially decided to have lots of kids. But over time, I kept having kids because they soothed and distracted that nagging loneliness for a while. Tommy lived for big groups and loud gatherings. I was the quieter of the two of us. Sometimes his extroverted lifestyle was too much, and I would go hide somewhere. I had always been one of those people that can feel lonely even in a crowd.

I got pregnant at nineteen, we got married, and I had Luke at twenty. Tommy was amazing. He supported me as I went through school and got my PhD in sociology. I worked my way into tenure at a local university. I had a full and busy life, but it was still marked with that alone feeling at times.

I remember asking Luke a few years earlier after he had left for college, how he would describe his dad's and my relationship. I wanted an outsider's view, maybe to confirm what I had concluded. He said that Tommy and I seemed unconnected sometimes. Tommy would do his thing and had his own relationships with each kid, and that I would do my own thing.

And Luke was right. I would try to sit down next to Tommy and tell him something, and he didn't really hear me. I would say something funny, and he wouldn't react. It was like he either didn't think it was funny or wasn't paying attention to me. It hurt. And it fed into the loneliness dialogue I constantly had with myself. *I am not worth knowing. The deeper parts of me are not worth knowing or at least trying to know. My sense of humor is maybe tasteless. I have nothing to offer.* We had good moments. And when Tommy needed me physically, I made myself available, just because I needed to be needed by him. And I would take those crumbs.

Tommy wasn't bad or wrong. He was moving up in his career, and he had a family he was responsible for. He enjoyed his career, and it fulfilled him. He didn't need much from me. He was a very successful businessman. He assumed I was happy and fulfilled as well, and I should have been. I found it ironic that I had married someone who made me feel just as lonely as my childhood had been.

And into my life walked Bo. We talked about everything. He was smart and not afraid to discuss God, church, and life with me. And most importantly at that time, he seemed to genuinely like me.

The odd thing is that I wasn't unhappy with my life. I felt the blessings of God all over my life. I had a husband who was good to me, worked hard, and was a great father to his children. He prayed with and for us. He made sure we made it to church every Sunday. I just didn't realize the extent of my own loneliness until Bo.

Luke elbowed me. It was time for the closing song. As I walked up to the stage, my eyes searched for Bo in the sanctuary. He was leaning against the back wall and staring at me intently. The music started, and we just looked at each other. I had to force myself to look away. He was staring at me in a way that confirmed every past moment we had experienced three years earlier. It was real. We had something. And now he was back.

Chapter 7

I WALKED OUT OF CHURCH COMPLETELY spent, emotionally, spiritually, and physically. My kids left after the first service and went to eat somewhere. I was glad to be alone and to think about how I was feeling after seeing Bo. The past reasons to not think about him or not cross any lines didn't exist anymore.

I had seen Bo talking to people and going in and out of the sanctuary. But I had not spoken to him again; I was purposely avoiding him. I just wanted to go home and escape, preferably for a nap.

I was almost to my car when I heard, "El!"

I turned, even though I already knew who it was. He was the only person who called me El. Even though I was tired, I couldn't help but smile when I saw him. But I was annoyed. *Why does he have to show up after so long and make me think about things I have pushed down years ago?*

He jogged up to me, all handsome and fit. "I am glad I caught you. I am sure you are hungry and tired after a long morning of singing. Can I take you to lunch so we can catch up?" He must have seen my hesitation. With a giant grin, he added, "I am only in town for a few days." He had a beautiful mouth with perfect lips.

I had my hands full, and I was digging around in my purse for my keys. It was a good way to not look at him. I put my bag in my car and turned around to answer. I should have just said, "No," but

I literally could not get the word out. Plus, I really did want to know what he was up to, besides confusing me.

After a moment of hesitation I said, "OK, sure. I can meet you at La Casita." Curiosity had gotten the better of me.

We both wanted to sit outside. It was such a gorgeous day, and the sun felt warm. We sat at a rickety table with plastic chairs and a faded umbrella. We both had sunglasses on, which allowed me to look at him without being obvious. We sat quietly as we looked at the menu. A few people came by and said, "Hi." Between the two of us, we knew half the town.

After we ordered, he leaned forward in his chair, looking at me. "El, I am so very sorry about Tommy."

Tears welled up in my eyes. Shoot, I was glad I had my sunglasses on. I managed to get out, "Thank you," which had always felt like a strange response to that sentiment. But I could never settle on anything else.

"How are you and the kids doing?"

"We are doing better each day." I paused. *How much do I share? How much do I let him in?* I just looked at him for a moment while trying to read him. I always had appreciated how he would allow a silent moment to pass.

"Honestly, it has been hardest on them. They have been completely devastated. I spent twenty years with Tommy, and I know he is heaven worshipping his heart out. Sweet Tea only got nine years. Anyway, thank you for asking." I started getting choked up again.

Bo tried to change the subject. "You have an incredible voice. Have you ever pursued anything more than church singing?"

"No but thank you. That ship sailed a long time ago. I sing because ever since I can remember, God has spoken to me through song. He draws me close to Himself and reveals Himself to me through singing. From what I can remember and have been told, my mother sang to me all the time. So singing is part of her legacy to me, and I think of her often when I sing." I have no idea why I just shared all of that. It was probably too much. Bo had always done that to me—made me share more than I ever intended. I asked him a question. "Where do you feel closest to God and like you can hear him clearly?"

Bo nodded. "Easy. Out in nature, all by myself, and with no one around, especially at night when I look at the stars. In fact, every year around February, I go for about five days to a remote cabin and just focus on God. It has always been life changing and path altering. I leave in a few weeks, and I can't wait."

I imagined Bo alone at night looking at the stars. I smiled. "Sounds incredible."

We ordered, and after the server left, I looked at Bo's tanned face, strong shoulders, soft brown eyes, and cheek bones. *Incredible*, I thought. After three years, he can walk back into my life and do what he has always done—make me feel comfortable in my own skin. I started talking again. "Today was the first time I sang in public since Tommy's service. It was harder than I imagined it would be to get back up onstage and sing of God's goodness while my children sat front and center, reminding me of the heartache of the last year and a half."

Bo had listened intently to me. There was a distinct ache inside me at that moment. I missed having someone listen to me. My life was full of me listening to my kids and being their soft place to land. I had amazing women friends, yet they were all busy with their spouses and kids. I had no one to really share my life with.

I changed the subject. "Tell me all about you, your business, and Florida." I knew a little bit about his Florida life. After he left three years ago, I did some Facebook stalking but quickly realized it was not healthy for me to be investing myself and my emotions in his life. I needed to be fully invested in my own life.

He proceeded to entertain me with stories and wild tales. He had always been able to make me laugh, and it felt good to laugh with him. He showed me pictures on his phone. He had a house on the water. The one next door was a rental for his excursion business. He had gutted and had renovated both.

"Bo," I said, "what a beautiful place to live and wake up to each morning. Texas probably can't compare."

"Texas is a different kind of beauty, which I couldn't find anywhere else even if I tried," he replied while looking straight into my soul.

I don't even know how I was sure that he wasn't talking about trees and shrubs; I just was. I sighed. And I was so mad at myself for noticing how good looking and in shape he was. We always have had that in common. We used to talk about what workouts and food plans we were following, so I asked him, "What is your workout and food regimen these days?"

By the time our food came, we had discussed the pros and cons of fasting and the best workouts. He didn't run but did a lot of weight training. I did the opposite—more running and less weight training. But as my body felt it's age, I was doing more weights and yoga.

He asked me about my work, if I had published anything recently, and how I liked the department. "My favorite thing to do is teach. I would rather do that than get sucked into a research project. I usually make my TAs do that, and I teach the classes."

Then he nodded toward my wedding band. "Tell me about your wedding band being on your left hand."

Shoot. I looked down. *Yep, it is on my left hand.* I switched it back and forth so often that I didn't even remember doing it. I moved it back to my right hand.

"Well, I am not sure I have a good answer or one that will make sense. I feel as though I am still trying to figure it out."

Bo nodded and leaned back. "Tell me more."

I continued to twist it around on my right hand. "I think that I am ready to move it to my right hand, but the moment I do, it feels like betrayal. Like I am betraying Tommy somehow. I know it doesn't make much sense."

I continued, "And a year after Tommy's death, everyone felt like he had the green light to court me or something. Men were asking me out, and it felt strange; I wasn't ready. So instead of saying, 'No,' and being in awkward conversations, I kept my ring on my left hand sometimes."

He then casually asked, "What do you think needs to happen for it to not feel like betrayal?" He said this nonchalantly and as if we were talking about the weather.

I smiled shakily. I paused for a minute. I took a breath. I knew that I didn't have to answer. I could say it was none of his business. But something inside me wanted to answer that question or at least to try to.

"I don't know how or when it won't feel strange to be involved with or to date someone. I do know that there are some moments when I think I might be ready to move forward—moments of loneliness. However, being a single parent to all my kids takes up so much of my mental, spiritual, and emotional energy. Not only do I think it would be unfair to someone to get the limited leftovers but also that my kids aren't ready yet. And maybe I am more worried they will think I am betraying Tommy." I paused. "I think it would take the perfect person for my situation. I take it back; not perfect but just someone who fits seamlessly into a complicated situation."

Bo commented, "Being a single parent does sound really exhausting."

"And," I continued, "I am not, nor have I ever been, big into dating. It feels like a lot of pretending. Like let's pretend to have it all together at specific dates and times. Then based on those manufactured moments, we decide to spend more time together when I find out the person is not someone I want to hang out with. Then I tell them that, and then I am the problem."

He laughed, and I joined in. "Well," started Bo, "as you can see, I am not very good at dating, nor do I do it often. Years ago, I did date just for fun, and it never ended well. Now, older and wiser, if

I ask someone out to dinner, it is to intentionally know that person better."

"*Intentionality* is a good word. But right now, dating sounds like one more thing to add to my already very full plate." I was intentionally giving him a warning sign.

He stopped and smiled at me. "What about the guy who ignored your ring trick and asked you out to lunch anyway?"

"Well, that guy said he wouldn't be around long, so I figured it was a safe lunch date. No commitment. No hurt feelings." Clouds had started to gather, so I pushed my sunglasses onto my head.

We were silent for a minute. Bo was looking at me, and I was looking at him. He was contemplating his next move. Everything got very quiet.

Bo said, "El ... I don't know how you do it, managing everyone, taking care of everything, taking care of yourself too."

Why does he make me feel like bursting into tears and laying my head on his shoulder?

As he was trying to lighten the conversation by throwing silly ideas at me regarding how to turn guys who ask me out down, I was really looking at him. He was here, back in Texas and in my town. I started to feel frustrated with him. He left, he came back, and he was leaving again. Any fantasy I had that I was in control of my emotions and thoughts, he completely obliterated.

I shouldn't have been frustrated. He had left because he was a free, single man who could. I had been married to a good man, and we had four kids. His only option for our mutual sanity was to leave us as friends. It was the right thing to do. *He did the right thing*, I kept telling myself. *And I respect him for it. And for some insane reason, I am angry. All these feelings that I worked hard to put in a box and lock up are back. I thought they were gone, but one smile from him, and I am in trouble. Am I really that weak? How do I get them back in the box again when he leaves?* It all suddenly felt unfair.

My phone started ringing. It was Katie. And my kids had been texting me nonstop. We were done with lunch. I stood up.

"I have to go. My phone is blowing up. My people aren't used to me disappearing at lunchtime with a man they haven't seen for three years." I tried to laugh it off, but that had come out way more accusatory than I had meant. "I'm sorry. I did not mean it the way it came out. You just ... you surprised me today."

"El," he stood up and touched my arm, "I am sorry if I was out of line in our conversation. I didn't mean to upset you." His brown eyes looked penitent.

I could not think of anything to say. Maybe if he had stopped touching my arm, my mind would have worked. But he wasn't moving, and the electricity that moved between us stunned me. We looked at each other for a long moment. He affected me like no other man ever had—ever. The thought of him leaving me to wrestle with my emotions again made me feel swallowed up in complete and utter loneliness. Tears started to come. *Ugh.*

Before he could say anything, I took a breath and said, "You know, I have spent the last year and a half sheltering myself and my kids from any type of surprises or discomfort. And I did not see you coming. Why didn't you text me and tell me you were coming back to visit?"

He dropped his hand from my arm and put his hands on the back of a chair. He was silent for a moment, and then he motioned to the parking lot. We walked to our cars. He leaned against mine in that appealing casual way of his and said, "You are right. I should have given you a heads-up. That was selfish of me. The truth is," he took a deep breath, "I am thinking about moving back here. No, that isn't true. I want to move back here. I want to buy some land out in the hill country and build a home."

"Mmmhmm," I responded, trying to be unmoved by what he had just said. He was coming back for good. I was letting it sink in.

He continued, "I have lived in some amazing places and been so blessed in my business, and I am ready to settle down permanently. You know my parents are a few hours from here, and my sisters and their families are too. I do miss them."

"Those are really great reasons to come back," I said. And I meant it.

He leaned on my car door and looked at me. My face was getting flushed again. My phone continued to buzz. I don't think he had answered my questions, or maybe he had. I paused and channeled my inner southern manners and said calmly, "I know that you will be successful no matter where you are." I smiled. "Thank you for inviting me to lunch. It was great to see you and catch up." I started toward my truck's door.

"El, wait. Please." he said and put his hands in his pockets. He looked at me sheepishly. "I came to church because that is where I thought I would find you."

He was looking for me. He wanted to find me. He watched me to see my reaction. I wondered what my face looked like at that moment.

"When I heard about Tommy, I felt so bad for you and the kids. You don't really post on social media. I didn't know how you were doing, so when I had an opportunity to be back in the area, I showed up, hoping to see you and how you have been. Imagine my surprise when I walked in, and you were onstage singing."

We both started laughing. I think we were both nervous as nothing was particularly funny except our situation. He had come to find and see.

"El, I am coming back for a wedding in March. I am in it. You don't have to come for the ceremony but please come for the reception. It will be fun, it is in a beautiful venue, and we can catch up more. Will you come with me?"

I smiled. I got out my phone and looked at my calendar. *Who am I kidding? I will rearrange just about anything to spend time with him.* "OK. That works. I will see you in March."

He walked toward me and gave me a hug. It felt so good to be wrapped up in his strong arms.

"You still driving this truck?" he asked. "It has seen better days."

"I think both my truck and I have seen better days. But she is sturdy and still runs." I laughed at my self-deprecating humor and turned to open my door.

"El," Bo said.

Lord, the way he says my name with that East Texas accent. Like it's the most amazing name in the world. I turned to look at him. Our eyes locked.

"I will see you in March."

And I climbed into my old Toyota Sequoia and waved as I drove off.

Chapter 8

"WHERE HAVE YOU BEEN AND with whom?" Katie's voice yelled through my phone.

I laughed. "Don't act like you haven't been tracking me on Life360 when I didn't answer your text right away."

"I waited an hour for you to answer, and then I went on Life360. Anyway, you are avoiding my question. Who were you with?" she demanded.

"Bo," I said more meekly than I wanted to.

"Oh, wow. Tea told me he was at church. I wasn't sure I believed her."

"I know," I responded.

I had barely told her anything about my feelings for Bo the two years I had known him. But after he left for Florida, I was so down and feeling sorry for myself that she knew something was up. I gave her a very brief synopsis, hoping she could help me figure out what was wrong with me being completely infatuated with a younger man while married with four kids.

She thoughtfully had said, "Ellie, did you really think that once you were married, you would never ever again feel attracted to anyone? Like that piece of paper and promise meant no one would ever walk into your life again whom you would really connect with? But you both did nothing with your feelings. You crossed no line."

And she had a point. And that is all we said about it, mainly because I refused to talk about him to her or anyone. It was easier that way.

"Well, what did y'all talk about?" she asked.

I told her about our conversation. I left out how he looked at and touched my arm. I was *not* just imagining something because I was lonely. I didn't tell her that there was this intense connection, chemistry, or something between us, which I wasn't sure even existed on Earth until he walked into, then out of, and now back into my life.

"He said he might be moving back in the spring. And he will be back in March for a wedding. He asked me to go with him. And that about brings you up to date," I finished.

Katie sucked in a breath. "Ellie, he came back looking for you. He's been waiting for you. He clearly wants to be in a relationship with you. He likes you. And you like him."

"I don't know how you got that from what I just told you," I said. "I don't think I am ready for that anyway."

"It's called reading between your lines, which I have been doing for thirty years now. He could be the one for you," Katie said.

"You have lost your mind? A relationship is the last thing I need," I quickly retorted.

Katie quickly responded, "What I am saying is what if there is that one person for you in the world, and you found each other? I don't think you remember how down you were after he left. You were miserable with a fake smile plastered on your face for a year."

I admitted, "I was struggling, but it was a lot of other things too. And stating that he is the one is a lot to put on one person. And shouldn't I be putting all of my loneliness and stress on the person of Jesus and not Bo?"

"Listen. God created Eve specifically for Adam. For Jacob and Rachel, Jacob waited a long time for Rachel. All I am saying is that He has done it before and that He can do it again. And," Katie said quietly, "Ellie, you are lonely. You need someone to share the day-to-day stress of life with. Maybe God is providing that person."

I didn't respond. So Katie kept going. "God gives us people to share our burdens with here on Earth because He knows it can be lonely, even with Jesus."

I was not so sure. And if there was actually a human that God specifically created to match me, I couldn't finish the thought. I was so tired. The last year and a half had almost finished me off.

Chapter 9

I HAD WOKEN UP THE NEXT morning and had revisited my
conversation with Bo. He was in my dreams along with Tommy.
It had been a fitful night's sleep. All the emotions, the way Bo had
always made me feel, the guilt for feeling that way, not wanting to
hurt Tommy, wondering what God was doing, all of it was so heavy.

I sat in my grandmother's old chair. I call it my chair of holy
contemplation. I had gotten that from something Charles Spurgeon
had written about his time with Jesus. I pulled out my journal and
Bible. I looked heavenward. *Lord, You always work for my good and
Your glory—always. I don't really understand why Bo wanted to come
find and see me. I don't understand these feelings. It took so much effort
and work to lay the feelings that I had for Bo at your feet three years
ago, and now you are giving them back to me. I need clarity. Separate
out each emotion and clarify for me the path to take.*

I felt nauseous. I wished all my stress didn't land in my stomach.
*Is Katie right? Has he been waiting for me since he left? How do I feel
about that?* It didn't feel wrong to go to the wedding with him, which
was two months away. *Lord, help me to hear you. I want what You
want for me. Help me to be humble and open to whatever you have
for me.*

PART 2

PART 2

Chapter 10

ARLY SPRING HAD COME TO the Texas hill country. It was a
beautiful Saturday evening in late March. The red bud and
Bradford Pear trees were in full bloom. The bees were creating a
low hum throughout the days. I parked my truck and checked my
makeup in the driver's side mirror. My curls were behaving due to
low humidity. Half my hair was up in a clip, and the other half was
past my shoulders. I added some lip gloss and grabbed my sweater.
The sun could be warm, but the breeze was cool. It still got chilly
once the sun went down.

Bo and I had chatted through texts and only a few phone calls
the last few months. It was nice to have adult conversations with
him. I enjoyed his funny stories and genuine interest in my life,
teaching, research projects, and kids. It had been a busy winter with
dance-competition season underway for Tea. And I was planning
both Luke's and Brooke's pending graduations. It truly felt as if
the fog of mourning was lifting for all of us and that we were all
moving on.

I walked up the hill to the outdoor wedding ceremony. I scanned
the crowd for Bo. I was incredibly nervous about seeing him and
more than I wanted to admit. I dressed in a light-green top that
matched my eyes and a navy-blue A-line skirt that had a lace ruffle
at the hem and twirled with me when I spun around. I had on my
light-brown cowgirl boots, which had sparkles of blues and greens.

I wore a brown belt to match. I hadn't danced in a while, so Luke and I spent last weekend two-stepping.

My stomach jumped. I saw Bo talking to and smiling at the other groomsmen. They all wore khakis, boots, starched white shirts, blue blazers, and cowboy hats, of course. They were all posing for the photographer. He looked incredibly handsome. On the drive out there, I had told myself to act friendly, to be cool, and that this was not a big deal. We are just slowly rekindling a friendship. That is all.

I found a tree to lean on and watched him. I wondered if he went to that cabin in the middle of nowhere in February. *Did he stare up at the stars and talk to God about me? Did God answer him? Because God has been silent with me about Bo. God is near me, and I know He hears me, but there has been no clear yes or no, which usually means wait.*

I regretted that I had said yes. I looked at all the groups of people laughing and talking. I knew no one. I thought I saw a girl Bo used to date, Holly, standing near him. My introverted side just wanted to drive back home, crawl under my covers, and read a book.

Bo had spotted me. He smiled and started up the small hill where I was standing. Holly's eyes followed him up to me. He grinned at me the entire walk up. And I smiled back. He was impossible not to smile at. He looked so good. His hat framed his face, and the white shirt showed off his tan from fishing year-round.

"Hi," I said. Butterflies were doing triple flips in my stomach. *So much for being cool.*

He looked me up and down and said, "Wow, El, you look amazing!" He reached for my hand, and I let him take it. *So much for being friendly. Why am I completely hopeless when he is near me?* He looked at me for a minute, almost like he was going to say something. He dropped my hand and then hugged me.

"It is great to see you again." He stepped back and said, "Your eyes are so green tonight."

I smiled big and said, "Thank you." I had never figured out

34

how to respond to a compliment. Katie always said I had hit the genetic jackpot and that I had a heart-shaped face, high cheekbones, medium-size eyes, and a perfect nose. I wasn't sure about that. When I looked in the mirror, I just saw me—the me I had seen every day of my forty-one years. I saw the wrinkles, the smile lines, the freckles, the ever-fading eyebrows, and the boniness of my shoulders and wrists. Occasionally, I would glance in the mirror, and I would be a little shocked that I looked so put together because on the inside, I felt like a disaster most of the time.

He guided me down the hill and into the crowd of people I didn't know. As I looked at him, his brown eyes always seemed happy to see me. I wondered if he realized how his eyes always showed exactly how he was feeling. I wondered if I was the only one who could see it.

Bo's parents were there, as this was a family wedding. His sister Micah was also there. His other sister Dinah was busy teaching high school, and she couldn't make it. We found a table with all of them, and I was introduced. We had a pleasant conversation about my teaching college students and my family. I felt overly self-conscious about my age and how many kids I had. They probably thought I was some kind of cougar trying to catch their son. It hadn't crossed my mind until that moment that people might think we were dating. *Bo is dating an older woman and a widow*, they were saying to themselves. I was truly mortified. I glanced at Bo, and he didn't seem to be bothered by any of it.

The bride and groom entered the building and had their first dance. Soft lights hung from the distressed wooden beams; white flowers graced every table. I loved weddings. Everyone was so happy or at least pretending to be. I could have just sat and people watched all night. It was the sociologist in me, but Bo had me on my feet and headed toward the dance floor before I could protest.

He held my hand and pulled me onto the crowded dance floor. The country cover band was playing "Take My Name"[6] by Parmalee.

Take my days, baby take my nights.
Go and take the rest of my life
Because I don't want to wait no more.
Take my name baby make it yours.

I started singing just by habit. I was brought back to reality as Bo's hand went to the small of my back. I suddenly realized that this was the closest we had ever been. It was the closest I had been to any man other than Tommy. I lightly put my right hand in his left hand and my left hand on his broad shoulder. I decided to concentrate on breathing rather than singing. Bo was a very smooth dancer. *Is he bad at anything?* I thought about how small and delicate his large hand made me feel. My face felt very warm.

He leaned down to tease me about the failure of my vegetarian diet to put any fat on me. "El, seriously, if a stiff wind blew in tonight, you would fly off like a feather. I could probably pick you up with one hand."

I laughed and said, "I am heavier than I look. That whole muscle weighs more than fat thing." It was true. I had been using weights for the last year, and my arms and legs looked more muscular than they ever had.

A few months after Tommy had died, I started to look for some way to gain back control over my life. I believed that if I could stay five pounds below my high school weight, it would all be OK. I don't know how my mind got there, but it wouldn't let go. Sixth months after Tommy died, I was 105 pounds at five feet five inches. I was underweight, and I knew it. At five each morning, I would weigh myself, and if it was 105, everything was going to be OK that day. If I got over 105, I was sure that everything was going to break that day and that I would have a full-blown panic attack.

Anxiety was that stage of grief they forgot to tell you about. I spent nights wide awake, staring at the ceiling and worrying about health insurance for all of us, getting the title of Tommy's car changed, reminding myself to call someone to mow our two acres, etc. It was like I was running on a never-ending supply of adrenaline and working hard not to drop any balls, which left me exhausted and joyless.

Katie called me out in her know-it-all doctor way. I refused to listen to her. It became an obsession and a way to control something in this life when every single thing felt out of control. Katie finally dragged me to a nutritionist and a therapist. It resulted in a diagnosis of anxiety and depression and a plan to add more protein and weightlifting instead of just running for exercise. I was not sure where I would be right now if Katie hadn't stepped into my mess. And I was not sure I wanted Bo to be in my mess at all.

Chapter 11

WE WERE UP DANCING AGAIN. It was a slower song called "Neon Moon"[7] by Brooks and Dunn. That brought me back to my college days. I was trying to think of anything but his hand on my back and his body so close to mine. Suddenly, I could think of nothing to say. I had no easy banter to counteract the physicality of that moment.

As we moved around the floor, I was working hard to completely ignore the sparks that were crackling between us. I couldn't stop thinking about how rock hard his shoulder was as my hand rested on it and how his hand on my back was light. Everything in that moment felt incredibly intimate. I could smell his aftershave, and my body felt warm from his touch. I had forgotten how intimate dancing could be.

While his hand was guiding me around the floor. I let myself remember the first time we had met. I was outside as all my kids played soccer over spring break. I used to play in college at a small private university. I was a right-wing striker because I was fast. And I loved the game. Luke followed in my footsteps and was so much better than I was. He started on his high school team as a freshman. He scored in his first varsity game. It was hard to believe that he would be coaching our favorite sport and getting paid.

We had just gotten a new puppy, Bingo, who was running around chasing the ball, and we were all laughing. The ball went flying, and the puppy ran across the street chasing it. Our neighborhood was a tree-lined, large two-to-three-acre lot with wide streets. I was closest to the runaway ball and pup, so I ran after them. They ended up in our neighbor's driveway under a large work truck. It was Bo's. I was attempting to crawl under it to get the stuck ball. I saw two work boots and heard a voice laughing at me. "You looking for this?"

I brushed myself off and introduced myself. I just remember his eyes. They were so brown and full of kindness and laughter. He reminded me of a blond version of Tim McGraw. We stood there and chatted until the kids got tired and went to finish the game. He held the puppy until it fell asleep. And we kept talking. We talked about everything.

We kept seeing each other. In our small town at stoplights, we would smile and wave. I knew I was in trouble when I was happy to see his truck across the street. I would even start walking over to talk to him. He was so interesting, and I kept telling myself it was harmless. He was a friend. And then he left for Florida. We went on with our lives. It was the right thing to do. And we each had really good lives. Then Tommy died, and everything fell apart.

The band at the wedding was playing old-school country, which I had listened to in college: Brooks and Dunn, Shenandoah, and Garth Brooks. We kept dancing for a few more songs. I couldn't help but sing along. Bo had always thought it was funny that I sang even if I didn't know all the words. I looked up at him, and we laughed as I missed a line.

We finished dancing. He kept his hand on my back as he guided me back to the table until a family friend grabbed him and asked him to dance. I was grateful to have a minute to regroup.

I watched Bo dance with several women and then Holly, the ex. I think she had been the one who had broken it off. But now she seemed more interested in him. I wondered why Bo could never get a girl to settle down with him. He probably had commitment issues. At this point in his life—his late thirties—he was too set in his ways to be married.

I finished a glass of wine and felt more at ease talking with Bo's parents. They were delightful, and they seemed to like me. I kept one eye on Bo and Holly. Then I thought, *He should be with her. He should absolutely be with Holly or someone her age. They should get married and have a family together. Why am I even here? I am older and not interested in having any more kids.* My body was so done. Any thoughts of a future with him just weren't practical. I settled back on my previous resolution. *I will be calm and friendly. That is all,* as long as I didn't have to dance with him again.

Bo came over to the table after the song had ended and invited me to go to the buffet with him. Our plates of food always were a discussion of opposites. He liked meat, fish, and dessert while I filled my plate with fruit and vegetables. We joked that together, we always created a complete meal.

He was a fisherman and hunter and ate everything he killed. He enjoyed the hunt. Sometimes I wondered if the reason he never settled down and got married was because he enjoyed the hunt too much. No girl wants to be stuffed and hung over the mantle! I laughed out loud at the thought of Holly over his mantle as he grinned at me over his plate of brisket and sausage. He was so warm and reassuring. I told myself, *I will not be up on his mantle either, no matter what.*

Chapter 12

I REALLY ENJOYED MYSELF AT THE reception. I especially liked getting to know his parents, other family members, and friends. I wasn't sure if it was the wine or just Bo's presence. He was always so self-assured and a friend to all. He was sitting next to me. He leaned back and stretched his arm behind my chair as he was talking to some friends. I leaned into it before I even thought about it. I turned to Bo, and he looked down at me. His eyes looked happy. I felt my cheeks get warm. *Cool and just friends*, I told myself again.

Bo danced with his sister. His dad danced with his mom. It was so sweet to watch them. *Bo looks so much like both parents. His eyes are all his mom's.* She had those big brown, expressive eyes as well. I pulled out my phone and found a text from Luke.

How's the dancing going? Tell Bo I said hi.

Luke had asked me who I was going with when I had asked him to come home for a weekend and practice two-stepping with me. I told him that Bo had asked me to come to the reception. Luke gave me a raised-eyebrow look. "Is this a date?" he asked.

I sat down and took a break from dance lessons. "I don't know. I think it's more like two old friends catching up on each other's lives where free food, drink, and dancing are available. What do you think?" I asked. I really wanted to know his opinion.

"A guy isn't going to invite you to a wedding if he thinks of you as a friend. A wedding invite has all sorts of underlying motives." Luke said it like it is the most obvious thing ever.

"Really? I hadn't thought of it that way. I was under the impression it was that he was in town and wanted to catch up," I said.

"Mom! How do you not see the unspoken message of a wedding invite? And you call yourself a sociologist."

I laughed. Luke had always made me laugh. "I haven't been asked out on a date in about twenty-one years. I don't really know what anything means. I just know that Bo is kind, and I have always enjoyed being around him. And frankly I could use some grown-up fun."

"Well, I like Bo a lot. I approve of the date," he said flippantly as he walked out of the room.

"I don't think it even counts as a date if his parents are there," I yelled to his back. He waved his hand at me like I was clueless. I laughed.

I replied to his text that the dancing was going well.

> I haven't fallen down yet.

Bo came back with Micah and sat down next to me. I shoved my phone into my purse. "Luke says to tell you hi," I said.

Bo smiled. "He is a great guy. I got to talk to him a little at church a few months ago. All your kids are pretty great."

"They have their moments," I said.

Later, Bo and I got into a funny discussion about country song lyrics. He jokingly accused me of being unromantic because I do not like the song "The Moon Over Georgia."[8]

"I like the song," I insisted, "just not the sentiment. A woman having to choose between two guys, one rich and one poor, with nothing to offer her but the moon. And she picks the moon. Of course, she did because she is young and doesn't realize that having money keeps you from having arguments and sleepless nights. She doesn't realize that you can still see the moon with someone who has money. In fact, you will have less arguments and more fun."

"That's a strong opinion." Bo raised his eyebrows at me.

It must have been the wine that was making me more brazen than I normally was. I argued that you could be more romantic with money. "I say this from experience. I have lived paycheck to paycheck while paying off college loans. And I have also lived with money to put into savings, college funds, and family vacations. If given a choice, being financially comfortable makes way for a lot more romance."

Bo looked at me with his arms folded and while leaning back in his chair. "Hmm. Well, we just might have to put your theory to the test."

I laughed that comment off. I was not entirely sure what he meant. I knew from past conversations that Bo had felt that some girls he dated only really liked his money. I wondered if he had married one of those. I did know from town gossip that he was married a while ago and that the marriage ended after a year. I think he wouldn't care that I knew; he just didn't want to talk about it. And frankly, I wouldn't either.

I saw Holly glancing over at our table several times. Throughout the night, I kept trying to convince myself that Bo got the raw end of the deal with me. I was older, had four kids, and was a hot mess. He was so difficult to walk away from, even as a friend. *How do I walk away from someone who seems to make life ten times better by just smiling at me? How am I in this situation again? Why didn't I say no to the wedding invite? Why can't I just let him go?*

Bo pushed back his chair and grabbed my hand. "We have to," he said with a laugh. "'The Moon Over Georgia' just started.

"I will," I said, "just to prove to you that I am not heartless." I gave him my biggest smile, and he laughed.

The first half of the song, we were both dancing and singing along. I became more comfortable dancing with him. And this was what Bo did well: made me so incredibly comfortable in his presence that I forgot any promises I had made to myself. And as much as I was fighting against it, I couldn't even hate him for it.

Bo really had a good singing voice. Then during the second half of the song, he said, "All joking aside; you have one of the biggest and best hearts I know."

As he said this, I realized that he purposely pulled me a little closer. It surprised me. I looked up at him and didn't know what to say. He met my gaze and smiled. *Ugh. That smile.* It was downright dangerous. I felt his right thumb over my hip and the palm of his hand on my back. His fingers stretched to my spine. The more I thought about his hand, the more I felt lightheaded. I sensed heat rushing to my cheeks, into my arms, and down into my belly. I hadn't felt that type of heat in a very long time.

I sighed inwardly. I felt myself surrendering. I suddenly couldn't find the fight in me to control the situation so that he or I could walk away and so that it wouldn't hurt. In his arms I just waived the white flag. I didn't realize until that moment how much I wanted it. I wanted him. I wanted Bo to hold me and tell me it was all going to be OK.

We stayed on the floor for the next song. Bo had pulled my hand toward his chest, and I could almost feel his heartbeat. My head was swimming, and it felt good to just let the song cover us as we danced across the dance floor.

When the music stopped, I was trying to breathe normally. Our eyes locked, and I slid my hand down his chest. *What am I doing?* I needed to step away from him and regain some control. I stepped backward and turned around, but his hand was still holding mine. Holly was staring right at us—at me. It felt as if the entire room of people was staring at us. I wasn't ready for this. Even if my heart wanted it, it hadn't communicated any clarity to my brain but only a bunch of mixed and confusing signals.

While I stood there for a second, some guy walked over and gave Bo a big hug. He had to let go of my hand. *Thank you, God. An exit strategy.* I grabbed my purse from the table while completely avoiding eye contact with his parents. I just needed a minute. I walked outside toward my car. I was overheated from the dance and the warm room. My curls were starting to slowly escape from the clip. Holly had much tamer hair. Holly—I was certain they could work out their issues and have a lovely marriage and babies together because we could not do this. I was emotionally overwhelmed.

Chapter 13

I FOUND MY CAR AND PUT my warm forehead on the side of my cool car door. My head was throbbing. The wine and the loud band probably didn't help. After a few minutes, I started to breathe normally. I heard someone walking up behind me. Bo leaned against my car. He was silent for a minute.

"You, OK?" he asked.

"I am. I just got overheated." My voice sounded weird. I still couldn't bring myself to look at him, so my head stayed firmly planted on my car. My thoughts were racing. I needed to think. I was so tired of making responsible decisions. I just wanted to make some decisions because they felt good.

Bo leaned against my car and looked up at the sky. He took his hat off, put it on my hood, and ran his fingers through his short blond hair. He was way too handsome, and he knew it. I turned around and leaned against my car next to him. I was overly conscious of how good he smelled. I crossed my hands over my chest just so that they wouldn't reach for his.

"Bo," I said softly, and then I couldn't seem to put a sentence together. After a long pause, I said, "I'm sorry." I was sorry. I was sorry that I had walked out of the reception. I was sorry that I flirted with him while married. It may not have been the hair-tossing, lip-biting type of flirting, but I was laughing and smiling with him. I was sorry that my own issues of loneliness resulted in a need for attention from him. I was sorry that it and I made him leave three years earlier.

Before I could conjure up something to say, Bo started. "El, I am the one who is sorry. Maybe I pushed a little too much tonight, and you told me a few months ago you weren't ready." I took a breath and started to say something, but he kept going. "When I was at the cabin last month, I prayed about you and me. I was very intentional about not hearing what I wanted God to say, but I focused on what God says over and over in His Word."

I looked over at him. I was incredibly curious as to what God showed him.

"You and I have something ... that I want to explore, but I also understand that you don't need an intense relationship with me. You just need kindness and gentleness and patience from me. And I am more than happy to meet you right there with what you need."

Bo took a breath and said, "I remember the first time I saw you. You were running across the street, yelling your dog's name, and laughing. Your long legs sprinted to catch your puppy. Your hair was flying everywhere. Your kids were all running behind you. And when you popped out from under my truck, your huge smile, green eyes, and freckles—"

I laughed. "Oh man, I was a mess." I sighed. "I still am. I—"

Bo started to interrupt me.

"Wait. Please let me say this. I want you to know that I feel ... I felt really terrible ... so guilty about ... being part of the reason you decided to leave three years ago. I know we were just friends from the outside looking in, but in my heart, it was more. I was thinking about you, wanting to tell you things, looking for you, more than happy to see you. And it was wrong." I paused for a breath. "And in a way, I was relieved you left. And now you are back. And my life looks so different. I'm just confused." My voice was shaking, and my eyes were filled with tears. Maybe if we just put everything out on the table, I could make sense of it all.

I didn't want to cry, so I sucked in my breath and swallowed. I couldn't tell him it took almost a year to get him off my mind. I did everything I could to focus on Tommy and our beautiful family. But there were quiet, dark moments when I would lay out my deep loneliness before God and think about Bo. I would put all my needs, struggles, and desire to obey in front of Him, and He would take it and walk me gently through the day.

Bo and I were still looking at the stars. Bo took a deep breath and looked down at the gravel. "El, please don't be hard on yourself. The opportunity to move to Florida and start this business came up. I knew as soon as I saw it that I needed to do it, to create some space between us." Bo thought for a minute and then said, "I think how I finally resolved in my head us and the connection we had was that it was a good thing we had but just at the wrong time. We never crossed any line, and God was opening a door for me to walk through."

I was thinking about his first impression of me: lively, active, and surrounded by a bunch of happy kids and a puppy. "I am not sure I know where that fun person from three years ago is. Life has ways of subduing you. You deserve so much better than me. Someone with less kids and baggage." I forced a laugh. We were both back to staring up at the sky filled with stars. Hard conversations were easier when we weren't looking right at each other.

Bo turned to face me. "Now hold on, El. First, you are who you are because of the kids and baggage. And I like that you. You are real and have lived a real life. Second, you have no idea what I deserve. The truth is," he sighed, looked down at his boots, and then slowly looked up at the sky, "I deserve the wrath of God. I have lived a good part of my adult years thinking I knew everything, and it was all about me. My life and my sin were particularly ugly. But God has poured out His grace on my life. All I did was whisper a prayer for help and mercy.

"And maybe you have changed some in three years, but so have I. And I don't think growing and changing is a bad thing. I don't know what you see when you look in the mirror, but I see an intelligent and passionate woman, who has, despite tragedy, continued to build her life upon God's promises. I see a beautiful woman, inside and out, and someone I want to know more about."

I laughed and looked at him. "Honestly, you render me completely—I don't even know the word." He was still looking at the sky and smiling. "You really want to spend time getting to know someone who is in the throes of parenting two teenagers and a tween?"

He answered, "I have lived long enough to have explored the world and the people in it. And you are who I want to invest more time in, not someone else. You are who I want to get to know better."

That statement, for the moment anyway, cleared away from my mind all the younger women I was planning to push him toward.

Chapter 14

WE STAYED SIDE BY SIDE, looking up at the stars. I had forgotten or made myself forget what being next to him was like. It felt like we had stood next to each other a thousand times before. Being next to him was so comforting that I just wanted to curl up in his arms.

We were silent for a minute. Then we could hear the MC tell everyone to meet outside to say goodbye to the happy couple.

"You should go," I said as I nudged him with my hip. He turned to face me with a look of concern in his eyes.

"I apologize, El, if I made you feel … conflicted or confused earlier."

"Bo, you don't make me feel conflicted or confused. Those feelings are all me. My life and responsibilities are all consuming, and I am still trying to figure out how to live with them.

He smiled at me. "I came to give you your sweater. You left it on your chair." He threw it around my shoulders and then touched my bare shoulder gently with his thumb. He smiled and said, "Ellie. What does Ellie stand for anyway?"

"Elouise," I said nervously. "My grandmother's name. I am told that I look like her."

His hand moved from my shoulder to my cheek. He brushed his hand on my cheek. I felt like I was literally melting into the gravel parking lot.

He opened my door, and I got in. Then he said, "I am headed back down to Florida to close out some things for a month or so. Let's keep talking and praying about us. Will you please text me when you get home? These winding roads in the dark make me worry about you."

"I will."

Chapter 15

I HAD AN HOUR DRIVE BACK to my house. I called Katie even though it was almost midnight. She answered on the first ring.

"I want to know every single detail!" she yelled.

"Katie, I am so tired." I sighed. "I am only calling you so I can stay awake on this drive."

"Please tell me how it went. I'm dying to know. It's just me, a middle-aged doctor living vicariously through your entanglements with a very hot, single man. That is all."

I laughed and told her about the dancing, Holly, and our talk by my car.

"That is a huge conversation. It sounds like he is madly in love with you. Just don't make him wait too long. I won't be able to stand the suspense."

"Katie," I chided.

"Oh, Ellie. I don't understand how you can't see it. But I will pray for your eyes to be opened," Katie half joked.

"I am just happy to have finally apologized to him and to have him tell me that God was asking him to leave. I feel relieved. Now I just need to process it. I mean, he literally said he wanted to get to know me more. I am not sure what to do with that."

"You take it, Ellie," Katie said fiercely. "You open yourself up to being known by someone—being really known. You are ready. Take down some of your walls. We are all built for connection, and you have someone offering to connect with you who loves and obeys God, is undeniably handsome, and has had a thing for you for years."

"Well, I'm pretty sure we are just as equally built for heartache, seeing as I have been feeling that for the last few years." I sighed inwardly.

"OK, negative Nancy. How about this, I believe that you are capable of feeling two big contrasting emotions. You can feel the heartache of losing Tommy and the beauty of something new. We are created in God's image, and He does that. He can be perfectly, justifiably angry at the evil in this world *and* kind and loving to those who turn from evil toward Him. So you can do it too."

We chatted until I was almost home. Then I texted Bo, went inside my house, and fell into bed.

Chapter 16

I WAS LOUNGING ON THE COUCH after a busy week. Tea was showing me her roundoff back tuck on a mat she had dragged inside.

Teadora was named after Tommy's paternal grandmother. Little Tea was strong-willed, athletic, and a social butterfly. She was a dancer, singer, soccer player, cheerleader, and always busy. She missed Tommy a ton. He would always give her so much attention. He played games and made up dances with her. He was her favorite playmate. *Lord, soothe her broken heart and guide her into all the good things you have for her*, I prayed silently.

Tommy had been half Romanian. His dad was an Olympic tennis player from Romania, who met his mom while training in the US. The marriage didn't last long, and Tommy's dad died of a heart attack fairly young. That should have clued me in to insist that Tommy go see a heart doctor. But with four kids' medical, dental, and orthodontic appointments, I didn't have the bandwidth to look out for Tommy's health. Maybe I should have. That was what a good wife did, right? I felt complicit in his heart attack most days. He was a big six-feet-five-inches guy with no desire to be athletic. I could have done something. I should have.

Whit was watching a movie beside me. Whit, who was named after my maiden name, Whitmore, was quieter and calmer like I was. He had my genes. He was not going to be very big—maybe five feet eight inches—like my dad. He was not competitive, but he liked being with his friends, as most fifteen-year-olds do. He was my musical child. He played piano and drums. Tommy had played the base guitar. Out of all the kids, he was the closest to Tommy. They did everything together.

Whit seemed shocked by his dad's death. It was like each day, he couldn't believe it. His big blue eyes looked wide with fright too often. Tommy was there one day, and the next, he wasn't. The proverbial rug was pulled out from under Whit and all of us. I felt his trauma deeply.

I had been so focused on walking my kids through their trauma that I had barely touched my own. I knew that one day, it would hit like a tornado. I kept holding it back. The stress I was under was toxic to my body. It was no wonder I was so tired all the time.

Brooke was lying on my other side, flipping through Pinterest on her phone. She was my artist, painter, and sketcher, who lived in her own artistic world and sometimes let me in. She was a senior, and she would be off to college the following year. Tommy hadn't been not sold on her going to college and being an artist, but I didn't have the energy to talk her out of it. And I am all for doing what brings you joy because this world can be harsh.

I started to think about Luke, my firstborn baby. He loved and followed Jesus passionately. We both loved to worship through music. Going to church and worshipping next to him and all my kids was my greatest joy. He put all the fun in our family. He could be ridiculously stubborn sometimes. But he came by it honestly. Both Tommy and I were so stubborn.

I was saddened when I thought about Tommy and I fighting. I wasn't sure we were going to make it some days. After twenty years, we had grown into such different people, or maybe we were always different but made it work. I wondered if I was bad at being married. It was like a skill set I just didn't have. I was an only child; therefore, I was selfish and self-centered most of the time. Any good that I had ever been was a result of Jesus moving in my heart, mind, and soul.

Easter was the next weekend. I was singing at church for three services. Easter Sunday had always been my favorite day of the year. Spring was everywhere, and people were dressed in bright colors. I would practice Jesus praise songs all week. Luke would be home. He had come home more since Tommy had died. I wanted to tell him that it was OK not to be there, but the truth was that I loved it when he was home.

As I was lying on the couch, Bo called. We had texted and talked a few times over the past two weeks. I answered on speakerphone. "Hey, Bo!"

Tea yelled, "Hi!" Brooke leaned into my shoulder, probably to listen.

"Hey, there!" He laughed at Tea in the background. "Quick question: Do you have plans for Easter?"

"Ummm, just having my friend Katie and her family over. It's a tradition. We eat, hide eggs, and have our annual family throw-down volleyball game. It's fun." Katie had three girls in between my kid's ages. A sixteen-, thirteen-, and nine-year-old—Kylie, Remy, and Landry. Her husband, John, was a great guy and a pediatric dentist. Katie and John had kept me going the last few years with their undying support and prayer. They kept my kids and drove them to school, activities, and church, all while I was trying to get through each day.

"Well, I have a realtor that wants to show me some land this weekend. It just popped up. I thought I would fly in and go see it Saturday and then go to church on Sunday with you, if you don't mind."

"Of course not! We would love to have you over after service also. I have to warn you that competitive play runs deep around here." He laughed.

Tea yelled, "You can be on my team!"

"I'm in," he said. "I can't wait. I will text you when I get to town."

We said goodbye and then hung up. I started making a grocery list and texted Katie to see what she wanted to bring. I couldn't wait for her to spend some time with Bo. Oh, and my dad was coming too.

Our house was the perfect place for entertaining guests. Three sets of French doors opened onto the patio and pool. While Tommy and I didn't agree on everything, we always agreed that our house was a gift from the Lord and that we would use it to bless others. Even when things were rough between us, we could always find some common ground to hang onto. We always said that at least we both loved going to church and worshipping. Some days it was the only thread that held us together.

Chapter 17

THE SATURDAY BEFORE EASTER WAS chaotic. In the morning, I went to rehearse with the praise and worship team for the Easter service. That afternoon, I was running around trying to get everything that Brooke wanted for props and such for the photographer. I had forgotten it was Brooke's senior portrait day. I had hired one of my friends to take photos. Because it was Brooke, it had to be artsy. By 3:00 p.m., I was sitting in my car in front of Tea's friend's house and waiting for her to come out. I was eating an old bag of cashews I'd found in the bottom of my purse and trying to keep myself from falling asleep. I had been up since 4:00 a.m. thinking about Bo's visit and my kids and wondering if everyone was really OK.

Bo called. He was done with seeing the property, and he asked if I needed any help. For once, I said, "Yes." I added somewhat apologetically, "I am really struggling being everything to everyone today."

He was going to meet me at my house to load up Brooke's props. I suddenly got a nervous stomach. I couldn't sit still, so I went into the garage and began pulling out all Brooke's props. I hadn't seen Bo since the night at the wedding. I worried that seeing him again was going to be weird and awkward. I stopped and reminded myself that he wanted to see me, prayed about us, and wanted to intentionally spend time with me.

But what if he has changed his mind and realized that everything he has said has been a mistake? What if he doesn't feel the same about me? Our phone conversations and texting had been light, probably because we had dug so deep into our relationship and feelings the last time we saw each other.

I looked down and realized that I was in workout clothes: black leggings, running shoes, a sports' bra, and a tank top, with a hoodie tied around my waist. My hair was in a ponytail, and my loose curls were everywhere. My attempt at bangs or something to frame my face usually just became an untamable bunch of curls flying everywhere. I was about to walk inside and change when Bo pulled up.

I stood in my long driveway with one hand up blocking the sun and the other hand waving. Seeing him always made me smile. He jumped out of his truck and walked toward me. He was wearing jeans, work boots, a light-gray T-shirt, and a baseball cap. Watching him walk up to me, happy to see me, and wrapping me in a big hug, I was pretty much ready to run away with him.

"Hi!" I said as he hugged me. "It's really good to see you. Thank you for coming to my rescue. I had completely forgotten about Brooke's pictures being this weekend."

Bo stepped back from me, looked at me, and smiled. "I am glad I could help. You know it feeds the male ego to be able to move things with his truck, right?"

I laughed. "I will try to remember that. I apologize for my appearance. The day has gotten away from me." I motioned toward my outfit.

"El, you look great. As my grandma used to say, 'You would look good in a paper sack.'"

"That is too funny. Well, my grandma used to say, 'Never leave the house without your hair done and makeup on,'" I said with a laugh.

Brooke walked outside, said hello to Bo, and asked me to come inside and help her bring all her outfits out to the car. Bo looked at me and mouthed, *All?* He has no idea what he had signed up for. And I laughed to myself.

Bo loaded everything for Brooke's session into his truck. He drove it to the art center downtown and unloaded it while I helped Brooke get her hair and makeup done.

Brooke and I met Bo and the photographer at the art center. Bo walked up to me with a vegetarian taco and ice water. I literally could have kissed him. "You actually paid money for food without any meat?" I joked. He laughed. I had made Bo laugh, and that was turning into one of my favorite things to do. I scarfed down the taco while he moved furniture and art pieces where Brooke directed. It felt so nice to have another adult helping me—really nice.

The light of the sunset and Brooke's vision for the photo shoot were absolutely gorgeous. She was stunning. I started to tear up and had to walk away. I wished Tommy could see her. He would be so proud of her. Maybe Katie was right; I could have two really big emotions at the same time—stunned by Brooke's beauty and maturity while being completely heartbroken for her loss of a father. Bo walked up with tissues, of course.

"I am so sorry. Tears sometimes come at random times. Did I mention I was a mess?"

"Several times," he commented while smiling at me.

"If you can hang with me and my emotions through the spring when both Luke and Brooke graduate, you will have earned your place in my world," I joked—sort of.

"If all it takes to hang with you is keeping you hydrated and fed and wiping tears away, I am here for it all," he quipped. We looked at each other for a minute. I had no clue what he saw in all of us.

"Mom," Brooke called, "I need help changing into my next outfit."

After the shoot was done, we grabbed the pizzas that Bo had ordered and took them home to the hungry masses gathering at my house. *Good grief; how is he so good at this?*

Chapter 18

W E WALKED INTO THE HOUSE, and my dad was there, along with Luke, his friends, Tea, and her little friend. Whit was practicing drums. *Yep. Bo is really getting a test run this weekend. Better to know upfront so he can get out while he can.*

I introduced him to my dad, and they hit it off. I knew they would. My dad is a small-town rancher, quiet, and wise. He had driven in from West Texas to spend a few days with us. He never liked leaving all his cows, horses, barn cats, and hunting dogs for very long. I smiled thinking about what an interesting childhood I had had. It was lonely except for all the animals.

I sat at the big dining-room table and watched Bo and my dad talk. The kids eventually pulled out Trivial Pursuit because they were determined to beat my dad. He never lost. I always said that he was the smartest guy I knew. Bo looked at me like, *Are you serious?*

I shrugged and said, "No pressure. My dad always wins."

"Not today!" yelled Luke.

"You say that every time, and he does," Tea challenged. She started to run but Luke caught her, picked her up, and threw her onto the couch. Screams were heard for miles. I smiled apologetically at Bo.

We taught Bo the Parker rules for speed Trivial Pursuit. Basically, if the person whose turn it was couldn't answer the question correctly, the person to his or her right could try. If that person got it wrong, it went to the next person. While I never seemed to be able to answer my own questions, I was uncanny at answering everyone else's. But my dad won again because he could answer both his question and everyone else's. Bo held his own in the chaos of the game. There was cheating, kicks under the table, pantomiming answers, and straight-up yelling. My kids were loud and competitive.

After the game and dinner, Whit and his friend played outside, and Tea and her friend sang and danced. Luke and Brooke sat down with me, Bo, and my dad as we talked about the ranch. Brooke loved to paint out there and planned to go keep my dad company in the summer. Luke and I had always liked to hike around and explore the place. I knew that Bo would absolutely love it.

Chapter 19

I T WAS GETTING LATE, AND everyone started to head home. Parents came to pick up the extra kids. I walked Bo out to his truck. He had kept a house he had renovated himself in our town. He stayed there whenever he was back for a visit. And I guessed he left his truck there too. We had never really talked logistics because there was always so much other stuff going on.

"Well," I said, "I can understand if you need to never come back. You have my blessing. I wish I could say it isn't normally that loud, but." I laughed nervously. I was nervous that he would say that we were too much and this getting to know you thing, whatever it was, wouldn't work out.

"El, it was great. I loved meeting your dad and watching all the family dynamics. Your dad and I could talk ranching and hunting all night long." He smiled. He seemed genuinely happy. We were standing right next to his truck—the same one I had crawled under to look for our puppy Bingo four years earlier. It literally felt like two lifetimes ago.

I looked up at him, and my stomach did that flutter thing. I wasn't sure what to do with my hands or what to say. I reverted to my southern manners and said, "Thank you so much for coming over and helping me get through this day."

Bo looked down at my hands. "Did you know that you start wringing your hands when you are nervous?"

"Oh, do I?" I looked down at my hands. I looked up at him. I felt myself blushing. "I guess I do. Remember, I did grow up as an only child and alone on a ranch. I sometimes wondered, throughout my life, if my social skills were a little off because of that. I joke I was raised by cattle and barn cats. I have a theory that I picked sociology to study, hoping it would give me some social interaction clues." We both started laughing.

Bo took my hands and said, "I will see you tomorrow. Thank you for letting me be part of your family today and tomorrow. I know it can't be easy letting someone in."

"It isn't. Thank you for acknowledging that." I looked straight into his eyes. And he gave my hands a squeeze. Then he waved as he walked to his truck.

Later that night, Luke came into my room and flopped onto my bed between a snoring Tea and me. "So, mom, what is the deal with you and Bo?"

I put down my book. "I don't know. I mean, what do you think?" I asked tentatively. I knew that I probably cared too much about what my children thought of Bo. I just wanted them to know that I heard and saw them when the rest of the world seemed to have moved on from Tommy's death.

"I like him." Luke smiled at me. "He is a good guy. I talked to him about all his jobs and adventures around the world. He really has lived his life. I think he's ready to settle down. How old is he?"

"Thirty-seven or thirty-eight, I think. And he has mentioned he is ready to stay in one place for a while," I answered.

"Mom, I think he genuinely likes being around you. You smile more when he is around. Y'all should talk about dating and pray about it."

"Honestly, just thinking about dating seems a little overwhelming," I said.

"Mom, if you need my approval, I approve. It would be nice to know there is a man around here to take care of you and the kids. I wouldn't worry so much."

"Oh, Luke, please don't worry." I never wanted him to feel responsible for me and all of us.

"Mom, stop. It is my job now. I know that God will release me from it someday," Luke said as he settled into my bed to watch a movie. I looked over at him. He was my responsible firstborn. I smiled and picked my book back up.

Chapter 20

I WOKE UP EXCITED ABOUT EASTER Sunday. I started singing as soon as my feet hit the floor. Tea was in bed next to me as usual. She rolled over and said, "Happy Easter, Momma!" I gave her a big hug. "What are you singing again?" she asked.

"I am doing mostly backup except for the last song 'Jesus Paid It All.'"[9]

"Do you yell sing that one?" she asked.

"Only a little," I answered. She mimicked the yell singing as she wandered into the kitchen. I was pretty sure she was trying to wake up everyone in the house. When she looked back at me, I put my finger to my lips. In defiance, she kept singing. That kid would probably give me a run for my money as a teenager.

She showed back up in my room all dressed in her new Easter outfit with breakfast in hand. "I am coming with you early," she announced. Knowing Tea, I was not going to be able to talk her out of it.

"Ok, but you can't run around like a wild child, so promise me you will find out who needs help setting up. And you look beautiful," I said.

"I know," she said as she pranced away in her dark-pink swing dress, jean jacket, and sandals.

Everyone else would meet us at the last service. I grabbed a plant protein smoothie. I was going to need it in order to get through three services. I warmed up my voice in the car. Tea warmed up with me. She had a very sweet voice with good pitch. Any type of singing she pursued would have to be her idea and not mine. I sighed. She was the epitome of the strong-willed child.

I had been told that I sound a lot like the worship singer Kim Walker-Smith. "Jesus Paid it All" was one of my favorites and a perfect Easter song.

> Jesus paid it all.
> All to him I owe.
> Sin had left a crimson stain.
> He washed it white as snow.

My favorite part was the refrain, "Oh praise the one who paid my debt and raises life up from the dead." *Yes, Lord. You raise up life. You change destinies, God. You rewrite stories. You take dead things and make them new.*

Chapter 21

DURING MORNING PRACTICE, I SAW Tea running around with her little friends with donuts in hand and then breakfast tacos. *Can those girls eat!* I wanted to get a picture of those cutie-pie girls in their Easter dresses, so I went to look for them after the sound check was done. The first service was starting in fifteen minutes. I caught my reflection in the glass of the foyer. My hair was behaving itself thanks to bobby pins. It was pulled back in a low ponytail. I had fun, new, dangling earrings framing my face. I was wearing a light pink, sleeveless, high-necked, lace shell with dark-gray pants and pink sandals with a three-inch heel. It was a higher heel than I would normally wear, but fashion trumped comfort on Easter.

"You look great, Ellie. Happy Easter!"

I turned around and saw that it was Randall Harmon. "Oh, thank you, Randall. I wanted to make sure I was put together OK since I will be on stage in a few minutes," I said with my friendly yet cautious smile. He was one of the several single dads I had been avoiding for a year. I felt as though I hadn't given anyone a fair chance, but the thought of dating just sounded exhausting. I had no idea what I was doing with Bo. Because he lived far away and was showed up randomly, it didn't feel like dating.

Randall and I talked about Easter plans. I could feel him directing the conversation toward the next weekend's plans. I kept smiling. I didn't want to say no to a date, especially on Easter. *Ugh, why does it feel like literally nothing has changed since middle school? Nothing.*

Randall weaved the ask into the conversation. "Next Saturday, if you aren't busy, I was wondering if you wanted to go see the new Avenger movie with my girls. Feel free to bring your kids along too."

"Oh, that is so nice of you to ask. I ... um ... I am ... I have no idea what is happening in the Avenger movies."

"Not to worry. We can go get dinner first and get you up to date," he said.

"Oh." I walked right into that one. And I used the word *oh* way too much when I was uncomfortable.

"Hi there." Bo came up beside me and put out his hand. "I'm Bo Channing." *Thank goodness.* I inwardly sighed with relief. Randall introduced himself, and Bo got him talking about fishing. I noticed the time and excused myself. Bo smoothly got out of the conversation and caught up with me as I walked into the sanctuary. He casually put his hand on my back, and we went through the double doors. Once inside, I started to laugh.

"Bo, he was asking me out. See what happens when I move my ring to my right hand? I am still an awkward middle schooler when it comes to that stuff. I get embarrassed so easily."

Bo leaned over and whispered, "I walked in and saw you shifting your weight and wringing your hands, but other than that, you looked perfectly normal."

"Ha, ha, ha," I said joking with him. The way he made me feel surprised me. When he was next to me talking or saying nothing, it was so comfortable like I had known him forever or we were good friends a long time ago. When we saw each other, we picked up where we left off.

"I didn't expect to see you this early."

"I was up and wanted to be in church. Happy Easter! You are going to do great." Bo gave me a quick hug.

"Thank you. And can you locate Tea for me and tell her she can sit with you or her friend? I'm fine with either."

"Got it. And you look beautiful." Bo winked at me and then went off to find Tea.

As I walked toward the stage, it struck me that all men made me so uncomfortable—even nice men who loved Jesus. They all did except for Bo. He just made me blush. I guessed that I trusted him a whole lot. I trusted that he would look to God's Word for direction regarding our relationship. He was humble enough to know he didn't have all the answers. And that quality brought me peace.

I grabbed my earpiece and microphone and walked onto the stage. Looking out over the crowd coming in for the service, I couldn't stop smiling. The band was warming up, and we all started clapping. *Thank you, Jesus, for Bo.* I didn't really understand what was happening, but I felt more hopeful and peaceful than I had in a long time.

Adam got to the lead mic and said, "Let's go!"

Chapter 22

I WAS PRETTY WIPED OUT AFTER three services, but I perked up when I came home to a beautiful Easter spread of food. I walked in and gave Katie and her girls a big hug. "Thank you for doing this. It means a lot."

"Thank you for singing your heart out today. That song was amazing. And I can't wait to hang out with Bo. I have questions to ask him." Katie raised her eyebrows, and I laughed. Since we were in sixth grade, we had always allowed our possible crushes to be interrogated by each other. Bo could totally handle it. Katie was a big softie when she wanted to be anyway. Later, I saw her corner him by the basket of rolls.

We were all sitting around my big dining room table. Katie's girls and my kids were playing inside. I loved all the noise, commotion, and the sound of silverware on plates and cups being placed down on the table. I had forgotten what it felts like to have a celebratory Easter full of family and friends.

After lunch we all changed and went outside to the sand volleyball court for our annual family, not-so-friendly tournament. Teams were picked, and my dad was the referee. Luke had designed the tournament and picked the rotating teams and prizes. For the warm-up, we played family versus family and then boys versus girls. Those games were hilarious. I laughed so much that my sides were hurting. Bo, of course, was a good player. And I was quick to the ball. The way Luke created the rotations, we played against each other first. Landry and I were up against Bo and Tea for the first round. Then it was the best two out of three. We lost two to one. We were off the court for a while as Luke and Kylie played against Brooke and Whit.

Bo found me by the bottled water and commented, "I had no idea you were so competitive! You have a very intense look about you on the court. You must have sand all over you, as many times as you dived for the ball." He seemed impressed.

I laughed and said, "The Parkers look calm and easygoing until there is a sporting event."

Bo smiled at me. His face was tan, his brown eyes twinkled in the sun, and his blond hair peeked out from under his baseball hat. He had a kind smile. I could just stare at him sometimes.

Katie and John walked over. "OK, OK, you two can stop smiling at each other." She gave me a hug. "So what are we all doing next weekend?"

I turned to Bo and said, "I think she likes you."

"Look, I am just happy that Ellie won't have to be the third wheel to John and me anymore. That is all. Do not get excited," Katie said snarkily. We both started to giggle.

John said, "Listen, Bo, you need to understand that with those two, it is a package deal." We nodded together. "Joined at the hip since the day I met them. I had to convince Katie not to invite Ellie on our honeymoon!"

Katie jumped in, saying, "Not true. Well, half true anyway."

John looked at Bo. "Consider yourself warned."

"I told you I would get the condo next door. I don't know why you still act like that would be intrusive." I pretended to still be hurt over it.

Luke said, "Team red to the court. I need Bo and Ellie to get over here before I forfeit on your behalf. And Katie, you need to get over here so it will look fair when I beat them." He had my competitive spirit.

Bo jogged up beside me and said, "Come on. Let's do this!" We raced to the court. We barely beat Luke and Katie. It was so much fun. I went and sat down by the pool with the kids. I was tired. I could feel the sun on my face, and I closed my eyes. Everything felt so good and so right—as it should. Nothing made a momma's heart happier than to see all her kids at home, laughing and playing in the backyard. After such a rough few years, we all deserved these moments. I soaked it in.

Chapter 23

I WAS STARTLED AWAKE. BO WAS sitting on my lounge chair by the pool. "I'm sorry to wake you." He was looking at me in his way, and I couldn't ever figure out what he was thinking.

"Oh. It's OK. I'm so sorry I fell asleep. I need to work on my hosting skills."

Bo smiled. "You have had a long day. I am going to head out in a minute. I just wanted to tell you what a great weekend I have had. Thank you for inviting me over today."

I rubbed my eyes and pulled my knees to my chest. I looked up at him and smiled. "I am so glad you came. What is your plan for the next month?"

"Well, I am going to go home and look at some numbers. I was talking to your dad about the property and how much it is worth. He is so wise."

I nodded in agreement. "He was a lifesaver in dealing with all the accounts, investments, and insurance after Tommy died. I surely would have drowned in a spreadsheet without him." *Shoot. Do I talk about Tommy too much? Is that a turnoff?*

Bo didn't bat an eyelash. "I'm going to put an offer on the property and hopefully start closing up my Florida business. Ultimately, it is in God's hands."

"Agree and amen," I replied. I noticed that we were sitting really close to each other. He smelled like sunscreen, sunshine, and a little leftover aftershave. I felt that pull and force between us. Just being near him made me want to be even closer. I looked at him, and I could tell he felt it too.

"Your nose got a little pink today. Probably from your nap in the sun."

"Oh shoot, it probably did," I said as I touched my nose. "I have to warn you that I am one of those people who can fall asleep anywhere. I think it stems from being a mom of four kids who didn't get a restful night's sleep for years. My body is trained to grab sleep wherever it can find it."

"So on car trips you are probably worthless?" Bo asked jokingly.

"I'm out before we get out of the neighborhood," I quipped back. We both laughed.

"I admire the fact that you went to school and raised kids. You did both things well. Your kids are great people. I see different pieces of you in each of them," Bo said and gently took the hand that was wrapped around my knees. I knew he was about to say goodbye. And I felt very emotional about him leaving. Having him near me for a weekend made it more difficult to watch him leave. And I was trying to keep my emotions in check so that I could approach this possible relationship rationally. My strategy wasn't working very well.

He looked down at my hand like he was thinking about what to say. I was looking at him intently when he lifted his head and smiled at me. Tears started to fill my eyes. He reached up to my cheek like he had that night after the wedding and moved his thumb down my cheekbone to my chin. "Goodbye, beautiful," he said. "I will see you again soon."

"OK. Goodbye, Bo. Be safe."

Chapter 24

A FEW DAYS LATER, BO CALLED and said that he had put an offer on the property he had come to look at over Easter, and the sellers accepted. He described it to me, and it sounded amazing. It was up on a hill, and it had a beautiful view of the sunrise and sunset. There were ten acres in the hill country of Texas—off the beaten path.

It did make me nervous when I thought of him being back in my town permanently. *What would that look like?* The long distance, no matter what it was, was a very emotionally safe place for me. *What if once he moves back and realizes he doesn't like me, but he just liked the idea of me?*

I felt a little nauseous. I had wondered if I was too much for Tommy. I cried, laughed, and yelled. I ignored, hugged, demanded, and gave. *Maybe all he wanted was peace and quiet.* I had too many kids and too many emotions. *Maybe all of it led to his heart attack. Maybe it was me. I caused it.* It seemed easier to blame myself for it because if it wasn't me, I didn't know who to blame.

I could blame God and wonder how He could allow something so cruel to happen to my children, or I could blame something eviler. I could blame the one who was said to wander this planet focused on killing, stealing, and destroying. I shivered at the thought.

In theory, I could say that I believed there was an evil one. But when the worst thing happened to your family, Satan could become very real, very quickly. It made this world seem so unsafe and so frightening. Therefore, I blamed myself, knowing that wasn't the answer that I would ultimately settle on.

It was near the end of April, and the sun was warm. I was sitting outside watching Tea on the trampoline. She was practicing her tumbling for cheerleading. My blue heeler Bingo lay down beside me. It was a perfect day.

Tea ran up for a drink. She sat down across from me and asked, "Mom, what are you thinking about?"

"Hmmmm. I am thinking about Daddy. I am thinking about life. I am thinking about Bo. Just trying to figure things out." I always tried to be honest with my kids so that when I asked them what they were thinking, they would answer honestly too.

"Do you think Daddy is missing us or not missing us like we miss him?" Her eyes began to fill with tears, and her bottom lip started to pout. I motioned her to come hug me. As I stroked her dark hair, I thought about what to say.

"I don't think he misses us because heaven is a place of no more tears and sorrow. I think he is excitedly waiting for us, to greet us and show us around. Maybe. It is hard to know exactly," I answered.

"Do you think Daddy would like Bo?" she continued. I stared at her heart-shaped face, light-blue eyes, and dark long hair pulled back in a ponytail. They were all of Tommy's features except that she had my face shape.

"Daddy met Bo when he was working across the street, remember? And yes, I think they liked each other. They didn't know each other very well," I said. I couldn't quite look her in the eye. My guilt had reared its ugly head.

"Then Bo moved away, and Daddy died. And now Bo is back. Is he your boyfriend?" she asked.

I took a deep breath. "Bo is back, but we are not boyfriend and girlfriend. We are good friends. I feel like I have known him forever like Katie. They are both really good friends to me. But I don't want to say that I will never date him. I am not sure. So I am praying that

God, who knows what is best for me and for all of us, will give me wisdom and knowledge. I truly want to do what is wise and best for all of us."

Tea listened intently. She paused for a minute and then said, "I think you should date him. You smile a lot when he is around. I think that means he makes you happy like Katie. But you can't date her, so."

There you have it. I laughed. I reached for her and gave her a squeeze. "You, my little love bug, make me so very happy too."

"Well, you can't date me either, so Bo is going to have to be the one."

"Mmmmm, well, we will see." Then she ran off to practice her back handsprings. She was the second kid to tell me that I smile more. *Have I hardly been smiling?* I wondered. I had really hoped I was projecting that I was more than OK. I wasn't as good of an actress as I had thought. I sighed.

Chapter 25

I CALLED BO THAT NIGHT. I had been holding back and not calling him very often. It wouldn't have been fair to him since I was still trying to figure out what I wanted. I had concluded that I did enjoy having an adult friend who was available to talk to. It had felt amazing when he had been there over Easter. I enjoyed having an adult friend to help me. I hadn't realized how much I missed that partner aspect of marriage. I had also concluded that Bo was so intelligent, kind, patient, and ridiculously handsome. I knew me—once I decided to date him, I would be all in. There would be no turning back. Or if there was any turning back, it would be incredibly painful.

I appreciated him so much. I most appreciated how he could tell me that he wanted to spend time with me and get to know me and my family more but could be a perfect gentleman and put no kind of pressure on me to reciprocate. Half the time, I just wanted to catch a flight to where he was in Florida and spend days and nights with him until I knew every single thing about him, spiritually, emotionally, and physically. *Yep. Everything.*

He answered the phone with, "Hey, there. I was just sitting on my back porch watching the sun set on the ocean and thinking about you."

"Sounds beautiful."

"I will send you a picture of it. Probably won't do it justice."

"Can't wait to see it. How are you? How are all your plans coming along?"

"Great! I am hoping to be back by the end of May. I will be staying at my house in town while I get plans drawn up for the house I want to build and slowly restart my custom building business."

"That sounds perfect. I am so happy for you," I replied.

We talked about my last few days, and I told him about Tea's and my whole conversation. "It makes me sad that she is watching me so closely, making sure I am OK, and seeing if I am smiling," I continued.

"El, all of your kids are watching you all the time. I see it. I think it shows how much they love and care for you."

I was listening to Bo's voice. His East Texas drawl and the way he called me El was so calming. It was such a pleasant sound. It made me want to curl up in it and take a nap.

"I am glad that you smile more when I am around. And I hate to be the one to tell you, but your face hides nothing."

"Nothing? Really, not anything?" I asked.

"Sorry, but no," Bo said.

"Well, rats," I responded as I laughed. "I tried, but Luke said almost the exact same thing about me smiling more when you are around. Anyway, I feel like I have some insight into how at least two of my kids feel about the possibility of us really dating."

"What are you afraid of with your kids and me?" Bo asked

"A lot of things. For one, I have never dated with kids. And maybe it isn't healthy, but I would want their approval—the green light. But also, I am afraid of having an audience watching me possibly stumble through a relationship, and it end badly. Any experience I had in dating was over twenty years ago. It ended real fast, as in pregnancy and marriage."

Bo responded graciously as always, "I hear you. Before seriously dating, it would be nice to have a 100-percent guarantee that it would all work out. I have fears too like what if I fail again at a relationship. Since I got divorced, I haven't been able to make any relationship stick. And it is probably me. You probably know that I was married eight years ago."

"Mmmmhmmm. If you are trying to make me feel better, this isn't the best way," I said as I laughed. He laughed with me.

"I'm definitely not helping my case. It is hard to know with any certainty." Bo sighed. "I do think the fact that we have known each other for a long time and that you want to just slowly move into a dating relationship is helpful, which gives us time to make prayerful decisions. Also, I see your heart for the Lord, in your singing, how you raise your family, and in your daily decisions. All of that offers me a peace that you are more than worth taking a chance on."

"What if I am afraid that once you get to know me better and see the sin side of me—because it is there, big and ugly—you will say, 'Never mind. You aren't what I thought,'" I hypothesized. "In a nutshell, I fear rejection. Because of that, I am picky about who I let into my life. Once I let you in, I am committed to building something that will last, be it a friendship or something else. You are the only male person I have let into my world besides Tommy and my dad."

"First, I am in the company of great men. And I mean it. Second, have you met yourself?" he asked, and I laughed. "You are beautiful and smart. You are funny and athletic. You love Jesus, and your kids are amazing. The line of those who have rejected you has to be very tiny."

"Hmmm, I wonder if in my mind, I think that death is a rejection of me instead of just death. My mom died when I was so young and then Tommy. I will have to think about that. Can you tell me more about your marriage?" I asked tentatively.

"Short version is we lasted for a year. She was from Dallas, and it was culture shock to her. I was not following God's word at the time. I would go to Dallas and stay with her every weekend. After we got married, I moved her down here. She didn't like the smaller, more relaxed, small-town life. And I didn't really understand why she was miserable. I didn't try to understand, I should say. I learned

81

some hard lessons being in that relationship. I am grateful that God showed me all the ways I failed, in His patient and kind way. But it was really humbling."

"Bo, I am sorry. That sounds really tough," I said. I thought that there must be more to the story, but it was his business and not mine; at least, not mine right now. "I think just being married is humbling because it is not all about you anymore. You realize how selfish and self-centered you really are and how much you need Jesus every minute of every day in order to share a life with someone," I added.

"Yep," Bo agreed. "And one big lesson I learned is that when physical intimacy comes before emotional and spiritual intimacy, you are playing catchup, and everything feels out of whack."

I agreed 1000 percent. "And then getting pregnant and married before you have any idea about emotional or spiritual intimacy makes the relationship a big struggle," I added.

"Mmhmm," Bo said, which wasn't a response I had ever heard from him.

Yeah. There is something there, but clearly, he doesn't want to tell me yet.

"Bo, thank you for being patient with me and not pushing me to make a decision. I want you to know I am praying about us and any baggage that I have from the last few years. I want to walk into a relationship with you with a heart of peace and rest. I am making progress. Some days I am getting a glimpse of that fun and joy-filled person I used to be. And it is usually when you are around."

We moved onto other topics, but I felt such a peace as we ended our conversation. While it was exhausting to talk about relationships, it probably did keep most of the heartache out of it in the end.

PART 3

PART 3

Chapter 26

IN EARLY MAY, BO WAS sitting at my kitchen table, helping Whit with his algebra 2 homework. It was an answer to prayer because I was useless with algebra. Bo was on top of it, and he explained all of it. I couldn't stop thanking God and smiling. I was sitting on my couch, grading final exams. I was wearing my fun jeans with two holes in the knees and sparkling patches inside the holes. and a white tank top. My bare feet were propped up on the coffee table. Bo's presence in my life was becoming very comfortable.

Brooke was in the kitchen with Katie's girls, baking cookies and planning her graduation party. She had always loved to plan parties and decorate, so I just gave her a budget, and she did everything. Tea was working on her birthday list. I couldn't believe she was going to be twelve and going into middle school.

My house was busy with voices, laughter, and cookie smells. I was in my happy place. I tried to focus on the last few finals. I had to turn in grades by midnight. Bo had been back for a few weeks. He had been busy with the closing on his new property and getting resettled in Texas. We had met for lunch a few times and had gone out to dinner, but we hung out at my house most nights because that is where my kids were.

A few minutes later, Bo snuggled in beside me really close. He smelled so good. It was slightly intoxicating. "Hey!" I said as

I looked at him and smiled. He put his arm around me, and the hand around my shoulder held a box tied with a white ribbon. I looked back at him, and he was grinning big-time. "What is this? "I asked.

"Well, a little birdy told me you have a birthday in two days, and I will be out of town." He looked like a little kid. He was so pleased with himself. Meanwhile, I had done everything I could to forget that I was rapidly moving through my forties.

"Wow! Hmmm, I wonder who the little birdy was that told you this?" I looked over my shoulder at my Teadora, who couldn't keep a secret to save her life.

"I said nothing!" she said vehemently. Then she burst into giggles.

All the kids came over to the couch and started chanting, "Open it! Open it!"

I untied the beautiful bow and pulled off the cover. Inside, there was a pair of diamond earrings in a white gold setting. They were stunning. I gasped quietly. I turned to look at Bo in shock. I had told Bo a while ago that I had lost my diamond earrings that my grandmother had given me.

All the girls were gathering around and oohing and awing. Whit was smiling like he knew already. Bo was smiling. He leaned over to my ear and whispered, "That was exactly the reaction I was hoping for."

"They are beautiful," I said as I stared at them.

"I am glad you like them," he replied.

"Thank you," I said as I put my hand on his thigh and intentionally looked at him. I surprised myself. It was just a natural reaction to touch and connect with him. It was the first time I had really initiated any type of physical touch.

"Now I need to know who told you about this birth date." I looked around and saw Tea duck behind the couch. Whit joined her. *Ah ha!*

I put the earrings on and started to feel uncomfortable with all the attention on me. When Katie walked into the house, thank goodness, all the attention turned her way. Katie came and sat down for a bit to chat. She always entertained us with her weird skin condition and rashes stories. I leaned back into Bo's arm that was up on the couch behind me. And I turned my head to look at him. He was so gentle and kind to me.

Chapter 27

I T WAS A SCHOOL NIGHT, and the kids needed to get to bed. I walked Bo out to the driveway. It was one of those late spring nights in Texas where the stars are bright, and a breeze brings a hint of summer warmth to come. And I didn't want the night to end. The cool night air felt intoxicating.

I thanked Bo again for the gift. I really did love them. I hoped I had expressed that. We hugged. He was going on a fishing expedition with some family and friends for the next two weeks.

"They look amazing on you. They catch that sparkle in your eyes perfectly," he said while he hugged me. I held on for an extra second. I realized I was usually the first to back away. I grabbed both his hands. "Thank you for everything tonight."

Bo took his hand and slowly went up my shoulder to my ears and then to my cheek. He moved it to my hair and tucked a curl behind my ear. "You know, a few months ago, leaving for two weeks sounded like a great idea. For the first time in my life, I am questioning my leaving to go do something that I love to do."

I took his hand from my cheek and held it. "We will all miss you. You will have a wonderful time, and I can't wait to hear all about it when you get back." I smiled big for him. He was just amazing. He hugged me again and then picked me up. I laughed.

He put me down and said, "Have an amazing birthday."

Katie kept texting me. She wanted to talk about his gift to me.

Chapter 28

KATIE AND I HAD MET at a forced gathering initiated by our dads. Katie was new in town, and my dad was worried about me. I was going into sixth grade, and I only had farm animals as my friends. I was quiet and shy, partly because that was just my nature but also because I struggled to relate to other girls because I didn't have a mom. It felt like there was a secret handshake, and I didn't know what it was. I always felt like I didn't fit in.

Katie's mom brought her over to our house on a rainy Saturday in August. I remembered looking out the window as they drove up. I was interested in making friends, but I was picky and naturally awkward with two-legged humans. I didn't remember my first impression of her except that she loved animals. So I showed her all of our animals as we splashed in mud and held our umbrellas. We sat in the hay barn with the cats and talked. We both liked to read, dance, and sing. And from then on, we did everything together.

We survived middle school and got to high school. We played soccer together, danced on the same dance team together, and sang in the choir. We would go to church and youth group together every Sunday and Wednesday. Her parents were warm and welcoming. And her mom, Barbara, became a safe place for me to be mothered. If I needed to cry or just a hug, I would walk up to her, and she would just envelop me in her arms.

In high school, Katie was the fun loud one, and I was the quiet wallflower. Katie was much more outgoing than I was and smarter. She had a billion friends. I felt lucky that I got to hang around her and them. Sometimes people thought we were sisters because we were about the same height, and we both had freckles. Her hair, however, was auburn and straight while mine was blond and curly. Katie would always put a hand on her hip and said, "Now do you really think I would hang out with my sister?" And we would giggle and walk away.

Since the day I met her, we had done every holiday together—even as adults. The only time we were apart was in college. We ended up going to different colleges because I was given a soccer scholarship at a small university, and she was doing premed at a big university.

While she was in medical school, I got married, became pregnant for a second time, and worked on my master's and PhD. We graduated at the same time and forced our husbands to move to the same city. It was the best decision we ever made.

She had been my absolute rock those last two years. But I knew it wasn't fair to put everything on her. She had her own family and medical practice. She never complained about me calling her in the middle of the night because I couldn't sleep, helping me get the kids to their activities, or standing beside me as I figured out how to do everything on my own. No wonder she liked Bo so much. She needed to not be that person for me anymore.

Chapter 29

IT WAS A STRANGE TWO weeks. I literally kept thinking that I was missing something. I kept checking my phone, wallet, and calendar for missed appointments, but I realized by the second day that I was just missing him. I was super productive, though. I had decided to take the summer off from teaching. I would still work on articles and research with my grad students. There was just so much happening with my kids, and I wanted to be a part of it. Tommy was always very responsible with money. He had good life insurance and left me with enough so that I could work and have extra. I paid off the house and all the cars with his life insurance. All the kids had well-endowed college accounts. God had taken care of us.

Tea's dance recital was the next weekend, along with Whit's music recital. Then Luke was graduating that weekend. And Brooke's graduation and party were over Memorial weekend. After that, we would head to the ranch for rodeo weekend. I was thinking about inviting Bo. My dad was the one who asked me if he was coming. It struck me as funny that those two had hit it off. My dad and Tommy had a stiffer relationship. Their common ground was finances, the stock market, and investments. Tommy and Bo were such different people. But I was also different from what I was twenty years earlier when I met Tommy.

I was thinking about all those things as I cleaned out my car. I really enjoyed vacuuming, dusting, and glass and leather cleaning. I was washing off the floor mats in the driveway when Bo pulled in. I didn't think I would see him until the following day. He must have just gotten home and come right over. I felt like my heart would burst with happiness when he stepped out of his truck. I turned the water off and ran up to him. It hit me as I was running over to him that I only had a tankini top, board shorts, and Tevas on.

I jumped into his arms, and he spun me around. We were both laughing. "You are wet," he commented as he let me go.

"I didn't think you were coming over today, or I would have been drier."

"I know. I just had to," Bo said. "It was just wild how much I missed you. I wanted to drive straight to your house from the airport. I did call."

"Oh, shoot, my phone is in the house. I am sorry I missed it." I was just staring at him and smiling. "I missed you too," I said.

"I didn't know about this hidden talent you have of cleaning cars," Bo said as he ran his hand over the hood. He washed his truck daily. I realized that I had found the way to his heart: clean cars. He turned to me and asked, "Can we go out to dinner tonight? My parents are in town since my dad went with us on the fishing trip," he said.

"Umm, sure. Where are we going so that I can dress appropriately?" I said as I gestured to my outfit.

"I like your outfit," he said while smiling. I started to feel warm. I couldn't look him in the eye. "However, you would probably be more comfortable in something else. We have reservations at the Italian place right outside of town."

"Oh yummmmm. It's my favorite."

Chapter 30

I LET BO PICK ME UP and drive me to the restaurant. It was like a real date. Almost every time we did something together, we would meet there. It was because of my busy kids and their schedules, but it was also because it felt safer to be in control of a situation by having my own car. I always told Brooke that if a guy you do not know asked you out, you met him at a restaurant. It was important to always have your own car. Then you had the control. I hadn't known to do that, so when I was young and in college, I had some incidents that I couldn't get out of as easily because I didn't have a car. Now there was Uber and Lyft, but I was old school. I wanted my car.

Bo pulled up, and I hopped up into his truck. I was wearing light-colored skinny jeans, little strappy tan-heeled sandals, and an off-white summer sweater where my shoulders peaked out. I had on the diamond earrings he gave me for my birthday and a bracelet with a matching necklace. I had my hair pulled up on the top of my head with curls falling around my face. I could tell he noticed that I actually took time to dress up a little.

"You look so great," he said as he smiled at me. I snuggled close to him. "You smell good." I really did miss him. I told him about feeling like I had been missing something for two weeks and how strange it was to see myself walking around the house and wondering what I was missing.

We talked about Tea's birthday party that weekend, which would be after Luke's graduation. And Bo was going to sit through some of the dance recital with me. Tea was on the dance team and performance teams, and then she had her own classes. It was a whole day, three shows, and a complete time suck.

Bo laughed as I described recital days. There were eleven costumes, eleven hairstyles, and eleven everything—makeup and shoes. It was absurd. We talked about Luke's graduation and his birthday on the following week. He would be twenty-two and off the Parker payroll. He was going to be a teacher and a soccer, track, and football coach at Riverview Christian Academy, mainly working with junior-high-aged kids. I knew that he would be absolutely perfect for that job. And it was only forty minutes away. I was just chatting away and sitting a little sideways so that I could look at him while he drove, and we talked.

Bo parked at the restaurant, looked at me, and said, "I am fairly certain this is the most I have ever heard you talk."

He was smiling at me, and he winked. *Cutie.*

"And I love that you are sharing all these plans and your excitement with me. I hope you aren't all talked out. We have a two-hour dinner ahead of us." He smiled.

"I am so sorr—

"No apology. I loved every minute of hearing what went on inside that incredible mind of yours. You are usually quieter and more contemplative, which I also love. But sometimes it's nice for me to get a look inside."

We laughed and continued to make fun of ourselves as we walked toward the restaurant, on the gravel path, around the fountains, and to the lighted restaurant. When I impulsively grabbed his hand and intertwined my fingers with his, he looked at me with a smile. I forgot what touching him did to me. I would get warm and feel outside of my head like I could fly. *Endorphins, I guess.* I felt as if I could handle anything if he was standing next to me.

As we walked up the hill to the restaurant, we were laughing. When we got close to the restaurant, there was a group waiting outside, and they were all staring at us. I smiled back and then realized Bo's parents were there. Some guy said, "Well, if it isn't Ken and Barbie." I must have looked confused because I was.

"Good to see you, Uncle Pat." Bo hugged him. "And you, too, Aunt Jane."

"My word, Bo, you and your friend here just sparkled as you walked up the path with that sunset behind you. We were all enthralled. You both look like you were out of a movie. Please introduce me to your beautiful friend."

I was introduced to Aunt Jane, whom I liked immediately. She had that way about her that made you feel like a long-lost friend. I met Uncle Pat and hugged Bo's parents, David and Sarah. It was so nice to see them again. There was also another couple who were old friends of the family, Sally and Joe.

As we were walking to our table, I hung back with Bo, turned to him with my eyes big, and whispered, "You did not tell me this was a family reunion."

He answered with a shrug and a smile. "I had no idea." He looked at his phone. "We were driving when they let me know who was coming so."

We all got settled. I was sitting between Aunt Jane and Bo and across from Sally and Joe. Aunt Jane told me so many stories about Bo as a child. He was shy and sweet, and he loved being outside all the time. I was not surprised at all. Sally was super interesting as she was a child-support investigator who went all over the country finding rich, worthless fathers and made them pay. They were such great stories.

I had a couple of Italian margaritas, which was a lot for me, and I was feeling flushed. I wished my cheeks wouldn't get so pink. I was thoroughly enjoying myself. I was leaning toward Bo and talking to his mom when Bo gently put his hand on my leg under the table. *Holy moly.* All he had to do was touch me once, and I melted into happy, warm little pieces of complicity. It really was not fair. I put my hand on top of his.

Bo's parents were asking about my work and classes, and suddenly, the whole table was listening. I felt like this was my interview for family approval or something like that. I was explaining sociology. "In its simplest form, sociology is the study of human social institutions and social relationships. I teach sociology of sport and social psychology, which deals with social interactions."

"Are you analyzing our social interactions right now?" teased Uncle Pat

"I am officially off the clock, so not right now. But I may jot some notes down later in the evening," I teased back.

"What kind of research are you doing?" asked Bo's mom.

"Well, I like to have my hand in several pots. I am working with some colleagues from the psychology department and school of public health on a research project. We are in the developing stages of research on how sports can be used to heal types of emotional trauma in children. I explained a little more, wondering if I was coming across too boring. Everyone seemed interested. They were nodding and asking questions.

Then Uncle Pat changed the subject to fishing stories. He was making me laugh so hard. Then he turned to Bo. "Bo, here's what I have learned about fishing that I can apply to life: be patient and wait for the right time, and you will hook the best catch in the water. You have caught a beautiful and intelligent lady. Take it from me, don't throw her back expecting something better. Cause there ain't."

Bo said, "Yes, sir," and Uncle Pat winked at me.

Oh, my. I was just compared to a fish. I started laughing.

Aunt Jane patted my hand and said, "You will get used to him, dear. He is loud but lovable." And we giggled.

Uncle Pat continued, "I tried to get her to throw me back cause I know she could do better. But that sweet lady has kept me for thirty-five years."

Wow. I found the topic of marriage and staying together so fascinating. My next project should be on the topic of the sociology of marriage. *How do people figure out how to live with each other when each one is constantly morphing into something newer, wiser, gentler, and different than before? How close has each of the couples here at the table been to divorce? And what made them keep going?*

97

Chapter 31

WE SAID OUR GOODBYES BY one of the beautiful outdoor fountains. Uncle Pat gave me a hug and said, "Bo is a good man, so don't throw him back either. I have seen a lot in my sixty-five years, and there is no man better than him."

I gave Uncle Pat a squeeze and said, "I couldn't agree with you more."

Aunt Jane hugged me and said, "I have such a good feeling about you two. You are just beautiful together."

"Thank you, Jane. It was so lovely to meet you."

I hugged Bo's parents. His mom was quieter than his dad. She had a very calming presence. She pulled me aside and said, "We are so pleased Bo is back in Texas. Thank you for being the one who brought him back. And we look forward to seeing you and your family at church on Sunday. I heard you were singing." She was so sweet.

I watched Bo hug his parents. In that moment, I realized that I respected him so much. He hadn't just turned away from temptation, he had fled the time zone. And I realized that I wasn't the temptation. Satan was tempting him and me. Satan wanted to use us to destroy each other and our families. And God somehow created something amazingly beautiful from it. Tears started to gather in my eyes.

I turned to look at the big Texas sky. I love the Texas hill country. There was nowhere else I would have rather lived. Bo put his hand in the small of my back as we strolled down the path to his truck. I loved how his warm hand felt and the kindness in that gesture. We were both looking up and out over the hills. His hand went gently up my back and over to my shoulder. Did he have to go so slowly and softly? *Sheesh.*

"You were amazing tonight. Thank you for putting up with my family," Bo said.

"Oh, my goodness, they were so much fun. Just maybe next time you could tell me we are going to a family reunion and that I will need to give my dissertation." We were laughing as we reached his truck. I was truly in awe of the stars, the magic of the sky, and how I felt as though I had found a safe, kind, long-lost friend in Bo—and maybe something more.

"El," Bo turned to look at me when we got to his truck. He took a long pause. "This is going to sound cliché, but given that my uncle compared you to a fish tonight, it can't be the worst thing said tonight." I laughed out loud. He grabbed both my hands and started to talk. "You. You are it for me. I have always only wanted you. I want you with all the kids and the whole package. I hadn't planned on saying this tonight. But there is something about being with you, next to you. It is absolutely nothing I have ever felt before. And from your nodding right now, you feel it too. The thing is that it has always been you. I don't think any other relationship in my life has begun or ended well because God knew that today, I would end up holding your hands and telling you what He has always known."

I nodded. I looked straight into his eyes. He was right. I knew exactly what he was saying. I wanted to back away from it. I didn't think I was ready for it. And at the same time, I wanted to run into it. Tears started to well up in my eyes. I wished I didn't cry so easily. I lifted a hand to wipe a stray tear away. He took that hand and continued.

"I just wanted you to know where I stand. I completely get that you might not be ready. And I am OK if you need more time. But if your fear is uncertainty about us and the future, I want to tell you that you are it for me—no matter what."

"I know exactly what you are saying. I feel it. I do," I replied. "But my life is very complicated. My heart has been through a lot, and honestly, it is barely hanging on some days. And while I don't think I am ready for us, a relationship, and all it requires, at the same time, I do want to try."

Bo paused and then said, "I promise I will be very careful with your heart and give you the time you need to get to where I am," he replied.

I leaned forward, put my forehead on his chest, and breathed him in. He was intoxicating. He let go of my hands and put his arms around me. He gave me a kiss on the top of my head. He was so very sweet. I had no idea what I had actually just agreed to, but I was warm and happy.

Chapter 32

WE GOT THROUGH LUKE'S GRADUATION that Friday and Tea's birthday party that Saturday. I was singing at church on Sunday morning. I was utterly exhausted. Ever since the first day I saw Bo at my church, he was there every Sunday that he was in town. He would always ask if he could sit with us. Usually, Katie and her crew sat behind us. She would always raise one eyebrow when she watched our exchange. Katie's kids and my kids loved seeing Bo there, and they were constantly chatting with him. He had built in the area for so many years that he knew almost everyone in our 1,500-person church. He talked more than me after church.

Since we had been seeing each other, I had felt more comfortable staying after church to talk. I realized that in certain settings, I needed an anchor. Katie had always been my anchor until Tommy. And after Tommy died, I felt very uneasy in social settings. I think I made people uneasy because they didn't know what to say to me, and I couldn't think of anything to say to anyone.

That Sunday morning, I saw Bo sitting with his parents and my kids. Everyone was introduced. They chatted over coffee and donuts while I was doing sound checks. It didn't scare me to see him sitting next to Whit and Luke with his parents on his other side.

I walked over to them a few minutes before we started. I was wearing a navy-blue mesh and cutwork shell with white jeans, navy-blue, chunky heels, and big silver hoop earrings. My hair was getting so long that I had it in a single braid with bobby pins holding my curls in place. Tea hopped up to me and gave me a squeeze. "What are you singing today?"

I greeted Bo's parents and gave them a warm smile. "I am so glad you are here. We are singing one of my favorites: 'You Keep Hope Alive.'[10] That song makes me cry every time I sing it. I hope I can get through it. Don't be surprised if you see a tear or two."

Luke knew that song well. Right after Tommy died, we would sit late at night and sing some of the lyrics over and over.

> There is hope in the breaking
> Hope in the sorrow
> Hope for this moment
> My hope for tomorrow.

The "hope in the sorrow" line would get me every time. Hope was what got me and my kids through it. God kept hope alive in each of us. It was solely by His grace that we made it.

Luke came over and hugged me. Bo's mom walked over to me and said, "Your children are just darling. I can see how Bo enjoys each of them. I am sorry this is such a short trip for us. Next time, maybe we can spend more time with you and yours."

I gave her a hug. "I would love that." I heard my name and turned to walk onto the stage.

Chapter 33

I INVITED BO TO COME WITH us to my dad's ranch for rodeo weekend and my childhood stomping grounds. Our small town had a rodeo that came every summer. All my kids had gone every year since they were babies.

We drove two cars. Whit and Tea rode with Bo and me in Bo's truck. Brooke and Luke drove my car with several of their friends. I knew Bo was going to absolutely fall in love with my dad's ranch. Bo hunts all fall and winter and fishes spring and summer. He shopped only at fishing and hunting stores and drove a big diesel truck. He was made for West Texas ranch life. I couldn't wait to see his face as we drove into my dad's place.

As we turned onto the dirt road that leads to the ranch house and drove through the gate, Bo took his sunglasses off and looked around. There was a field to our left full of sorghum. To our right, there were pens for cows and hay-bale storage. The big water tank was straight ahead, and the giant workshop was behind it. Next to the workshop was the barn, and a few barn cats scurried out of the way. We turned left toward the house.

My childhood home was a standard ranch house with a big front porch held up by big white pillars. There were faded green shutters on the windows upstairs. And the front screen door slammed as my dad walked out to greet us.

My dad gave Bo a tour of all one thousand acres after we

unloaded. Bo was in heaven. It looked as though my dad was happier to see Bo than any of us. I had brought dinner, so I got cooking, and all the kids were outside playing with the hunting dogs, barn cats, horses, and new calves. We used to have goats, pigs, and a donkey, but it was too much for my dad. He was turning seventy that year. It was hard to believe. The ranch kept him young and active.

At dinner, all Bo could talk about was the ranch. My dad was so happy to finally have someone to talk about all the ranch things with. I was never very interested in running the ranch or staying in this very small town. But I always loved coming back. My kids loved being there and spent a lot of time outside exploring. When they were younger, we would hike, and everyone would pick the spot where he or she wanted to build a house when older. Tommy did not make it out there often. He worked so much of the time. And I know that he felt pressure to provide for all of us. Working hard was how he loved us.

Bo and I went to sit outside after dinner to watch the kids play a chaotic nighttime game of hide-and-seek around the house and barn. They had invented it when Luke was fifteen, and since then, they have played it every time. There was a lot of screaming from the girls throughout the game.

"El, this place is amazing," Bo said as we rocked in the rocking chairs. No southern front porch was complete without rocking chairs.

"I knew you would love it," I responded with a smile. I really enjoyed seeing him happy.

"I am envious of your childhood," he said while looking out toward the barn. "Growing up out here. I can just see you running around with cowboy boots on, blond curls and freckles, chasing barn cats, and riding horses. I saw your first buck hanging in the house. Your dad said that was your first and last buck and that you never liked shooting too much."

"Yeah, I just did not like guns. But I would go sit with him, my cousins, or uncles, drink coffee, and watch the sun rise."

He looked at me and smiled as he grabbed my hand. "So you will go hunting with me in the fall but just to keep me company in the deer blind?"

"Exactly!"

The next day, I showed him the town. It only took an hour. We sat and watched the annual rodeo parade down the main street. Then we met Katie and her family for lunch at the local drugstore, which served the absolute best milkshakes and burgers. We made plans to meet up at the rodeo in the evening.

Being home always filled me with peace but also reminded me that I had no mom to come home to. I was dreading the rodeo that night, just because all the people that I grew up with would want to talk and catch up. It was an exhausting exercise for an introvert. But I was always glad I came.

I tried to hide next to Bo that evening at the rodeo, but eventually, I had to get up and go to the ladies' room. I joked to Bo that it would take me an hour to make my way back, as I would be stopped by old classmates and friends. He and my dad were busy talking about the price of wheat or something else.

After the rodeo on Saturday night, there was a dance. It was for only eighteen and older, so Katie and John, Bo and I, and Luke and his friend Trent ended up dancing. It was an outdoor dance pavilion with a live band, and we all had such a fun time. I took turns dancing with John, Luke, Trent and Bo. A few guys from high school noticed me not wearing a ring and asked me to dance. Bo was a good sport about it.

The last time we had danced at the wedding, there were so many sparks. And when he pulled me close at the rodeo dance, they were the same sparks, with the added comfort of knowing him better. I didn't worry when he pulled me closer or pulled my hand up to kiss it. I just enjoyed the moment. We got home at midnight and crashed.

Early the next morning, I grabbed some coffee and went to sit out front with my dad. It was our routine and time to talk. He told me several times about how much he liked Bo. He asked what our plans were.

"I am not sure. I just know that we really enjoy each other. He is a good man, dad. But I am not making any decisions. It has taken a lot of work for me to get in a good place, finally getting Tommy's estate settled, and the kids are all OK. I just want to enjoy it for a while with no other life pressure added." And I just wasn't ready to let go fully and love someone. And Bo would be so easy to love. It scared me to even let myself think about it. Maybe it was because the thought of losing someone else—I couldn't even go there.

"Dad, I am going to go see mom and then go by and see Katie's parents."

"OK, honey." He patted my hand. "And there is nothing ever wrong with taking your time getting to know someone if they are willing to stick around for it." I nodded. I noticed how much grayer his hair had gotten in just a few months. He seemed more hunched over and tired. I silently whispered, "Please don't leave me too, Dad."

I got in my car and drove to the cemetery. I pulled up beside the Whitmore family plot. It was right next to the Heath family plot, my mother's family. A giant oak shaded almost both plots completely. When I was younger, I would climb the tree, sit, talk to her or God, and imagine what she would look like a year older. She had red curly hair and blue eyes. She was taller than I was. I was more of the blond, scrawny Whitmore side except for my freckles and curls. I did love that Whit got her red curls. I leaned against the tree and tried to tell her about all her grandkids, me, and Dad. I was worried about him out on that ranch all alone. But all I did was just end up crying. The old feelings of the unfairness of it all crashed over me—of my mom dying from breast cancer when I was five. I knew deep down that she was there for the first five years, the most important years of a child's life. She sang to me all the time. She taught me about God. She read my favorite Bible story over and over again—Joseph and the coat of many colors. Music and Jesus were her legacy in my life.

And I was grateful but also so sad. My heart ached for Mom. I could feel my physical heart hurt when I came to the cemetery.

I wiped my tears and drove over to Katie's parents' house. All the memories of us coming home from school washed over me as I drove down the long driveway to the small brick house. I walked right in out of habit.

"Hello!" I called. I then saw everyone in the backyard. I pushed the sliding glass door open and walked outside.

"Barbara! My second momma!" I went and hugged her from behind. She always smelled like lemons. Both she and Katie's dad, Brad, were retired teachers. She was the high school librarian, and Brad was the junior high principal. Barbara stood up, looked at me for one second, and said, "You were out to see your momma this morning."

I wiped my eyes. "Is it that obvious?"

"Only to me, sweet girl." She wrapped me in a big hug. As I started to shed a few tears, in walked Katie and her youngest, Landry.

"Auntie Ellie, don't cry," said nine-year-old Landry. And she hugged me from behind.

"I might as well pile on," said Katie, and we all ended up giggling.

I sat with Brad and Barbara and had a cup of coffee. They always wanted to know how all my kids were doing. We normally all stopped by, but I needed to be alone this morning.

Katie sat down to join us as Brad got up to leave us for our ladies' chat.

"Now Ellie, I want to hear about this Bo person," Barbara said. I laughed. She always said someone's name and added person whenever she was skeptical. I looked at Katie.

"I have said very little. Not my story to tell." She stuffed a muffin in her mouth so as not to say anything. Clearly, she was dying to talk.

I turned to Barbara and began, "Well, I have known him for a few years. Just as friends. He was living in Florida when Tommy died. He came back recently, and we have been getting to know each other better. That is about it."

Katie started choking on her muffin and then in her dramatic flair declared, "Mom, she is a bold-faced liar. He is hot, he's rich, he loves Jesus, he's younger than her, and is 1000 percent in love with her." I gave her a look, and she said, "I said what I said," and crossed her arms. I threw a napkin at her.

Barbara rolls her eyes. "Nothing has changed with you two. The truth is usually right in the middle." We all started to laugh. She was right, though. I had given the reserved version, and Katie had given the overly imaginative version. After about an hour, I headed back to our ranch.

When I got there, Bo was out in the shop, helping my dad fix something on the trailer. "Hi. I'm back. I am going to go shower and start packing." I had poked my head through the doorway.

Bo walked over to me. He was already sweating in the West Texas heat. He was also wearing a tight T-shirt, and his muscles were showing. Katie was right. He was hot. And I had to work really hard to pretend I didn't notice.

"You, OK? Your dad said you went to see your mom." He looked intently at my face for any signs of tears.

"I am OK. I did see her. and it was good." I wasn't sure if I was talking about my mom or Barbara. They always kind of merged together. I smiled at him. Any resolution I had to keep things between us very chilled went away when he walked toward me as if I were the most interesting person in the world. And the muscles, sweat, and manliness were not helpful.

On the drive home, Tea and Whit fell asleep. I grabbed my pillow and lay down with my head close to Bo. We started talking quietly, and he made me laugh. We ended up talking about parenting styles. He was the youngest, with two older sisters. I was an only child. Both of us spent our childhoods getting our own way on most things, yet we both liked peace and quiet.

I went to a therapist several years ago, and she asked me to describe my dominating emotion as a child. It took a few minutes, but *lonely* was my word. Once Katie and her family came into my life, I wasn't lonely very often. But when I went to college where I knew no one, that heavy feeling of loneliness came back. I knew that my dating Tommy, becoming pregnant, and getting married quickly had to do with not dealing with my own loneliness. I put Band-Aids on it. Interestingly, I married someone who made me often feel lonely in our marriage, which was probably why I had four kids. They filled the void. Then the friendship with Bo for a few years filled a void too. I told him that.

"I am really sorry you were lonely. Maybe I picked up on it and liked being able to fill that space up for you. Do you still feel lonely?"

"Not as often as I used to. When Tommy died, I faced my worst fear: being left alone. And that space is where God met me and taught me that I am never alone. I was never alone. When I looked back over my life, I saw Him always there. He never left me or forsook me."

"Amen," Bo said. "I wanted to tell you that you are a really great mom. I have watched you parent over the years in different situations, and I am always amazed at how much your kids love and respect you, and you them."

"I have great kids. But I had so much insecurity with Luke. I couldn't just call my mom for advice. I really struggled as a first-time mom. I felt like I had no direction. I was the first of my friends to have kids. I was reading my Bible, looking for answers, and asking God how He parented us. I found some help in Proverbs 16. I can paraphrase: Patience is a fountain of life. Wisdom allows for patience. Gracious words are a honeycomb, sweet to the soul and healing to the bones. I came to the God-inspired conclusion that like God says repeatedly, 'Kindness leads to repentance.' I always try to lead with kindness and grace-filled words with my kids, along with a lot of patience. I haven't been perfect. And of course, kids remember, despite all the good, the times when I lost it." I laughed.

"I have noticed you intentionally working with Tea," Bo stated.

"She has been tough lately. I knew she would be as a preteen who has always been the baby and pretty much gotten away with a lot, especially for the first year of Tommy being gone. I just let her have her way because I couldn't deal with her, but I am paying for it now. I may seem calm on the outside, but I was able to practice on three people before her. Sheesh. Her attitude and the way she talks to me sometimes." I rolled my eyes.

Chapter 34

THE MONTH OF JUNE WAS complete insanity. After the rodeo, we all helped Luke move into his new place. Then Brooke had a beautiful eighteenth birthday party. It was what our family calls birthday season because from April through June, most of us have a birthday. With graduations and birthdays, I was feeling exhausted and broke.

Bo had been so amazing. He was getting a small amount of attention from me, and I missed him. He helped Luke move and set up the parties. He was present, and he had no expectations of me. He had been working on his custom-built business, but he was focused on building his own house also. I had barely even asked him about it. I told myself that I needed to do better.

My fear was becoming reality. My kids took up a lot of my time and energy, as they should. Bo was fifth in line. I wondered if he was second-guessing his decision to be all in with me. I had tried to warn him. I started thinking that Bo deserved a younger woman who didn't live like the old lady in the shoe poem: "She had so many children she didn't know what to do." He deserved a calm life and not my hectic one. He deserved someone who could put him first and shower him with attention. He was probably done with me, but he didn't know how to tell me. I shook my head, trying to get rid of the negative thoughts.

I suddenly did not feel well. I was unloading the dishwasher (for the millionth time it felt like) and got a chill and a headache. I went to get some Motrin, and I felt dizzy. My throat had been sore since that morning, but in that moment, it felt like fire. I went to lie down on my bed for a minute.

"El," a voice called from the kitchen. *Oh, no!* I had forgotten Bo was coming over to just hang out for a little bit. I realized my little nap had turned into an hour-long one. I heard Tea tell him I was in bed. *Awesome.* He most definitely deserved a younger woman who wasn't bedridden. I pulled myself up. I was freezing, and my throat was angry. I grabbed a blanket and wrapped it around myself. I shuffled out into the den.

"Bo," I croaked out, "I am so sorry. I am not feeling well at all."

He turned around, and his smile turned into a look of concern. "El, your face is red." I kept shivering. He walked over and put a hand on my head. "You are hot. Back to bed. Where do you keep your thermometer?"

Tea peeked from behind Bo and said, "I will get it! You do not want to see my mom's bathroom." I tried to yell that it was her fault that my bathroom was a wreck because she slept in my bed and used my bathroom. She was a tornado with clothes, socks, and shoes.

Bo guided me to my bedroom, and I crawled into bed still shivering. My temp was 101 degrees. Tea grabbed my phone and said, "Call Katie. That is what we are supposed to do when Mom is sick."

I heard Bo and Tea in the kitchen talking to Katie. I wasn't sleeping, but I was not fully coherent either. Bo gave me some Tylenol. My throat hurt so bad that I couldn't even talk.

Katie came over. After she looked in my mouth, she said, "Strep. I will send a script over to CVS after I get back to my office." She and Bo walked out of my room and kept talking. At some point, I took the antibiotics.

The next thing I knew, it was dark, and the house was quiet. I felt very disoriented but slightly better. I found my phone. It was

5:00 a.m., so the antibiotics had had twelve hours to work. I walked into the den and saw Bo sleeping on my couch.

Wow. This guy is all in with us, and I can't begin to understand why. All I was offering him was a messy house, a bunch of kids, and my contagious self. I just wanted to curl up next to him. I walked over to him, crawled onto the couch, and lay down beside him. I was still shivering a little, so feeling the warmth from his body just made me instinctively snuggle in closer.

"Hey, there," he said groggily.

"I am so sorry I messed up our plans," I whispered. He pulled me closer to him. "I am also sorry that you had to sleep on the couch. We have an extra bedroom."

"No more apologizing. I wanted to be closer to you in case you needed anything," he mumbled, still half asleep.

I couldn't sleep anymore. I just closed my eyes and enjoyed being wrapped up in his strong arms. I thanked God over and over for bringing Bo to us and to me. We—no, I—needed him more than I ever would have admitted. I finally got up and took a shower. I had forgotten that I had sweated half the night due to my fever. I probably did not smell very good. When I mentioned it to Bo, he said, "You always smell like sunshine." He was making it very difficult for me not to fall in love with him.

Chapter 35

WE DECIDED TO ALL WATCH a movie together after dinner. Bo had cooked something for the kids. I was resting because I was still very tired. I was not particularly hungry. Brooke made me hot tea, and we all watched the musical *Oklahoma*. My kids loved musicals. I raised them all on *The Sound of Music*, *The Music Man*, *Mary Poppins*, *Hairspray*, *Hamilton*, *My Fair Lady*, and I could go on. Bo was not so sure about watching one. We all promised him that he just had to watch one, and if he didn't like it, we would never make him watch one again. Bo's face was hilarious.

He said, "Deal," and we watched it. I was sitting next to him with a blanket covering me. I was so proud of all my kids singing along. I gave myself a pat on the back. My job as a parent was done. Just sing your way through life, and you will be OK. Oh, and lots of Jesus too!

I fell asleep halfway through it but woke up for the end. I turned to Bo. "So what do you think? Are you going to join our musicals are the best club?

"I can probably go one a year, if that." We all laughed.

The kids all went to hang out with friends, so we sat on the couch and talked. It felt like it had been a month since we had caught up. I looked him in the eyes, grabbed both of his hands, and said, "I am so grateful for how much you have cared for my family, helped us move, stood on ladders to hang balloons, grabbed my curbside groceries, and so much more over the past month. Thank you."

His smile was so worth every word I said. "You are welcome, beautiful."

"I don't really understand why you want to jump into this chaos we call family. But I see the work you put into having a relationship with each of my kids, and it means so much to me. You are such an amazing example of a man who follows Christ in word and deed."

"El, your kids, your life, the chaos, I have loved every minute. I can tell by your face that you don't quite believe me." He grinned at me.

"It is hard for me to imagine that you, your steady presence, and your calm and laid-back way would even tolerate the hot-mess life we lead. You could have a calm, quiet life with a younger woman who wants to start a family with you and not a life with an older woman who already has a family of needy and sometimes obnoxious children." I was joking but also not.

Bo quickly responded, "El, I have told you before, and if I have to say this to you for the rest of my life, I guess I will. Please hear me. I want to be with you. I want to be part of your family. I had a quiet peaceful life for many years. And I am sure there may be moments when I need some peace, just like everyone. That being said, I have had more fun and laughed so much the past few months. I can't imagine going back to my quiet life. And also, please stop saying you are an older woman. You are barely four years older than me, and you look ten years younger anyway."

Wait, I thought, *did he just say "rest of my life" and that I "look ten years younger than him"?* It was those pervasive freckles that ran across my nose. My head was spinning.

"OK. I hear you. I just was giving you an out in case you needed an out." I took a breath. "Here is what I have been thinking. I have lived almost two years doing everything myself. Though it has been utterly exhausting on every level, I am proud of myself. But pride is lonely. And it hit me the other day that I need help; I need a partner.

And God has given me you. You are such a gift to me. I am tired. I am staring at you, and I realize I need you. I don't think I wanted to admit it before. But yesterday and last night when I was sick, it was such a relief to have someone else take over. It's like I have been bearing so much on my shoulders that I didn't how much it was until you came and took some of the load off." I was smiling at his kind eyes, and I felt so very tired. I turned and leaned on his chest. His arm was wrapped around my shoulder. It was dark outside and in the house except for a few lamps that were on. It felt so very peaceful.

"El," Bo said quietly, "despite the occasional chaos, you have handled everything so well. Your kids are some of my favorite people. You have done an amazing job raising and guiding them through the last two years. I think I like them so much because I see the best pieces of you in each of them." I smiled. He was so thoughtful and kind to me. I had this urge to give him everything of me.

His phone rang. It was Katie. They talked like they had known each other for years. He yes-ma'amed her and hung up. My mouth must have been hanging open.

"She didn't want to call you in case you were asleep." Bo said, trying to defend himself.

"You are stealing my best friend. One weekend together, and y'all are besties." I was laughing and trying to look shocked at the same time.

"I admit that we have been talking a lot. Mostly about you, though." I gave him the side eye. He smiled and pulled me back beside him. "I am so grateful that you have allowed me back into your life, El. You know, when I decided to come back to town, it really was to solely see you."

"What would you have done if I wasn't at church, was there but seeing someone, or said no to your lunch invitation?" I teased.

"I am a planner, and coming into town was the most unplanned thing I had ever done. You had been on my mind so much in the previous month that I think I was just looking for a sign that you were OK, or you had moved on and were dating someone. I just had this intense desire to see for myself. If you weren't there, I guess I would have gone by your house, which sounds a little stalker-like. So I probably would have called you. If you had said no, I'm not sure what I would have done. I purposely didn't think of it as an option. But when I walked in and saw you on stage, and you started to sing, it literally blew me away. I watched you walk off the stage and graciously hug everyone. I realized in that moment that no matter what happened next, I had to just go all in with you, four kids and all. And I have not regretted one second."

I hugged him as tight as possible as I nestled into his chest. He touched my face and said, "You are still warm." I shivered on cue. I wanted to tell him that I was ridiculously, madly, no-holding-back in love with him but not yet. I was content to just fall asleep on his chest.

Chapter 36

B O CALLED AND INVITED ALL of us—Katie's family too—out on his boat for the Fourth of July. Katie and I had decided to rent a house on the lake for the weekend, so it would be perfect. I was ready to just sit in a chair by the lake.

The lake house had five bedrooms. One room had two bunk beds, so Tea, Landry, and Remy took that one. Brooke and Kylie took one bedroom. Luke and his friend Trent took one. That left me one and Katie and John one. Bo was going to sleep on his boat, and Whit was thrilled to do the same. It struck me as funny that in order to get my own room, I had to rent a house. Tea had to get out of my room at home. Once Brooke left for college, I was redoing her room for Tea. Maybe that would help.

Bo asked if Luke and I wanted to drive to the boat. Then Luke would take Bo's truck back to the lake house while Bo and I brought the boat over to the house. It was a gorgeous Thursday evening. Friday was the fourth, and we were staying at the lake through Sunday. I was in such a happy mood. All day, I sang or hummed whatever song came into my head.

On the drive over, Luke took over the music and had me listen to some new songs. I had lost control of the sound system about ten years earlier, and I hadn't had it since. "Mom," said Luke, "don't use up all your voice. We do have the annual July 4th karaoke competition tonight. And it is my turn to pick the theme."

118

Bo looked confused and slightly panicked. "Competition? Theme?"

"Don't be alarmed, Bo," I said. "We can have partners. Then I asked Luke, "What theme did you pick?"

"Country music, bad breakups." Luke smiled, all happy with himself.

"Ohhhh, good one." I laughed and turned to Bo. "And don't worry Bo; John can't sing a lick, and we still love him." Bo's face was so funny. I put my hand on his arm. "I'm kidding. You can be the judge." Bo looked relieved.

We got to the boat slip and waved goodbye to Luke. Bo got the boat ready, and I just sat in the front looking out into the lake. "All right! You ready?" Bo asked.

"Yes!"

I loved being at the front, where water would spray and where wind would blow. I had my hair up in a tight bun. I wore a black-and-white-striped, strappy tank top, black summer joggers, and Tevas. We drove for a good twenty minutes, and then Bo slowed it down as we got close to the lake house. I stood, walked over to him, and slid under the arm that was steering to hug him.

"What have you been thinking about for the last twenty minutes?" he asked. I told him I wasn't thinking about anything in particular. I was just letting my mind rest and was enjoying all the natural beauty. "You seem really happy today," he observed as he took my hand and kissed it. We hadn't kissed yet, but our physical affection had been very touchy lately. We had talked about how kissing was so intimate, and I wasn't quite ready yet. That was about a month ago.

He was so patient with me. He never teased me about my timeline or blew off my guilty feelings about Tommy or the kids. He just trusted that God would heal me at some point. He demanded nothing from me. He said he would never want me to do anything I was not 100 percent comfortable with. And in that moment on the boat, I thought that I was at a good place to be more intimate.

However, I was actually super nervous to kiss him because we already had this intense chemistry. *What if we have to struggle to stop? What if part of me doesn't want to stop? What if I just want to give into every emotion instead of practicing restraint?* But marriage sounded really scary too. I told Katie this, and she thought it was hilarious. She said, "So basically you would rather have a salacious love affair then get married?" *Pretty much.* But I knew there were always consequences when we didn't do life God's way. Marrying Tommy while four months pregnant was proof of that.

"I am happy. I have a lot of joy today. I love being away from my house, with all the to-do lists and dishes staring at me. Being with you and my friends and family for a weekend away makes me happy."

As he drove slowly, he said he wanted to show me a quiet spot. We maneuvered into an alcove, and it opened into a place with stunning cliff walls all around it.

"Wow! It is so beautiful." I literally couldn't stop smiling. Bo had turned off the boat and looked toward me to see my reaction to the scenery. He was looking at me with that look he gave me sometimes. I wondered what would happen if I just leaned in a little.

I put my hands on his solid chest and moved them up to his built-out shoulders. I was watching and feeling for his reaction. I was looking at his beautiful brown eyes with lashes and perfect nose. I ran my hands slowly up his strong neck, knowing with every part of me that I was moving this relationship to the next level. The cove was so quiet that I could hear his breath. The tension that had been between us since the day we had first met was about to break open. The anticipation between us felt heavy. My body was firing in all the places.

He moved his hands to my waist. He pulled my body toward him. He had one hand at the base of my back and the other on my cheek. He ran his thumb over my lips. He hesitated for a second. We were centimeters apart. I couldn't breathe. Then he tilted my chin and put his lips over mine.

Every part of my body was responding to him. This was exactly what I knew would happen. I was completely undone. All the heartache, stress, and tension completely left my brain and body. I couldn't seem to stop kissing him. He then started to kiss my face and my neck. He was working his way down my neck, and it felt so good. I gasped. I was trying to think as he worked his way down my chest. I could just melt into his arms and forget about everything. I could take him down into the boat cabin and end up on his bed.

As much as I did not want to, I pulled his face up to mine. I looked at him and smiled. Before I said anything, he said, "I know." He kissed my lips slowly. I didn't want him to stop. I found it hard to let go of him. He picked me up, put me into the captain's chair, and leaned forward on the arms. Our faces were so close again. I wanted to touch him, so I lifted my hand to his face.

"Wow, El." He took a breath. "I am going to need a minute." He turned away from me. I wanted to pull him back and to go back to that place where I didn't care about anything except his mouth.

"Same," I said, slightly out of breath. He turned back toward me and looked at me with his still very charming smile. He went to sit down at the front of the boat.

I pulled my knees up and put my head on them. *God, help. That was intense.* Up until that moment, I had only kissed Tommy. I tried to conjure up what it felt like to kiss Tommy, and I couldn't remember. I guessed that if I had to put a word to it, kissing Tommy was comfortable and was all I had known. But I don't think I could ever forget this kiss with Bo. I was so close to letting him take me downstairs to bed. "Ugh." I looked up. Bo was laughing at me.

"Did I say that out loud?" He nodded, and I started to laugh. Then I pointed at him. "You are going to have to stay away from me," I joked, but I wasn't really joking.

Bo leaned back against the boat while looking at the sunset and said, "Trying to avoid you all weekend is going to be tough." He was still smiling.

I put my head back down on my knees. *Ugh.* I wanted him to come back over and kiss me again so badly.

After a few minutes had passed, he came back over to me and kicked me out of his chair. "I need to focus on driving this boat so that I do not think about your body." He said this like it was the most natural thing in the world.

I went to sit a few feet away in the other chair and looked out at the water. I could feel him looking at me. I heard him say, "You look like you are pouting."

I laughed and turned to look at him. "Well maybe I am," I said and turned away from him.

"Are you pouting because I didn't take you downstairs?" I turned away with my arms folded. I started to giggle, and then I couldn't stop laughing. Bo smiled as he steered the boat. I watched his muscular arms steer all the way to the lake house's dock.

We docked, and before all the kids came running out, he walked over to where I was sitting. He took my hand and kissed it. I blushed, and I couldn't quite look him in the eye. He looked at me and said, "I love you. I have been in love with you since the first day I met you. And one day soon, I promise, I will take you to my bed, and," he paused and continued, "you won't be pouting." He winked at me and finished tying up the boat.

I covered my mouth's mocking shock. "I cannot believe you just said that," I looked at him, and his eyes were laughing. He started to whistle and walked toward the dock.

Lord have mercy. That was the sexiest thing anyone had ever said to me. I stayed in the boat for a minute to recover.

Chapter 37

AFTER WE ALL FINISHED DINNER, Katie and I began cleaning up as the guys started getting set up for the singing challenge. I had already had several glasses of wine. I was working hard at forgetting about the kiss.

"What is with you tonight?" Katie demanded. "You have had two glasses of wine and have been very quiet. Yet the looks you and Bo have exchanged are, dare I say, sexy?" I smiled slowly. "Oh, Lord, did you kiss on the boat? I knew it! Y'all took way too long."

"No, we didn't," I protested. "It was maybe fifteen extra minutes."

"Well, I have been praying for you two to kiss for months," Katie said.

I started to laugh. "You are so weird! Who prays for that?"

"Me. Because he is the real deal, and as soon as you kissed him, I knew you would finally be all in. I mean, he is a stud. How could you not be all in after kissing that face."

"You really are deranged," I responded while laughing a little too hard. It was the wine.

"You are deranged for taking so long to kiss him. And stop changing the subject. I want details."

"I will give you one detail."

Katie thought for a moment. "I can live with that. Tell me."

"It was the hottest, most intense, most physical kiss I have ever had—ever."

"I knew it. Your cheeks are so red. What else did y'all do?" Katie was following me around the kitchen.

"No more. Anyway, we have to pick our karaoke song for tonight. Luke said the theme is country, bad breakup."

"Ohhhhhh. What are you thinking?" Katie asked.

"How about 'Bye-Bye'[11] by Jodee Messina? You can sing it, and I will sing around you."

"Isn't that how we always do it?" Katie said.

"Always!"

Chapter 38

THE NIGHT WAS FUN. THERE was so much laughing that my sides hurt. Bo decided to be the judge, which was fair. It would be asking a lot for him to sing in front of us. The winner was Luke, Remy, Landry, and Tea doing Taylor Swift's rap version of "Bad Blood."[12] Then we all had s'mores around the little fire. Eventually, Katie and I went in and got the girls in bed and settled with a movie. Brooke and Kylie were watching an *Avenger* movie with Whit, Luke, and Trent. I walked back outside to the dock and Bo. Katie and John had gone for a walk.

"Hey," I said as I sat down next to Bo. I was still in a little shock over how kissing him affected me. He woke up places in me that I had forgotten about or hadn't had time to think about in a long time.

"Hey, beautiful," he said like it was the most natural thing in the world. I smiled at him, and he took my hand. I lay my head back on the Adirondack chair. I was so tired that I could just close my eyes right there. "You had too much wine."

"You are so right. What did you think about our annual July 3 karaoke contest?"

"It was fun. But sometimes I think I have joined the Partridge family, with all the music and singing involved."

"Ha, ha. Not true. Well, maybe kinda true."

Bo put some music on his phone and said, "Let's dance." He pulled me up from my very comfy seat and in close with those magical hands. I leaned into his chest. I could hear his heart beating. His hand was on my back. "You know, I have touched your back so often, I feel like I have it memorized."

Who taught him how to be so gentle and soft with women? Maybe I didn't want to know.

"So," I said, "if you were blindfolded and had to identify me by my back, you could?" I was flirting. My hands were on his shoulder and neck.

"Definitely," he said. We were looking at each other and smiling.

"Hmmm, so confident. I let you kiss me once, and you get all cocky," I teased.

"Let me? I am pretty sure you pulled that trigger." He was still flirting.

"So you driving into a very private spot on the lake was just you showing me the scenery?" I asked.

"Yep."

We were both laughing, and then he got quiet. "I am serious about what I said." He stopped dancing and looked at me. His hands were resting on my hips. "The more I get to know you, your heart, your mind, I am overwhelmed by your presence in my life and so grateful you have allowed me to stay."

"Oh, Bo." I didn't even know how to respond to that. "You have been nothing but patient and kind to me and my family. You have brought laughter and joy back into my life. Things were pretty dark and heavy for a while. And so hard. But coming out on the other side has been really beautiful."

"Beauty from ashes," Bo responded.

"Yes. And thank you for saying such nice things about me to me. I am really humbled that you feel that way about me."

"El, I am here for you, for as long as you will have me."

We were looking at each other. It was quiet for just a moment. I could hear the water lapping at the dock. I heard his breath and mine. There I was again, feeling utterly powerless in his gaze.

I moved toward him, and we kissed. This time it was slow and gentle. His hand moved up my back and into my hair. He was so good at this kissing thing. I pulled back, and we kept dancing.

Then I said, "I was really hoping you were serious about what you also said on the boat when we docked." I was smiling.

He looked confused for a second and then remembered. "Wow, I really am enjoying this sexy, flirty side of you."

"Oh, I have all kinds of sides and surprises." We were going to have to do a better job of staying away from each other that weekend, or I was in trouble.

Chapter 39

I GOT UP EARLY ON FRIDAY. I pulled my hair back and put it into a ball cap. I put on my running shoes. I was warming up when Katie came out.

"I'm coming too," she said. I laughed. We had run together since we played soccer in high school. It was where our best conversations happened. It was July and warm. At least it was cloudy, but by the time we finished our three miles, we were drenched in sweat. We raced to the end of the dock and jumped in. We popped up in the water and began arguing about who won. Bo was on the boat getting it ready for the day. He shouted out that I won.

"See, I told you," I said to Katie, sticking out my tongue.

"What? He is so biased. I bet he just wants to be kissed again." And she took off swimming for the dock.

I yelled as I chased her down, "You are dead!" I tried not to look at Bo as he was laughing at us. My cheeks must have been crimson. We ran barefoot up the dock chasing each other. She made it to the sliding glass door and locked it.

I turned around, and Bo was clearly amused at the whole thing. I shrugged and tried to convince nine-year-old Landry to open the door by stating that I would not actually harm her mom.

We were out on the boat all day Friday except for meals. The kids got on the tube, and we pulled them around. Then we got out the skis, and everyone tried it. Bo was so good and such a show-off.

I hadn't water-skied in years, but I got up on the third try. Katie just rode the tube because she had pulled a muscle sprinting away from me that morning. It served her right.

The guys wanted to rent Jet Skis later in the afternoon, but everyone else wanted to go in and rest before the fireworks. As we waited for it to get dark enough for the fireworks, Trent brought out his guitar and started to play. Landry was on my lap snuggling with me. She was upset about something her sisters did. Bo was sitting across from me. Trent was next to me with Luke next to him. John had a chair, and Katie was in front of him. The rest of the kids were on the floor. I was in my happy place of family and friends all together.

Trent and I discussed songs to sing. He started with Cademon's Call's "We Delight."[13] Luke and Katie joined in as we harmonized our way through such a great oldie. Then Katie and I taught the kids the classic Young Life songs from the nineties. Then we started to talk about what songs we would do at Vacation Bible School (VBS) on the following week. Our church had put me in charge of kids' music, so Luke, Brooke, Whit, and Tea were all leading the singing. Katie and sixteen-year-old Kylie were helping with serving snacks and drinks. John and Bo were setting up and tearing down. We started making up dances to teach the kids at VBS, and it got really silly. I will always remember that evening before the fireworks, singing, dancing, and laughing with my family, friends, and Bo.

Bo and I had been exchanging smiles and looks all day. He would squeeze my hand if I walked past him. We were getting the kids ready for the boat, and he walked over to me. We turned and walked toward the boat with his arm around my shoulder.

Then thirteen-year-old Remy popped in between us and said, "Uncle Bo, Mom says to ask you if you need more ice for the boat cooler."

He answered her, and I mouthed, *Uncle Bo?* He grinned. I loved how it sounded.

Chapter 40

VBS WENT OFF WITHOUT A hitch. As the children's minister, Macie said, "The Parkers did it again." And all of a sudden, it was the end of July. Brooke was working at a boutique, and Whit and Tea were at camp for two weeks. Luke was running soccer camps and getting ready for school to start. I had the house to myself, and it was amazing. I got caught up on work and emails. I did some deep cleaning and touch-up painting. I worked with a voice coach on my range and explored some old gospel hymns. Bo had been busy with his house. He kept telling me that it was almost ready for me to see.

I was sitting inside and waiting for the hottest part of the day to pass when Bo walked in. "All right, El, today is the day. Let's go."

I looked up from the kitchen table and smiled. "Where are we going?"

"To the house before the sun sets. I want you to see it from the property." He was like a kid. "Grab your boots; it's kind of a mess."

He almost pulled me out of the house. The twenty-five-minute drive took us up into the hills. We turned onto a tiny two-lane road, which wound up, down, and around. It was such a pretty road, as oak trees created a canopy over it. We finally turned on a gravel road that ended at a gate. After getting through the gate, we went up a dirt road that switchbacked slowly up to the property. Once we pulled onto the newly cemented driveway, I could look around. The view was breathtaking.

"No way! This is amazing!" I shouted.

He smiled and took my hand. The foundation was poured, the walls were up, and the roof was in process. The front porch didn't have stairs yet, so Bo lifted me up onto the slab. He pulled out the floor plan, and we sat down to look at it. He designed that house. It was big, and I loved the layout. It was not lost on me as I looked at the house plan with five bedrooms, a workout room, two offices, and amazing front and back porches that he was not just building it for himself.

We went to the back porch, and he showed me the design for the pool, patios, and trail to the top of the hill where he cleared out trees so that we could watch the sunset. Bo pulled his truck around, and we sat down to watch the sun set on the river below. I was wearing a mini, light-pink sundress with the cowboy boots he insisted that I wear. My hair was pulled back into a messy bun. I had on the diamond earrings he had given me and a little bit of leftover makeup from that morning. I had quickly put on some lip gloss before I left the house with him.

I realized that he looked nicer than I did. He had on jeans but also a collared, starched white shirt. We were sitting at the end of the truck with our legs dangling and our arms holding us up from behind. As I was watching the sun set and enjoying the moment, he took my hand as usual. He squeezed it. "Come on. Let's walk."

So I hopped down, and we walked toward the edge of the hill. Further down, I could see cows grazing. I looked at Bo. He was so handsome. I looked back at the house, and it truly was amazing. He had been building for so long that he knew exactly how to blend the house into its surroundings. I turned to smile at him. He pulled me close.

We hadn't been really alone since July 4. We were joking on the way up to the house that we scared ourselves with all our chemistry. There were still sparks, but we made sure we weren't alone very often. And frankly, our lives didn't really create a lot of space for it.

That was probably for the best since I lost all conviction when he kissed me.

Bo took both my hands and pushed me back so that he could see me. "El, I love you. Each day, I love you more than the day before. You know that I find you fascinating—your strength in difficult situations, your faith and trust in God, and your perpetual glow of inner peace despite what is happening around you. El, there is no other place I want to be other than near you for the rest of my life."

He gave my hands a squeeze and then let go to pull out a ring box from his pocket. He kneeled down and opened the box.

Oh. Wow. I knew it might be coming soon, but I was still surprised.

"I have prayed for someone I could share my life with, and God has shown me you and your family. I have prayed about you and us, I have talked to your dad and Luke, Brooke, and Whit. I was told not to mention it to Tea." I laughed. Then I teared up, and my nose started to run. I was sniffling and wiping away tears before he could get out the next sentence. "I want to be with you forever. I cannot even imagine going back to my life before you. This house is for you and your family. You are a gift and a light. I want to be wherever you are from now on. At least within a few miles." He smiled and opened the box.

Oh, God. The ring was stunning. Of course it was. Bo was not frugal.

"I know you have been cautious and with good reason. And I am willing to wait any amount of time. I know, with all that I am, that you and I are meant to be together forever. You are who my heart desires." I was nodding and wiping my eyes with the back of my hand. "Elouise Ruby Whitmore Parker, will you please marry me?"

I kept looking from the ring, to Bo, and back to the ring. As scared as I was of all the unknowns, I knew I would never say no to him. Finally, I said, "How can I say no to the kindest, smartest, sexiest man I know." I started to laugh. "I love you, Bo." It was the first time I allowed myself to say it. It had been sitting in my throat and waiting for the perfect moment.

Bo started wiping his eyes and then slid the ring on. It was a perfect fit. I am positive Brooke had made sure it would be. I realized that it matched the earrings Bo had given me for my birthday.

Bo lifted me off the ground and twirled me around. I threw my head back and laughed. I looked at the house again. It was perfect. I absolutely loved it. I loved all that God had done. He rebuilt something out of the ashes of my life. And it was good.

PART 4

PART 4

Chapter 41

THE NEXT WEEKEND, BO WENT with me to pick up the kids from camp. It was just a two-hour round trip. Bo reached over for my left hand as we drove. "That ring looks so good on you. Whoever bought this for you must really, really love you." He winked. I rolled my eyes in a playful way. He was so proud of himself. He let go of my hand and put his hand on my bare thigh, right below the skirt I was wearing. I started to feel warm.

"Umm. Excuse me, but the guy who bought this ring would not appreciate you touching my leg like that."

He laughed and moved it up an inch. I feigned shock. We had been flirting so much, and it was fun. His hand on my thigh was making my body feel all the feelings. I can't imagine what it was doing to him. "So when are going to marry this guy and put him out of his misery?"

He made me laugh so much. "Well, I need a house to move into, so he will let me know when that will be." Truthfully, Bo was positive it would be mostly done by November. He wanted to have the wedding at the house in the amazing backyard he had designed. And I was fine with that. In fact, he, Katie, and Brooke were in charge of the wedding. All I had to think about was my dress.

Bo looked over at me. His hand was still on my tanned bare thigh and almost under my black skirt. "Lord, help me. You are gorgeous."

We got Whit and Tea's trunks and then went to find them. They ran up and hugged us both. We got to see their cabins and meet their counselors. On the drive home, we grabbed some lunch. They told us all the fun they had experienced for two weeks. We were almost to my house when I heard Whit and Tea whispering. Tea peeked over the seat and screamed. Her eyes were as big as saucers.

"Mom! Are you getting married to Bo?"

I answered, "Yes. What do you think about that?"

"I'm so happy!"

Phew! Bo told them all about the house he was building and how they each would get to help design their rooms and pick out the paint colors. They were so excited they started talking about colors right away. This time, I put my hand on Bo's leg. I loved how he loved my kids.

Chapter 42

I T WAS THE MIDDLE OF August and the hottest part of the summer. It was the time when Tommy had died. As the August heat became oppressive, I started having little panic attacks. I knew what they were and when they were coming. Last year, I had to go on anti-anxiety medication just to get through the month. Now it had been two whole years, and Bo was in my life. Bo and the kids were my life. But I didn't know how to bring him into that really difficult and disorienting time—the anniversary of Tommy's death.

Tea's behavior seemed to escalate in August. She was just angry, and she didn't even know why. I decided to take the kids to the beach again that year. I had rented a beach house the previous year. I found the same one with a bedroom for everyone. We all needed each other but space too. There were no rules for the kids. They could eat what they wanted and watch movies all day. There was no real bedtime. They could play in the waves, sit in the sand, cry, and pray.

Daily, I found myself sitting in the wet sand at the water's edge, where my toes and fingers could dig into it. On the last evening, the sun was setting in pink and purple hues. It was indescribable. It felt as though only God and I were sharing the beauty of it.

I once heard someone say that grief feels like a weighted vest like the lead ones you wear when getting X-rays at the dentist office. I felt the heaviness so acutely when I allowed myself to think of Tommy. I also felt the guilt of all our silly arguments and hurt feelings. *Why did I struggle some days with just loving the one I was with? Why was that so hard?*

Chapter 43

B O AND I GOT BROOKE all moved into her dorm. She was at the sweetest school with a lovely art program. Bo had already commissioned her for some artwork in the new house. Those two were thick as thieves, constantly texting about the wedding. I was not overly interested, mainly because I knew it was all in good hands. Bo and Brooke were so much alike that they could see something in their minds and create it with their hands. And anyway, I had done a wedding for myself before, so why not let them have fun with it. All I cared about was that all the people I loved would be there to celebrate.

Bo couldn't get over the fact that I was not all that interested in the house. I mean, all I really cared about was a big pantry and laundry room. He was the cook, not me. So the kitchen was all him. He kept telling me that I was the easiest person in the world to be engaged to. I laughed. He was easy to make happy.

Summer was over, and Whit was officially in tenth grade, and Tea was in sixth. I had them both in a private Christian school. My desire was for them to have a firm foundation in God's Word and to understand their identities in Christ before they launched into the big, scary world. Tommy had been public school all the way, and so was I. But that was thirty years ago, and it was a different time. There were no iPhones, and we had no cable TV. We made our own fun, and we were innocent of the harshness of the world for a little bit longer.

My teaching and research had started back up, and it felt like the days were flying by. Most mornings, I would get up at 5:00 a.m. and go for a run in our gated neighborhood with my blue heeler Bingo. Sometimes I would drive to the gym. And sometimes I would run to the gym, workout, and run home if I had time. The gym was only a mile and a half away. I would run out of my neighborhood, which was about a mile to get through the gate. Then the half mile was all downhill. I cut through a neighborhood and ran on a little trail through the woods until I got to the open baseball fields. The gym was on the other side of the fields.

I woke up at four thirty that morning. I couldn't get back to sleep, so I knew I would have time to run to the gym, workout for forty-five minutes with weights and yoga, and then run home. I would be home by 6:45 a.m. and have time to shower and take the kids to school. After drop-off, I would come home and have my quiet reading and journaling time with a big cup of coffee. Then I would leave for campus at around nine.

I got to the gym pretty quickly. I felt good; nothing hurt or was sore. I walked into the gym, and the usual crowd was there. I walked over to some weights, and someone bumped into me. It was this guy that seemed a little creepy. I had seen him at the gym over the past few months. It seemed like he was staring at or following me around the gym, but I wasn't quite sure. He smiled, and I said, "Hi." I was brought up as a Texas girl with manners, and we say, "Hi," even if someone sets off little alarm bells. He couldn't do anything to me at the gym. He probably couldn't help it that he was a little strange. I did notice that he dyed his hair. Again, that was strange. I had my earbuds in, so I just listened to a podcast and did my workout. Occasionally when I looked up, he was staring at me. It was so strange. *Why would he stare at me, a middle-aged woman with a giant diamond on her left hand?*

I finished my stretching, got my music going, and walked

outside to begin my run up the hill. It was still pretty dark. There were some intense dark clouds covering any light. I started running. I was pretty sure I was going to be drenched before I got home. A breeze kicked up, and I started across the deserted baseball fields.

I was thinking about Bo and this life we were starting to build together. I thanked God and prayed for him. I prayed for my dad, who just seemed significantly older than he had been a few months earlier. I prayed for each of my kids. I turned up the music because I was about to hit the steep part of the hill. I was running down the sidewalk between the four baseball fields, which led to the hilly, little path in the woods. It was only fifty yards through the woods, but the woods extended for a mile on either side, so I had to run through it.

I was about to head onto the wooded path when I suddenly felt cold in my bones. I looked up at the clouds, and an inaudible voice told me to "stop and look." I slowed down and looked behind me. I jumped back in surprise. Someone was riding a bike right behind me.

I immediately stopped and decided not to go into the woods. As I started to look for another way to run, I realized that the guy had hopped off his bike and was quickly walking toward me. I began to panic. In an instant, he was coming at me, and I tried to run left or right, but the fences from the ball fields were surrounding me. All I had was the sidewalk between the fences and the wooded path. I chose the sidewalk.

I tried to run past him, but he grabbed me. I tried to scream, but he threw me to the ground. When I landed on my left hand, pain seared up my arm. My next scream was drowned out by rolling thunder. I tried to get up, and he kicked me in the ribs. The breath was knocked out of me as I doubled over. I was trying to crawl away. I looked toward the gym, but I couldn't see anyone. I was in a complete panic. *Jesus, help me. Jesus, help. Please.*

I felt an arm around my throat as he dragged me along the sidewalk. *Oh, God, he is taking me into the woods.* I was trying to remember what Brooke had taught me from her self-defense class that past summer. All I remembered was to relax, not to fight against it, and to use his momentum. I made myself stop fighting against him. I felt the darkness of the woods envelope me as he dragged me into them.

I had never been more frightened in my entire life. Going against every instinct I had, I used his momentum and pushed off the ground to launch myself into him. He fell, pulling me down with him. His grip loosened as I fell onto him. I rolled off him. Pain from my rib and wrist made me cry out. I gasped from the pain. Tears were coming down my face, and I couldn't see a thing in the dark. I scrambled up to my feet. I lunged toward the other side of the wooded path where the houses were. I knew I could run faster than him if I could just get away. I took a step, and he tackled me.

*Jesus. Please. Please. Ple*ase, was all my mind could say, over and over. He rolled me over, and for the first time, I saw his face. "Oh, God," I said. It was the guy from the gym. His face was right above mine, and the look was bone chilling. I closed my eyes and fought, scratched, and kicked. He was heavy and was on me, putting pressure on my rib that I was sure was broken. I started gasping in pain. I didn't realize that I was saying, "Please," over and over again out loud.

He was yelling at me to stop moving. He said that he wasn't going to hurt me if I gave him what he wanted. I felt bile coming up my throat. My right arm got loose. I hit him and tried to roll out from under him. Suddenly, my head just exploded. He had punched me in my eye. I couldn't see or breathe. He was laying on top of me with his arm across my throat. I felt the will to fight leave me. His other hand was trying to pull my shorts down.

Jesus, please help! I can't die and leave my kids. Jesus, please! I was sobbing as I gasped for air. My right arm was still free, so I started searching with my right hand for anything to hit him with. I found something: a branch. It was big, but my hand fit around it perfectly. With more strength than I thought I had, I heaved the giant branch and hit him on the head. And I kept hitting him until I was out from under him. Then I ran.

My legs were moving faster than my mind could follow. I was so scared he was right behind me. I made it out of the woods and to the houses. I ran up the hill of the subdivision. I turned around finally, and I didn't see him. Instead, I saw a man walking to his car in the driveway. I yelled for help as I ran toward him. My whole body was on fire. I could barely take a breath. I fell to my knees as the man walked toward me.

The police and ambulance arrived. I couldn't stop shaking, even with warming blankets over me. I realized our church's children's pastor's house was right next door. Her husband was a police officer, and with all the commotion, he had come over. He walked over to me as the medics were checking me out. When he realized it was me, he ran back to get Macie.

Of course, I knew the medics. Chris went to our church. The other was a high school classmate of Luke's. They were all taking care of me, and I felt safe with them around. There were several police cars with lights on and multiple police officers. I kept looking down the hill at the wooded area and making sure he wasn't walking up the hill in the chaos. I couldn't stop shaking.

Macie was sitting with me in the ambulance when she called Katie. I could hear Katie on the other end of the phone saying that she wanted to talk to me. I shook my head no to Macie. If I talked to her, I would start crying, and I didn't think I would stop.

An officer took my initial statement. Several police officers were walking down into the woods. A photographer and crime scene investigator showed up as the ambulance pulled away. Luke's friend was trying to be professional, but he couldn't get an IV line into me because I was shaking so much. Macie was just holding me as I shook in the back of that ambulance. I will love her forever for that. Chris was concerned that I was in shock. He finally got an IV line in, and he was talking to me. I had no idea what he was saying. I couldn't see out of my left eye. He splinted my wrist and looked at my ribs.

Katie was the first person I saw when they took me into the ER. When the curtains finally closed to give us privacy, she looked at me with her face in disbelief. She brought her arm up to her eyes and choked out a sob. She turned away from me to gain composure. Katie did not cry. I could only count on one hand the times, since age twelve, that she had cried. We joked that I had cried enough tears for both of us.

I touched my face. My eye was swollen almost shut. I was waiting for her to say something. She turned around, leaned on both hands at the end of my bed, and finally said, "Dear God, what happened?" I then started to cry uncontrollably. She walked around to my side, wrapped her arms around me, and started to cry and pray with me. Mainly, she prayed that God "will find that mother you-know-what and kill him before Bo finds him."

Katie held me until we both calmed down. She told me that John had my kids. He took them to school, and Macie would pick up Whit and Tea and get them to their activities. She said they could stay with her for as long as I needed them to. She said she would tell them someone tried to rob me and that I had gotten hurt. I agreed to all of it, but I would need to call Brooke and Luke.

The doctor came in, sat down next to me, and did a full physical. I started whimpering because every part of my body hurt. Katie was holding my good hand. He ordered pain medication through my IV. He ordered X-rays of my ribs and wrist, along with a CT of my head.

The nurse came in and asked if I had been raped. I said that I wasn't, but I was not sure that she or Katie believed me. A tech came in to swab my eye for DNA and cleaned under my fingernails. He took pictures.

"Your shorts are ripped, Ellie. You have road rash, cuts, and bruises everywhere. Your face is a mess. You may have a concussion. Maybe you were … maybe you blacked out?" Katie was in doctor mode now.

"No!" I said louder than I meant to. "I would remember. Trust me. I remember everything." My voice was shaking as I forced the attacker's face from my mind and then started to tremble. "Where's Bo? Please call him."

Katie came back over to my side. "I did." She checked her phone. "He is on his way. He was out by San Antonio, so he is fighting morning traffic to get back." I started to feel the pain meds kicking in. "Let's clean you up a bit, or he might lose his mind over the state of you." Katie and the nurses changed me into a gown, got all the dried blood off me, and cleaned all my cuts. I literally felt like the traveler in the Bible story of the Good Samaritan. I was the one who was beaten, robbed, and thrown to the side of the road. I felt it in my bones. Those women gently moved me around to clean my face and body. The gentleness brought me to tears.

Jesus. Jesus, I prayed, *What have I done wrong that so many bad things have happened in my life? In my kid's lives? I don't understand it and don't think I ever will.*

The plastic surgeon came in to stitch my eye. Katie said he was the best and that there would barely be a scar. I lay back and tried not to see the numbing needle coming at my eye.

Bo walked in. I couldn't see him while the doctor was stitching me up, as I was facing away from the doorway, but I heard his boots, his walking, and him stopping short at the door. "El," I heard him say. He sounded out of breath and scared. I started to tear up.

"Ellie, we are almost done. Hang on. Just breathe," said the kind plastic surgeon. I heard Katie and Bo move down the hall to talk.

Once the doctor was done, the tech was trying to move me into a wheelchair when Bo walked in with Katie right behind him. "Bo." I was so glad to see him. He came right beside me to help get me into my wheelchair. I didn't want to sit in it; I just wanted him to hold me. Katie shooed the tech away so that we could have a minute. I put my head gently onto his chest. I visibly winced as he tried to hug me.

"It's OK, El. It's OK. You are going to be OK." I didn't want to leave him, so they let him come with me to get my X-rays and CAT scan.

I started having a panic attack during the CAT scan. I didn't know where my phone was. I lost it somewhere in the woods. *What if he took it? What if he knows where I live? What if he comes to finish the job?*

The technician put Bo on the speaker to talk me down off my ledge. "El, you are doing great. Just hang in there a few more minutes. The police are looking for the attacker. He is more concerned about hiding from the police than getting into your phone. It's password protected." He kept talking to me. It felt like his voice was the only thing keeping me sane.

Bo got a text from Katie that a room was ready for me. They wanted to keep me overnight. I was holding onto Bo's hand the entire way up to my room. I wouldn't let him go, but I couldn't look at him either. I didn't want him to see what this person had done to my face and my body. This body that Bo had been so very careful to protect and wait for was now a bloody and broken mess. The attacker had stolen from me and Bo our happy, exciting, and innocent engagement. Everything suddenly felt very dark.

Katie walked in. "Well, you have a fractured wrist and cracked rib. The orthopedic doctor will be up here in a little bit. As soon as your CAT scan results come in, I will let you know." Katie came over and kissed the top of my head. Then she headed back to her office. She had always been my rock since we were twelve. I realized in that moment that she was stepping aside for Bo to be my person, partner, and rock.

While we were alone, Bo finally got me to look at him, and I started to cry again. I wanted to tell him not to look at me, but I was crying so much I couldn't get anything out. He gently lifted my head up, and I saw his eyes going over my cuts and bruises. So many emotions flashed across his face. Tears started to fall out of his eyes. "I'm sorry," I managed to say.

He shook his head. "El, do not apologize. I'm the one who is sorry. I am trying to wrap my head around what happened. I can't understand who would do this to you. Why would someone be so, so violent?"

What if Bo decides I am just a walking disaster? Someone who runs outside when it is dark and wears ear pods with her music turned all the way up? Why would he want to marry someone so foolish?

He finally said, "I am so angry, El. I have never felt this way. I want to kill him with my bare hands. I want to do to him what he did to ..." He got up and walked over to the window. His arms were quivering as he leaned against the windowsill. "He could have killed you, El." His voice cracked at the end of that sentence.

In walked a police detective. "Ellie, I am detective Jonas. I am here to take your statement while the events are still fresh in your mind."

I barely got out an, "OK."

Nick, Macie's husband, walked in and shook Bo's hand. They knew each other pretty well from church and around town. Detective Jonas pulled out his laptop but then sat down in front of it to hear my story. He would type it up later. I started from the beginning. Bo sat beside me and held my hand as I told the story. When I got to the part where the man punched me and then lay on top of me with his arm across my throat, choking me, Bo got up and threw his chair down. Nick walked over to him, and they stood in the corner. Bo leaned into the wall with his arm across his face.

"You are doing great, Ellie. Keep going," Detective Jonas said in his reassuring voice. I wondered how many times a week he had to use it to calm victims. I didn't want to say the next part. I started to choke up.

"At that moment I realized he was capable of killing me. I started praying, begging God to help me. He, he, he." I stopped to wipe my nose. *Oh, God*, I prayed, *please keep Bo calm.* "He started to pull," I paused and took a big breath. "He started to pull down my shorts." I could feel Bo losing it from behind me. Nick was saying something to him.

"I'm going to throw up," I said weakly. Someone passed me a bowl. I started to shake like I was reliving it. Bo came over to hold my hand. I started again. "My right arm was free, so I started feeling around for something—anything—and." I stopped mid-sentence. I saw God. I saw Him right there in that horrifying moment in time. He came. He had answered my plea for help. As I sat there talking to Detective Jonas, I began to have this sense of peace flood my body from deep within.

I continued with a sense of calmness. "I have no other way to explain it except to say God placed a perfectly shaped and weighted tree branch in my hand." I paused and looked at my hand. I could still feel it in my hand. I looked up at Detective Jonas and finished. "I swung it and hit him with everything I had. I am not even sure where I hit him. I was aiming for his head but honestly, I don't know. And then I just kept hitting him and pushing myself out from under him. I got up and ran the fastest I have ever run in my life." I started to shake uncontrollably again. Bo grabbed a blanket off the chair and tucked it around me. Bo then parked his chair right beside me and made everyone leave me alone. I scooted as close to Bo as I could while lying in the bed.

Chapter 44

LATER IN THE AFTERNOON, I woke up, and Bo wasn't there. The orthopedic doctor was talking to the nurse. They put a black Velcro brace on my wrist. My CAT scan came back good. There was no brain bleed but only a minor concussion. My ribs were being iced. The psychologist came by to chat. He talked to me about PTSD. I told him that I knew all about PTSD because I taught it. He said it was one thing to have head knowledge, but it was entirely different to experience it. *No kidding.*

Bo finally came in and smiled at me. "You are looking better every hour."

"Please don't lie to me," I said. "And don't make me laugh. It hurts. Everything hurts." I hated how whiney I sounded. "Does Katie have the kids? I need you to call Luke. I can't. I might cry. I don't want him to see my face all beat up. And Brooke. Can you ask Katie to call Brooke?"

"El," Bo sat beside the bed, "it is going to be OK. I will call Luke right after I text Katie to call Brooke."

While Bo was out calling Luke, Detective Jonas walked in. "Hi, Ellie. How are you feeling?"

"OK." *Terrible actually. Like a giant truck ran over me.*

"Here is your phone. We found it in the woods but needed to process it. Is Bo coming back in?"

"Yes, he is just making a phone call."

"I think we have a lead on who attacked you. We checked the video and check-ins for the gym during the time you were there."

Bo stuck his head in. Nick was with him. Detective Jonas continued. "Ellie, we went to his house, but he wasn't there. We put out an APB on his car, and they have pulled over the driver." Detective Jonas pulled out six pictures of men that all looked similar. "I need you to do this photo lineup and see if you can identify the guy who attacked you."

He placed the pictures on the table just like in the police shows on the True Crime Network. I saw the man, and I visibly jumped. I could see him in my mind at the gym. Whenever I randomly looked up, he stared right at me with a small smile. Maybe it was a sneer of some kind. I never really could figure it out. I remember my stomach clenching a little bit when I accidentally met his eyes. Was he watching me all the time and just waiting for me to look in his direction? He was creepy. *Why didn't I tell anyone? But what exactly would I have said? Excuse me, but there is a creepy guy who stares at me with a strange smile during my workouts. Can you please remove him?*

"Ellie, just take your time and point to the person who attacked you if you see him. If not, that is OK." I pointed and signed the back of the picture. Detective Jonas jumped up and left in a hurry. I shook my head. I was so tired. Every part of me hurt. I got more pain meds, and I gratefully fell asleep.

Chapter 45

I WOKE UP GROGGY AND THEN remembered what had happened. I tried to move too fast. I moaned and lay back down. It was dark outside, and I needed to go to the bathroom. Bo was sleeping on the couch. My mouth, skin, face, and body felt so gross. More than anything, I wanted a toothbrush and a shower. I moved slowly to the bathroom and shut the door. I saw all my toiletries: my toothbrush, face wash, and soap. *God bless Katie.*

I took off my wrist splint and turned on the water. I just let my mind focus on scrubbing everything away. All I saw were cuts and scratches everywhere. It was the first time I had a chance to examine myself. I had only been wearing a tank top and running shorts. The sticks, rocks, and who knows what else had done a number on me. Washing my hair and body with one good hand was time consuming and just plain difficult. I wanted to get all of it—all of him—off me. I felt like throwing up again. I forced myself to focus on drying off, which was not easy with one hand. I put my hair up in a towel and got clean PJs on.

It was so ignorant to run with earbuds in at a time when no one was around and so naive. After I brushed my teeth, I lifted my head up to look in the mirror. I audibly gasped at my face. My left eye was purple and green. There was a cut above it where the plastic surgeon had stitched four perfect little stitches. And there was a bruise on my throat.

"El, you OK?" Bo asked from the other side of the door.

"Yes," I answered. *Not really.*

I combed my hair out and dried it with a towel. Then I came out into the room. Bo had turned on the lamp on the far side. Katie had pulled some strings; we had one of the bigger, nicer rooms at the hospital.

Bo was sitting on the couch with his elbows on his knees and head on top of his folded hands. I walked gingerly over to him, and he looked up. "Feel better?" He forced a smile.

"I do. I am sorry if I woke you up. I just needed to shower—at midnight. Can I sit with you?" I felt like a little kid.

"Of course. And I wasn't sleeping anyway. You kept crying out in your sleep. After a few times, I realized you were dreaming. But," he trailed off. He sounded tired.

I climbed very carefully into his lap. I didn't cry. I was sure I had no tears left. I placed my head on his chest, and he held me as gently as possible. We just sat there quietly for a while. I couldn't sleep. My eyes just wouldn't close. I kept looking at the door hoping nothing would come and get me.

Then I started talking, and I couldn't stop. "Bo, I was so scared. I was so, so scared. I have never felt that frightened in my life. I'm certain I peed my pants. I thought he was going to kill me. And I just kept thinking, *I cannot leave my kids this way.* And then I felt that stick and hit him. I have never hit another person with anything—ever."

I felt Bo breathe in sharply. "I am so sorry I wasn't there to protect you. When I think about how scared you were, I just get angry at myself for not helping you."

"Oh, Bo, how would you know where I was or what I was doing?"

"I could have asked you the night before. I could have gone running with you."

"It was so clueless of me to run by myself when it was dark. I know better. I do. I wasn't aware of my surroundings, and I had my ear buds in. I'm sorry to put you through this."

"El, this guy is messed up. Don't apologize! And if the law would let me, I would take him out, El. It is a scary feeling to know what I could be capable of."

I sighed. "Why does everything and everyone feel so broken right now?" I asked him. But I was not really asking him, and he didn't answer. He carefully held me tighter. And this was why he was the love of my life.

"Bo, why do you think that when I was finally not focusing on my personal losses or my kids' losses that someone came to steal from me? Why does it feel like I can't catch my breath before there is another tragedy in my life?" I was quiet for a minute. "I think what I am asking is why does it feel like God isn't protecting me? Like I know this sounds immature, but it feels like today, God doesn't even like me."

Bo was quiet for a minute. "I think there is another way to look at things. There was the loss of your mom, and God provided Katie and her parents for you. There was the loss of Tommy, and God provided Katie and John and a whole community to help you. This world has evil forces in it, and that evil force comes to kill, steal, and destroy. It seems fair to say that you have been the recipient of that and that you have a target on your back. But it's not because God doesn't like you. You have a target on your back because Satan knows that God loves you."

I sighed. Bo was right. I sat with that for a while. "Bo," I said.

"Mmmhmm."

My chin started to quiver. "My face is a mess. It looks so bad. So ugly. I am too vain. I know it's silly."

"You will heal," he said gently. "I keep thinking how you could have given up at any point yesterday while fighting for your life. And no one would have blamed you. The brutality of it. I have pictured you fighting this guy, and I am blown away. You," Bo paused, trying to fight back tears. "I could have lost you. You could have given in. But you did not stop fighting. I have never been prouder of anyone than I am of you. And I am so grateful that you kept fighting for your life, us, and our future. I hope I prove to you that we are worth it every single day." I was bawling like a baby. And he just held me.

Chapter 46

I GOT DISCHARGED FROM THE HOSPITAL a day later. Bo took me to the police station where Detective Jonas wanted to talk with me again. I had a baseball hat on, hoping to slightly cover my blackish-greenish eye. Bo walked me down the hall to the detective's desk. Detective Jonas shook Bo's hand and asked us to sit down.

"Ellie, it turns out that this guy is from California. He moved out here with his girlfriend six months ago. The San Diego PD had been looking at him for several unsolved murders. Most of their evidence had been circumstantial until some DNA came back last week. They are able to link him to one of the murders."

I said, "A murderer. He is a murderer?" My mind was not grasping this well. I started thinking out loud. "I used to see them at the gym together. He gave me a bad vibe, but I never assumed he was capable of something like this." I felt Bo stiffen.

Detective Jonas continued, "They believe his MO was stalk, attack, rape, and murder."

I leaned forward and put my head down on the detective's desk so that I wouldn't pass out.

"Ellie, he was arrested last night. The San Diego DA wants to transfer him to California and move forward with a grand jury indictment. If you agree, it means there will be no trial or anything done to hold him accountable here in Texas until after California is done with him."

156

I was perfectly fine with letting California have him. I never wanted to see him again. I just wanted to move on with my life. I didn't even want justice or to be a part of it. If he could be in jail for the rest of his life in California, it would be all right by me.

Bo was acting funny. He was not talking but just walking beside me. When we got into his truck, he was not OK. I realized I just hadn't known him long enough to have seen this reaction from him before. I reached out to his leg. "Hey, what is going on? Are you OK? I am fine with him going to California."

"You didn't tell me you knew him," Bo said very tight lipped. I looked at him closely. He was upset.

"I don't know him," I said, instantly defensive. "I told the police initially that I had seen him before at the gym." I tried to explain. "At first, he would randomly smile at me, and I thought maybe I knew him. But I couldn't place him. And then he started following me around the gym and staring at me strangely. But I," I faded off. Bo wouldn't look at me.

We drove home in silence. I had no idea what to do or say, and my head was starting to pound. After we pulled up to my house, he just sat in the driver's seat, not moving. "Why didn't you tell me some guy was being creepy at the gym? I could have done something about it."

"Bo, please don't yell at me. Please. I'm sorry that I didn't tell you," I said, working hard to stay calm. "It didn't seem important. I can see why you are upset, but—"

Bo hit the steering wheel with his fist. Like all the emotion from the past twenty-four hours was exploding out of him. "You could have prevented this whole thing from happening!"

I gasped. "What are you saying?"

"El, you have to tell me these things," he said a little calmer. His voice was still raised.

I looked at him. Tears poured down my face. "I told you I was sorry. I can't remember everything that happens in a day. It just didn't seem like—"

"And look where that landed you!" Bo replied.

All of the sudden, I was tired of him interrupting me and yelling at me. I didn't even recognize this person sitting next to me. I started to get angry. "Are you blaming me for this?" I looked at him, and in his eyes, I saw it. *He does blame me.* I felt sick, so I did what any injured animal would have done; I fought back. "Guess what? I have guys hit on me all day and have to ignore that just to get my work done. I didn't talk to him, flirt with him, or anything. It isn't my fault.!" I was crying and yelling.

Bo sounded very patronizing when he said, "You can't just walk around ignoring red flags."

"I cannot believe you are blaming me for this."

"How can you not see this? He was stalking you. Probably following you. He knew exactly where you were going. If you would have just told me." Bo got out of the truck and slammed his door. He walked toward the trees on the other side of the driveway.

My heart suddenly felt ripped to shreds. I felt like I was having a panic attack. I couldn't catch my breath. It felt like everything in my life exploded a few days ago and like it would never go back together.

I opened my door and climbed out with my bag. It was more like I slid down his tall truck. Nobody was home at my house, so I opened my garage and went in. I dumped my bag on the counter. I wanted to keep arguing and to make him say that it wasn't my fault, but I was too exhausted. And besides, trying to make someone say something never really works. I lay down on my couch, and Bingo came to lick my hands. I closed my eyes hoping for some kind of relief from my aching ribs, wrist, and heart.

After about five minutes, I heard Bo walk inside. I couldn't stop crying. I was wiping my tears and nose on a blanket. He crouched down by my head and took my right hand. I jerked my hand away from him and said, "Please go away." I wouldn't look at him.

"El, I completely exploded on you. I am so, so sorry." He took my hand and pressed it to his bowed head. He was silent for a minute. "I hurt you. I never wanted to hurt you, and I did. It was misdirected anger. I am angry at him and not you. Please believe me. Please forgive me. I was wrong.

"El, please look at me." I wouldn't. I had stopped crying, but my face was still buried in the blanket. "It is not your fault. And you are right. I have no idea what it is like to walk around as a woman and decide who to ignore and who to take seriously. I am so sorry. I know you are hurting. Please forgive me. Please, El."

I was to blame. It was all my fault. In fact, Bo needed to leave me right there on that couch. I reached for my ring and took it off. I still couldn't look at him. I sat up and handed it to him. "Take it. Do not marry me. There is something wrong with me. Death and destruction follow me around." I put my head into my hands and curled up in a ball on my couch.

Bo quietly took it. He stood up, and I prepared myself for him to walk out. Then I felt him sit down beside me. He took my left hand, splint and all, and placed the ring back on my finger. He lifted my hand up and kissed it. I still couldn't look at him.

"El, there is nothing wrong with you. You are not broken. You did not cause anyone's death or bring any of this pain on yourself. This world is broken, unfair, and scary. You are a fighter. You made it through childhood without a mother. You made it through two years of a big loss. You fought to keep your family together, your faith never wavered, and you figured out how to live without a partner. You are the strongest and bravest person I know."

We sat there in silence for over five minutes. "Bo, I am scared," I finally said.

"You are not alone. We will get through this together. I promise, I will never let anyone hurt you again—ever."

"You scared me," I whispered through tears.

"I'm sorry, El." Bo's voice caught. "I do not blame you. I am so sorry I said it. Hang on, El. We are going to make it through this. We are." Bo sat next to me and gently stroked my hair—the only part of me that didn't hurt.

PART 5

PART 5

Chapter 47

IT HAD BEEN FOUR WEEKS since the attack, and Bo and I were standing in the kitchen chatting with Luke and Brooke. Tea, Whit, and Katie were in the den talking to Peter Burke. Peter was our family counselor. Both Bo and I had seen him individually once, and this was our first family session. Peter was such an insightful, God-focused counselor. That day, we were going to talk about the attack and help the kids and Katie process what had happened.

We started walking toward the couch. Bo was holding my hand. He turned to me and asked, "You doing OK?" I nodded and smiled.

Luke piped in, "You look good mom. That eye is only a little green, and that cut is barely noticeable." When Luke came home the day after I came home, he walked in, saw me, and started to cry. He had always been my emotional kid. When Brooke came home, we just sat on the couch and hugged for an hour. Bo was so great with them. He talked them through what had happened because I wasn't ready to keep telling the story. It was emotionally exhausting.

Bo sat with Luke late into the night. Now all my kids were back to sleeping in my room just like when Tommy died. When Luke wasn't there, Bo slept on the couch. We were all just a little jumpy and traumatized.

I had been waking up in the middle of the night scared and not able to get back to sleep. I would walk out to Bo, and he would let me lie down beside him and calm me down. Poor Bo; he was probably glad Luke was home for the weekend so that he could go home and sleep in his own bed.

Peter asked everyone to sit down and get comfortable. We all went around the room and introduced ourselves to Peter. He had us play a silly game to warm up. Then he started with a prayer. "Lord, You are good, and Your mercy, grace, love, and goodness endure even in times of sorrow, confusion, and pain. Pour healing out on this beautiful family, turn their mourning into dancing, and trade all their sorrow for Your joy. Do only what You can do. Amen."

Peter took us all through that day. The emotions were high, and we were using Kleenex. But it was good. Everyone was able to voice their fear, frustration, and love for one another. I think Bo really saw how Tommy's had death affected my kids and that the attack on me sent them back to that trauma. We were all in need of grace from one another at that moment.

At the end of our session, Peter looked at me and asked me if I was OK. I smiled. *How can I not be OK?* I had a room full of people who cared about me. Most people didn't have that, and I would forever be grateful to God for those who surrounded me, despite all the heartache.

Then we lightened the mood with some laughter and jokes. It was very emotionally draining, but it was good to hear everyone's thoughts and perspective on the events. It was absolutely a step toward healing for all of us.

Peter stayed to chat with me, Bo, and Katie. I was going back to work on Monday, and Bo was going to go hunting with some friends. He wanted to cancel, but I wouldn't let him. He needed to get away from all this. I know I had been more than needy with him, and I hated that I was. It wasn't how I wanted to be, but I couldn't seem to stop myself. Katie was going to spend the night that week if I needed her.

I told Peter that I was nervous about parking in the garage on campus because it was always dark in there. I was still very jumpy. I had my mace and an alarm on my key chain. Peter agreed that

I needed to try. He recommended a Bible verse to say and a song to sing. I had told him I was learning some old gospel songs, so he wrote down one he thought was a good one. Bo and I would see him on the following Friday morning for some pre-marriage counseling.

I said goodbye to Peter and Katie and walked Bo out. He was leaving in the morning for his trip. He took both my hands, even though my left one was still in a splint. "I don't feel good about leaving you," he said with a concerned look on his face.

"I have Luke and then Katie, plus my dog and kids will all be in my bed anyway." I smiled, trying to make light of the situation.

He touched the scar above my eye and then brushed my stray curls behind my ear like he always did. "You are doing great. I am really proud of you, El." Bo gently and slowly slipped his arms around my waist. He was careful not to put pressure on my ribs. I wrapped my arms around him, and he kissed my head. "We are going to make it through this, El."

I started to tear up. I hoped so. "Please have a good time. You have taken such good care of me for the past four weeks. I want you to go enjoy yourself. I will miss you." I leaned into his solid chest. It was like a rock. He had been my rock.

Chapter 48

IT WAS FRIDAY, AND BO and I were in Peter's office. It was our first session together. We were doing pre-marital counseling. Peter was asking how the week had gone for me. "Baby steps" felt the most fitting word to use. "It was scary parking in the garage, and I had to just breathe when I felt my heart rate skyrocket. My finger was on the mace all the way to my office. But I did it.

"I got up in front of my students and talked a little bit about what happened. When class ended, I had a line of young women wanting to tell me how sorry they were, how they had a similar experience, or how they knew someone who had a similar experience. It was very moving, and we all shed some tears. The amount of physical violence in this world astounds me.

"That night, I slept in my bed without Luke or Bo in the house. Everyone else was in my room. But we did it." I was saying all of this, yet I felt like I was drowning, like I wasn't OK, but maybe this was the new OK. My brain felt like mush. I was having trouble focusing.

Peter was nodding his head and looked at me. "Ellie, how would you describe yourself before the day of the attack?"

"I would say strong, smart, confident, and fun, I guess," I said nervously. I didn't know why I was nervous. Maybe it was because I was never actually any of those things and always had been and would be a mess.

Peter looked at Bo. "Would you agree?"

Bo said, "Absolutely."

Why do I suddenly feel like crying? Why do I cry all the time? It was so exhausting.

Peter then asked me, "How would you describe yourself the past five weeks?"

"Basically, the opposite. I don't feel strong because I haven't been able to work out at all with my rib and wrist. There is nowhere to go because I am not going back to my gym or any gym. And I feel unintelligent for getting myself in that situation."

Bo tried to interrupt, but Peter held up his hand. "Let her finish."

"I don't feel confident in my decisions. I second-guess myself a bunch. I never used to do that." I sighed and stared at my hands in my lap.

Peter looked at Bo. "How do you feel about what Ellie is saying?"

"Terrible. I feel responsible for all of it." Bo sighed and looked defeated.

Peter asked, "How are you responsible?"

Bo ran his hands through his short blond hair. "I should have been there to protect her."

Peter leaned in. "Listen to me. You both need to forgive yourselves. Bo, you need to forgive yourself for not being there. And Ellie, you need to forgive yourself for running by yourself with ear buds in. And when I say forgive yourself, what I am really saying is stop condemning yourself. You are in fact telling God that condemning His Son for your mistakes was not enough and that there needs to be more punishment and mental and physical anguish for everything to be made right."

"When you each accepted Christ, you were accepting that all the punishment for all your junk was finished. It was over. Sitting in self-condemnation is keeping you both from moving forward." Bo was looking at Peter, and I was crying silently. Peter asked me what I was thinking.

"I think you are right. I am focused on punishing myself to the point that I am convincing myself that Bo definitely does not want to marry me anymore and that his rejection is my punishment for a bad decision."

Bo looked like he was about to come out of the chair. "El, I tell you all the time that you are who I want to be with for the rest of my life. There is no other woman on this planet. I wonder if my punishment for not being there is that you don't trust me, and I keep having to tell you that."

Peter looked at us and smiled. "Do you see it? You are both walking in self-condemnation and are looking for a punishment to atone for your mistakes. You have decided that your punishment is basically to blow up your relationship."

Bo and I both stared at Peter. "Wow," I said. "Are we hopeless? Because I could really use some hope."

Peter exclaimed, "There is abundant hope for you both. So this week I want you to work on taking those self-condemning thoughts captive, placing them at the foot of God's throne, and saying, 'God, help me to accept You and what You have already done.'"

Bo and I had been so desperate for some real healing that we did just that. All week, we held each other accountable and asked each other how many times that day, we took those condemning thoughts captive. It was a great way for us to talk about all of our thoughts during the day.

Chapter 49

THE NEXT WEEK, PETER ASKED us what one thing was that we wished we could change about the last six weeks. Bo said that he wished he was there in that moment to protect me because he was fearful that he had failed me. I said that I wanted to be who I was before that day because I was really fearful that I would never see her again.

After some discussion, Peter said this to Bo, "Think about this. In your saying to Ellie, 'I will protect you,' you placed yourself in God's place. Bo, you were not created to be her protector. You were created to pray for her. You were created to trust Him. But you were not created to be God. And when you place yourself on that throne as her protector and the only giver of good things, you are trying to be God to her. All you will end up with is a huge anxiety problem as you recognize that you can't keep her safe 100 percent of the time.

"Now I am not saying that she can't come to you and say she is frightened by something. She absolutely can, but your job is to pray with and for her that she finds the peace of God because there is nothing else on this earth like the peace of God. You cannot replicate it for her by monitoring her every move or buying guns and the latest and greatest security system. It just won't work."

Then we talked about my answer. Peter said, "Ellie, you are making your desire to be like you used to be an idol. Your standard for your behavior has become something like how close to being like the old Ellie did I get to today instead of how close to being like Jesus did I get today. The Holy Spirit will not get you closer to the old Ellie, but He will get you closer to Jesus."

Bo and I started coming to Peter with notebooks. We took notes. We joked that he was really tearing us down so that our only choice was to build ourselves back up using more truth and wisdom than before. We started praying together, and that was bringing us closer on a whole other level.

Chapter 50

THE HOUSE WAS REALLY TAKING shape, or so I was told. I wasn't allowed to see it. Tea and Whit went with Bo every weekend to work on their rooms. Brooke came home most weekends to work on the wedding. We were five weeks away, and I was assured that the house, garden, and pool would all be ready. It felt freeing not to oversee anything because I was having to make some hard decisions.

All the kids agreed to put our house on the market. It was tough because all our memories of Tommy were in that home. But it was old, and it needed a lot of work. I was getting it ready to sell, and some of our furniture was slowly being moved to the new house. I had given Luke a lot of our furniture for his place. Going through all our stuff felt cathartic. I was boxing up Tommy's and my wedding album, old pictures of us, and my wedding ring. It was sad. There is no other word but sad. However, building something new was exciting, and it felt like everything was going to be OK. I hadn't felt like that in a long time.

I was asked by Adam if I wanted to sing at church in two weeks. I wanted to talk about it with Bo, Peter, and then my kids. I owed my church family so much.

Katie had told me that right after Macie had called her about my attack, she had gotten on the phone to the church. There was a prayer chain that started immediately. Food was delivered to the house for a week to feed all five kids plus John and Katie. There were also volunteers who drove the kids to their activities and school so that John could go to work. Once I was home, we had dinner for two more weeks. I was overwhelmed by my church family. And I told Bo that I did not know how people made it through devastation and crisis without a church family. It literally broke my heart to think of people going through life and all the heartache it can bring without people surrounding them with prayer and support.

Chapter 51

B O AND I WERE SEEING Peter together. He was doing a few family-blending counseling sessions with all of us. We talked about what the kids wanted to call Bo, how they would introduce him to their friends, how we would handle any discipline, what to do if my kids and I got in an argument, and how Bo could be involved. It was such a good time of bonding and hearing one another. It brought us so much closer as a family.

I wanted to sing again. I told Peter and Bo that I realized that the reason I hadn't wanted to do it up until now was because I didn't feel worthy enough to lead people in worship and that I wasn't leadership material because I made unwise choices. But I also realized that I was only worthy to sing to God because I had been made worthy through Christ. And I sang out of thanksgiving for the grace of that gift.

Bo had such a big smile. Peter nodded and asked, "What are you going to sing?"

"Fight My Battles"[14] and "Tremble".[15]

Bo said, "I have heard her practicing, and it will blow up the place."

Peter responded, "I may have to visit your church next Sunday."

"I would absolutely love for you to," I gushed. "Plus, I really want to meet your wife and thank her for letting you come to our house on Saturdays to work with our kids."

I also thought that I was physically ready to start working out.

I only had three weeks until the wedding, and I needed to build up some muscle and endurance. But I had to create a different way of doing it.

As engagement gifts, Bo bought me an elliptical, treadmill, and a weight set. They would be moved into our new house right before the wedding. I was so excited that I could not stop hugging him and squealing. Katie was there and joked, "It takes a really special woman to not take those gifts the wrong way, especially before the wedding." Bo was coming over early in the mornings to show me some new workouts. It was fun to workout with him, more than I thought it would be.

Chapter 52

WE WERE FINISHING UP OUR time together one afternoon. It had been a particularly difficult week for me. My attacker was indicted by a grand jury, and a trial date was set for one of the rapes and murders in California. The reality of it all just hit me hard. And I was angry, which Peter said was good and normal.

Peter turned to me. "Ellie, desire for justice is a God-given emotion because we are made in His likeness. But only He can exact perfect justice for your attacker. We just make a mess of it. I know you are tired of crying, of death and destruction in your life, and of the work of repairing. You feel that you already had to do so much when your mom and Tommy died. And now this. But no one can wipe away tears like the God of love. And He is coming to do it for eternity. That is where your hope is. Hold onto it."

Chapter 53

KATIE AND I WERE OUT shopping for something to wear for the rehearsal dinner and some pajamas that were a little sexier than leggings and an old T-shirt. I said, "Will Bo even care?"

Katie said, "Yes, all men care." John explained it to her once. It was the fact that you made the effort, even if it only stayed on your body for less than five minutes. I rolled my eyes but decided to buy a few things.

We found my rehearsal dinner dress. It was made of a light-gray, shimmery material, and it was long, sleeveless, and with a square cut top. It made my eyes look lighter and more gray than green. And it had a slit up to my thigh. We found sexy, strappy, glittery heels. Katie and I laughed that he was going to struggle to make it through one more night before he could have me.

I told her I was a little nervous about our wedding night. I had only ever been with Tommy. Bo just seemed to have a lot of experience with women.

Katie smiled knowingly. "Ummm, you will be fine."

I laughed. "OK, but also, I haven't told him that I had a boob job yet. There just hasn't been a good time to tell him."

Katie was laughing so hard that I couldn't help but laugh with her. After I had Tea, my breasts became flat sacks of nothing. And the fact that my mom had breast cancer made the decision easy. I loved my new ones. They looked so young and perky and not tired and sucked dry.

"Maybe don't tell him until after the wedding night. I am sure he won't really care," Katie said.

"I just feel like I am being deceptive."

"How about tell him all about your boobs after the rehearsal dinner while wearing the dress that has a slit that runs all the way to your butt. He won't be sleeping at all with those things on his mind."

"I don't know. I am real happy that you find all of this hilarious," I said. And then we both giggled the rest of the afternoon.

Chapter 54

THE NEXT SUNDAY, BO'S PARENTS came into town. I hadn't seen them since before the attack. His sweet momma hugged me hard. She looked me in the eyes and asked, "Are you doing OK?"

I felt like I could honestly answer that I was. "Thank you for raising an amazing son who has been such a rock throughout this ordeal." We both had tears in our eyes. "I am fully aware that I have some PTSD. But with Bo's support, we are going to make it."

Peter came to church on Sunday with his lovely wife Anna. I liked her immediately and spent some time talking with her. Luke and Brooke walked in with Katie and her crew. Everyone sat in a row together: Bo's parents, my dad, Katie and John, the girls, my amazing kids, Peter and Anna, and Bo. It was all the people who have loved me, prayed for me, led me through the last few months, and were walking with me into my future. I could not be more grateful.

I took the microphone and thanked all the people in the church for their willingness to help us the past few months. Then the band started to play, and I began to sing.

> Peace, bring it all to peace,
> The storm's surrounding me.
> Let it break at Your name.

Still, call the sea to still,
The rage in me to still,
Every wave at your name.

Thank You, Jesus, for being the only One in this world who makes darkness tremble and silences fear. Then we launched into "This is How I Fight My Battles."

Afterward, Bo met me backstage. He hugged me hard, and it didn't hurt. "You are amazing, El. A gift to everyone here today."

I buried my head in his neck. "Thank you for seeing me through. I cannot wait to marry you in a few weeks." He put his lips on mine, and I kissed him back.

PART 6

Chapter 55

THE DAY BEFORE THE REHEARSAL dinner, everyone was in town. Bo's two older sisters, their families, and his parents, David and Sarah, were there. We had his entire family over for the day to get to know everyone better. My kids and his nieces and nephews were outside playing. The weather was gorgeous—a Texas November with chilly mornings but clear skies and sunny afternoons. I enjoyed getting to know Micah and Dinah. They all had Sarah's eyes; they were soft, kind, and deep-brown eyes. While Bo was blonde, his sisters had their mother's dark brown hair and smaller build. Their kids were Tea and Whit's age, which made for a lot of cousin mischief.

After spending a day eating, talking, and hanging out in the backyard, Bo's parents wanted to pray a blessing over us. Everyone gathered around and formed a circle. Bo's dad, David, said, "Future things are hidden from us; the next second, minute, and hour are all hidden except blessings. God tells us what we need to do for His blessing, smile, Spirit, grace, and full revelation. It is walking in obedience. Both of you have walked in obedience to Him throughout this engagement process. Ellie, we are so happy for you to join the Channing family. We already know you will be his better half. And Bo, we thought this day would never come, but we realize that you were waiting for God's perfect person for you." David prayed Psalm

128 over each of us and our marriage. We all hugged and said we would see one another on the following day.

Bo had already moved in, and he was staying at the new house. He didn't want me to see it until the next day. Even then, I couldn't look around at our bedroom or the upstairs. It was all a surprise. I was beginning to realize that Bo really loved to surprise me.

The next day, I had my friend Jenna come over to do my makeup. She did makeup for the rich and famous, model shoots, and weddings. She was absolutely gifted. She was doing a light version of makeup that night, and then on the wedding day, it would be the full show. I showed her my dress for that night, and she was so excited at the prospect of putting shimmery eye makeup on me. Katie and my entire family were helping set up for the rehearsal dinner, so it was just me and Jenna. We had a fabulous time catching up on each other's lives while she inserted helpful hints like I needed to use more than lip gloss as makeup. I protested that I did use tinted moisturizer with sunblock and occasionally mascara.

Chapter 56

I DROVE UP THE WINDING ROAD that I had last seen when Bo had asked me to marry him. *Wow!* That felt like a year ago instead of a few months. I was absolutely wowed by the house as I pulled up and drove through the circular drive. It was gorgeous, and it had perfect landscaping and even rocking chairs on the front porch.

I parked in the garage—my garage. Everything—the air, my footsteps, and the lighting—felt magical. I walked through the garage door as directed, past the guest room, then by my office, and into the kitchen. I was so nervous to see Bo. My stomach was doing flip-flops. My glittery high-heeled sandals clicked on the tile floor.

The house looked so beautiful. I wished I had better words. There were so many windows, each filling the room with light from the sun. I felt a well of emotion as I saw the kitchen and living area. Bo had a better eye than I did for decorating. The furniture and the colors of white, tan, blue, and green were just lovely. I felt like a princess walking around in her new castle. God was so good to me.

"El," Bo said from the staircase, "you look incredible." He walked toward me, smiling. I knew I looked pretty amazing thanks to Jenna. He took my hand and kissed it. "I do not want to mess up your very shiny lips."

I laughed. "You look so handsome." His beautiful dark blue-gray suit complimented my dress, and his tie matched perfectly. Jenna had picked it all out.

"Come on!" Bo said as he took my hand. "I cannot wait to show you the backyard. The last time you saw it, it was a mud pit." We walked onto the screened-in back porch, which was giant and had ceiling fans, comfy chairs, and pillows. Out the screen door and three steps down from the back porch was a beautiful, large stone patio, which had six round teak wooden tables with white chairs around them for dinner that night. Then three steps below that were the pool and hot tub, with a bridge going across and separating the two. Then three more steps down were the grass with a crushed-granite pathway downward toward the edge of the hill where the sun would set. White chairs were set up for the next day and a beautiful white, curved trellis covered with flowers and vines. All of it was breathtaking.

I told Bo that, and he said, "I am so glad you like it." I kept looking at him, smiling, and complementing everything. We sat down by the overlook, where he had proposed, and chatted. We were still holding hands and laughing about silly things when people started to arrive. We pulled ourselves up and walked back up the stairs to the guests—our families. I could not stop smiling the entire evening. Bo and I had decided that we would be next to each other all evening. There would be no separating to talk to people. We would let the people come to us.

The photographer took some pictures. Then we ate a beautifully catered meal after rehearsing. Then it was toast time. My dad got up and quoted Proverbs 23:24, which said, "The father of a righteous child has great joy." He paused and then said, "Ellie, you have been a great joy to me each year of your life. I am so happy for you to find someone who brings you just as much joy. God bless you both." I was dabbing my tears so that I didn't ruin my makeup. My dad loved Bo so much. He had loved Tommy too but just differently.

Then Bo's family got up and talked about me and how happy I had made their son. They were just the sweetest words I had ever heard, all poured out over us. Of course, Bo's friends stood up and roasted him. It was hilarious. Then my four kids stood up in order of their heights. Luke began. "Bo, we like you. We like you so much, we feel it is our duty to tell you some things about our mother that you might not know yet. And these truths may make you reconsider."

Oh no, I thought. Everyone was already laughing. I put my hands over my face.

Luke pulled out a long piece of paper. Everyone laughed. "Things you may want to know about my mom before you get married. She always drives ten or more miles over the speed limit but is *always* able to talk her way out of a ticket. More like flirt and smile, but we can say talk."

Bo was totally playing along like they had rehearsed it. Everyone was laughing.

"She can drive while putting on lip gloss, texting her friends, and singing to music, so one would think she can multitask, but no, at least not in the kitchen. She had to take the batteries out of the smoke alarm closest to the kitchen. Once we could all read, she left us to our own meals and the microwave. She does occasionally make a mean box of mac and cheese."

I was so embarrassed but laughing hard. Each kid of mine was taking his or her turn.

"She cries at every movie or show, even the news."

"She is late almost everywhere."

"When she is mad at you, she might use a bad word or two."

"She can only chew gum for five minutes and then starts to gag, no matter what kind."

"She hates to do laundry. Once we could all use a stool and reasonably reach the bottom of the washing machine, she handed that over to each of us. So at about eight years old, we all were doing our own laundry."

I was covering my face with my hands. Bo was laughing with his eyebrows raised in surprise about some of them.

"Let me tell you how amazing she is, just to be fair," started Luke. "She listens to every word and every story we ever tell her. All you have to do is call and tell her you need her, and she is there."

"She has a way of placing a gospel truth in conversation that leaves you wanting more of her wisdom."

"She has the best sense of humor and laughs at all our jokes, good or bad."

"She is always up for a change of plans."

"She is the smartest woman we know."

"We love you so much mom. And Bo, Godspeed."

I was laughing so hard that I was crying. Bo was up next. He took the microphone. He thanked my dad for agreeing to allow him to propose. Then he thanked my kids for loving me well and allowing him to come into their lives and love me.

It was my turn. "I want to thank each of my kids for their honest public assessment of my parenting. I think you all turned out fabulous, despite me. Thank you for being generous and loving when I introduced you to Bo. You are each so precious to me and have been anchors for me in the difficult times. You each are world changers. And I cannot wait to see what God has next for you." I continued thanking my friends and family. It was such a joy to be able to publicly acknowledge each of them.

Then my kids and I had a treat for everyone. We got up and sang a worship song together with Whit playing the piano. We sang "Great are You Lord" and led our family and close friends in worship. Then Bo joined us, and everyone gathered around us to pray. I couldn't stop the tears.

Jenna fixed my makeup, and everyone moved toward the house except us. We just sat back down at the table to talk and flirt a little. He was holding my hand almost the whole evening.

"I always wondered about the gum thing," Bo said, smiling at me.

I shrugged. "It's a weird quirk."

"Any other weird quirks I need to know about before tomorrow night?"

"You are just going to have to find those out for yourself," I said in a very flirty way.

"Oh, I plan on finding everything out about you tomorrow night," Bo said playfully back.

Here was my opening. "So I need to tell you something about my body, but there has been no good time to bring it up."

Bo looked beyond intrigued. I told him about my mastectomy and reconstructive surgery after Tea. Bo responded by kissing the hand he was holding and said, "Thank you for telling me. I am grateful you are here and healthy."

I continued, "And since we are having an awkward conversation anyway, I am super nervous about tomorrow night. I have only been with one person ever. I feel very inexperienced suddenly. I just don't know if you have any expectations of me. I wanted to tell you how I was feeling."

Bo looked at me with the kindest eyes. He looked down at the hand he was holding and played with my engagement ring for a minute. Then he looked up at me again. "After my divorce, I swore myself to celibacy until God brought the right woman to me—the one I would marry. I have been celibate for eight years. A long time. Some days, it felt like a hundred years. I have no expectations of you. I love you. We will figure it all out together, OK?"

"OK, and I love you too," I said.

Bo leaned over, brought his hand to my chin, and tipped it up toward his mouth. It was the sweetest kiss ever.

Chapter 57

I DIDN'T SLEEP VERY WELL THAT night. I was up wandering my house in the early morning hours for the last time. It was really a bittersweet moment. This house was Whit and Tea's only home. They all grew up here and had all their friends over. We had multiple parties and celebrations there.

I walked out to the backyard. It was full of giant old oak trees. The new house was so different from this one. My house was old and familiar. My new house was new and completely unknown to me. I was certain I would love it. But both were built with so much love. I sighed.

Almost everything was out of this house that had been my home. The buyers would move in on the following week. I was going to the new house around noon to get ready. All my books, journals, papers, files, and even my laptop were in my office at the new house. My clothes, makeup, and jewelry were in my new bathroom and bedroom, which I hadn't even seen. All I had were my phone charger, skin-care products, a towel, and the leggings and sweatshirt that I was wearing, plus Tea and my dog. Everyone else had slept at the new house. Brooke was in her room, and Whit was in his room. Bo's parents were in the guest bedroom, and his sister and family were in a nearby hotel. Tea kept me company on the previous night. I still had no desire to sleep alone.

The master-bedroom set would be left with the house. The

people who bought the house wanted it, and I didn't want to bring it into our marriage. It was the bed where Tommy had died, we had made love hundreds of times, and we had fought, laughed, and snuggled with our kids.

Katie texted me and said she was on her way. I washed my face and brushed my teeth. I sat on the front porch's steps and waited.

Katie walked up. She smiled as she handed me a Starbucks strong coffee.

"I love you," I said.

"How are you doing?" she asked as she sat down next to me.

"I feel like I am mourning a little bit. Leaving all these memories. I am probably just overly emotional because …"

Katie gave me her annoyed look. "You are not leaving Tommy, or exchanging Tommy, or whatever your head is thinking. So grieve right now for Tommy and that life you had, the good and the bad. You have time. And then when you are done, you are getting in my car and getting ready for the next part of your life. It isn't one or the other; it's both. Both men are a part of you, and that is OK."

Katie was right. I didn't have to get rid of Tommy to marry Bo. Tommy would always be part of me. And whoever I was because of Tommy's influence in my life, Bo loved that person. But I did wish life was simpler like a straight path instead of all the twists and turns where I couldn't see what was around the corner. But it wasn't. It never had been and never would be.

Chapter 58

I was in the guest room of my new house. I hadn't seen Bo, and I was surrounded by women doing my hair, makeup, and nails. The one decision I did make about the wedding was to not have any bridesmaids. I just wanted it to be simple. Katie, Brooke, and Tea would stand beside me. And Luke, Whit, and Bo's close friends would stand beside him. Brooke was coming and going quietly, checking on her project wedding, and literally living her best life. Tea kept running back in and out. Katie was feeding me and making me hydrate. Bo's sisters and mom were helping Brooke put the finishing touches on the decorations. After more coffee and a few glasses of champagne, I was laughing at all the chaos and just loving each female in my life. Women are the most amazing humans on the planet.

By late afternoon, the house got quiet, as everyone was outside. It was a beautiful November day. I kept getting up and looking out the window that faced the backyard. Bo wanted the service to be right before sundown. Luke was outside putting the last touches on the hanging strings of lights. There was a dance floor brought in just for that night. My dad was talking with Bo's dad as they walked around the property. I saw Bo's Aunt Jane and Uncle Pat with Sally and Joe. I saw Momma Barbara with Katie's girls. Tea and Whit were handing out programs. Bo's mom was talking to Bo. They hugged as she wiped tears away. So much sweetness and joy were all around me.

A little bit later, Bo knocked on the door and asked if I could stick my hand out so that he could hold it and pray. Jenna gave me a look and said, "No crying." I gave her a thumbs-up. But as soon as Bo held my hand, I started to melt.

"Jesus, all good things come only from You. Thank You for this beautiful woman. For the good she has brought into my life. Give her peace and joy as she walks into her new life with me. I am sure that parts of this day will be difficult for her. Pour your blessings over us today. Thank You for loving us before we loved You. Thank You for Your mercy and grace, which allows us to call out to You. Shine Your favor and light over this home and family. Amen."

I tried to hold back the tears and only sniffled once. Jenna motioned me back into my chair. This cued the touch-ups.

I was finally ready. I stepped into my Loni Morgan wedding dress. It was ivory with white gold and a classic A-line dress. It was covered with Alencon lace and medallion details on tulle with crystal beaded trim. It had a scalloped hemline with a deep V back and covered-button detail. Jenna put my long hair in waves and a small, thin crown on top. My earrings matched the top of the crown. I slipped my high-heeled, ivory shoes on and waited for Luke to come get me. I sat by the window. I was people watching at my own wedding. I felt like a princess who was waiting for my prince.

Katie walked in. She covered her mouth as tears filled her eyes. I had been working hard not to cry until I saw her tears. "Oh, my goodness, Ellie, you are stunning. Bo is going to lose his mind." She grabbed and hugged me. "To have watched you go through the last two years was so hard. I wanted to take away all your pain and stress. And I felt so useless to you."

"Katie, you were what kept me going. I am so incredibly proud to be your best friend. I can't even fathom my life without you in it." I started to weep. Jenna was giving me the side eye and unpacking her bag to touch me up.

Katie gave me one last squeeze before she left and said, "God has turned mourning into dancing. He has turned graves into gardens.

He builds beauty from ashes. He is the only one who can. And He always will."

Jenna refinished my face, and then the photographer came to get me for front and side yard shots with my family and the wedding party. She had just finished with the guys. Taking a photo with all my women partners in this life was so meaningful. We had raised our kids, cried, rejoiced, and laughed together. We had laughed at ourselves and this life. I would cherish those pictures forever.

Luke came for me. My dad was waiting in the kitchen. They would both walk me down the aisle. We started down the porch steps, the first-tier porch, and to the pool. Then we went across the bridge and down to the path. The sun was setting because, of course, Bo had everything timed perfectly. I felt like I was walking directly into the sunset. It reminded me of the verse from Malachi: "But for you who revere my name, the sun of righteousness will rise with healing in its rays." *Healing.* The walk toward Bo was light, warmth, joy, clearness of vision, and healing.

Bo looked so handsome in his blue suit with an ivory shirt and boots. He was smiling at me as I continued to walk. I got closer and closer to him, and I could see tears in his eyes. Luke saw it too and began to sniffle. I even heard my dad clear his throat a few times. I couldn't take my eyes off Bo. He was such a gift to me. He was handsome, kind, and trustworthy.

I could hear gasps and murmurs, and I looked around and smiled at everyone. It was the dress, and it was worth every penny. I literally felt like I was floating. I got to Bo, and his eyes were red and filled with tears. He took my hands and looked straight into my eyes. I remember smiling so big at him. "Ellouise Parker, you were worth waiting for," he said as he wiped away a tear from his eye.

I didn't hear a word our pastor said. I was trying to, but I was so distracted by the magic of it all, the amazing sunset colors, and my daughters and best friend standing beside me and my boys behind Bo that I felt completely covered in blessing. And when Bo put my wedding band on, I gasped. It matched the engagement ring perfectly, and it had so many diamonds on it. I looked at him with my mouth open. He just laughed.

I loved putting his ring on his finger. It was so moving and powerful to stand in front of everyone and make a vow before God. And when our pastor said, "You may kiss your bride," Bo kissed me and then picked me up and swung me around. I threw my head back and laughed. We did it!

Chapter 59

WE TOOK THE OBLIGATORY PICTURES but had some fun with them. They weren't all posed pictures. Bo kept kissing and telling me how beautiful I looked. We danced our first dance to "Prayed for You,"[16] which was so classic, but we couldn't think of another song that summed up our journey to each other any better. The dance was precious, and all the love I had for Bo filled every part of me.

I looked up at him while we were dancing and said, "I can't believe you chose me. Out of all the women in your life, surrounding your life, you picked me."

He pulled me close and whispered, "I pick you every day of the rest of my life. And, El, I don't want to forget to tell you, you are stunning in that dress. I will never forget how you looked walking toward me. I don't think I can explain it except to say you looked like an angel."

I had this desire to beg him not to die or to ever leave me. "I need you in my life every single day. Please don't ever leave me." I smiled at him through tears.

He looked at me, and he was quiet for a second. "As much as I can prevent it, I will not ever leave you. I did just pledge my entire life to you in front of God and everyone."

We danced through another favorite song, and then Luke and I had a surprise choreographed dance because well it was Luke.

He was a fantastic country-western dancer, and he could twirl me around the dance floor so well.

Next up was eating at our table, but we never actually got to our table to sit down. So many of our amazing friends were there, and they were all so thrilled for us. We stopped to talk to each one.

I finally sat down because my feet and back were beginning to ache—a hazard of being an older bride. I saw Bo grab the microphone on the stage. Someone poured champagne at every table. Of course, Bo had some surprise planned. He was Mr. Surprise.

Bo got up to toast me. He first thanked all the guests for coming to celebrate with us. He told a few jokes. Then he looked at me, and there were tears in his eyes. I had never seen him that emotional. "Ellie Parker Channing," he said and then took a long pause. He was looking at me and swallowing. "I catch my breath when I see you walk into a room. You are beautiful." He then looked out at all our guests. "But what I have had the privilege to see the last nine months is the striking beauty of your heart. You are patient and kind. You bring joy and faithfulness to others. You chase after the peace and blessing of God like no one I have ever known. You show goodness and love to all you meet. You truly consider others better than yourself. You hold fast to God's Word and believe it to be true."

He turned back to me. I could barely see through all my tears. "I will be forever grateful that you said, 'Yes,' to my proposal to be with you for the rest of my life." He paused, looked around, and said, "I am 100 percent sure I am getting the better end of the deal. And I know each of you would agree." There was some laughter.

Not true, I thought.

He raised his glass. "Here's to the most amazing woman in the world, who said, 'Yes,' to me."

After carefully wiping tears away, I stood up and walked over to him. I took his hand and raised my glass to his. We all cheered and drank. He pulled me close to him, and I leaned back so I could look into his face. He leaned down and kissed me. Then I said, "You will have to wait until later for me to show my appreciation for that speech."

He smiled and said, "I am so looking forward to it, Mrs. Channing." He leaned down and kissed me again.

Chapter 60

THE KIDS WERE DRIVING AWAY. Luke was headed back to his place and job. Brooke was staying with Katie and was headed back to college the next day. Whit and Tea were with Katie and John for the next week. Tea and Whit had taken me upstairs to see their rooms before they left. The rooms were perfect—Tea with her bright colors and Whit with his love for music on display. I gave them each a huge hug and told them how much I loved them. Then Bo shook hands with Luke, Whit, my dad, and John. He hugged Katie and Tea. Katie gave me a big hug and whispered, "Have fun tonight."

We waved as they all drove away. Down the hill at the driveway entrance, there was an automatic gate with a high-privacy fence all around and up to the house. The back had an electric fence for Bingo, so she couldn't leave but deer and wildlife could come in. Bo had bought ten acres of property. When we looked out from the back porch to the left, there were several hills. Bo planned to use them for cattle fencing and a barn. He had promised Tea sheep, goats, and a hen house. To the right, there were trees and brush. There was a lot of work to do, but the main thing was that I felt safe. It was like a castle on a hill. You could look out from the front porch and barely see the front gate. You couldn't see the main road at all. And calling it a main road was being generous. It was an unlined, barely paved country road. I wondered if Bo was trying to lock me up in this tower castle so that I could never leave again. But the town was only fifteen minutes away. The college I taught at was forty-five instead of thirty minutes away, but this house was worth the drive.

I walked back up to the front porch and took a seat on one of the two black rocking chairs with blue throw pillows on them. The front porch had six white columns holding up an eighteen-foot ceiling. There was recess lighting and two scone lights by the double front door. The other side of the porch had a hanging-bench swing and another rocker. Giant potted plants were placed around the porch. I hoped Bo had a plan for who was watering them because I was terrible with anything green.

I looked around, and the only people left were the caterers, who were cleaning up. Bo was somewhere—probably helping them clean up. He was so kind and good to anyone who worked for him. I placed my empty glass of champagne on the side table next to the rocking chair. Everyone would be gone soon. And then it would be just Bo and me. We were alone for one of the few times in the past nine months. I started to feel very nervous. I wanted to be cool, calm, and relaxed for him, but I was overthinking everything. So I did what every nervous bride does, I started looking around for more champagne.

The caterer was loading up, and I saw Bo talk to him for a minute. I leaned down and took off my shoes. It had gotten chilly. I found a blanket on the living room couch and brought it outside. I really had no idea where anything was in the house. I laughed to myself because it was like a treasure hunt. I had all week to figure it out.

Bo and I had decided to stay at the house for a week by ourselves. We wanted to enjoy his hard work, and I knew he wanted to show it off to me. The house was his wedding gift to me to all of us. We would go on a honeymoon trip after Christmas.

I sat and rocked myself with my bare feet while watching Bo talk to the cleanup crew. I kept repeating to myself, *I just got married. I get to live in this gorgeous house. I have a handsome and kind husband.*

I could tell the champagne was taking effect because the more I said it, the less scary it sounded.

He came back up to the porch as the last car drove away. He looked at me and smiled. "Before I sit down with you, I am going to run in and do something really quick. Don't move."

"Not planning on it," I said back. I was tired enough to close my eyes. It must have been after midnight. He came back out with more champagne. "Thank you. You read my mind," I said as I took the glass. Bo sat down in the rocking chair next to me. The night was cool with a southern breeze. Bo took my hand, and we rocked together peacefully.

Finally, Bo said, "Promise me that we will always find time to do this, even if it is after midnight. We will always sit out here together and hold hands." He took my hand and kissed it.

"I promise. Bo, my wedding band is beautiful. And you and Brooke did such an amazing job putting this wedding together. It was seamless, and all the important people in our lives were here. Thank you." I meant it from the bottom of my heart. He blew me away with his vision and creativity.

"El, thank you for marrying me. Today has been the best day of my life." He held up his champagne glass, and we toasted. He loved me so well; he always had. Soft music was playing throughout the house on the speakers that he had installed inside and outside. He had literally thought of everything for this house. He told me that he had been designing it for years in his head.

We kept talking about the night as we finished off the champagne. Then we decided to go inside. As we stood up, he reached for my hair and softly brushed it off my shoulder. Slowly, his hand made its way down my arm, and he said, "Let's dance first."

I put my arms around his neck and stood up on my toes. He took his hand and followed my arm down to my shoulders and then my side to my hips. I was literally melting inside like mush—really warm mush.

"Your touch is so soft," I whispered in his ear.

His hands moved up my back and through my hair to my head. "I have been waiting a long time to run my fingers through your hair," he said.

I gently pulled his face to mine, and we kissed. Suddenly, he picked me up and carried me across the threshold of the front door. I laughed. "Welcome to your new home, Mrs. Channing." He carried me to the kitchen, sat me on the counter, and grabbed two bottles of water. Then he had me walk with my eyes closed toward the master bedroom. I had not seen it yet because it had been clothed in secrecy up until this moment. He opened the door. The lights were off, and there were lit candles everywhere.

"Bo, it is so lovely. It's perfect!" There was a big fireplace with two big, comfy chairs in front of it. A big bed with a tall headboard, two dressers, and two nightstands were there. Everything was in white and blue. My favorite color was all shades of blue, and he knew this.

I was overwhelmed with the sheer loveliness of the dark room and glowing candlelight. I placed my hands on his face and looked at him. "I love you in a way I have never loved anyone else. I want you to be sure of my love for you."

All he said was, "You are going to have to help me with this dress." We both started to laugh. I turned my back to him and pointed at the fifteen covered buttons. "I promise it is not Fort Knox."

He went slowly. He finished the last button, moved my hair, and began to kiss my neck to my shoulder. He moved the straps of the dress out of the way and turned me around. We were smiling between kisses. Then things sped up as we both became incredibly desperate for each other.

PART 7

PART 7

Chapter 61

WE DIDN'T GET TO SLEEP until around 4:00 a.m. And since I had barely slept that week, I was out cold. When I woke up, Bo was already up somewhere in the house. *I know he is an early riser, but man.* On the previous night, I had dug around in the dark and found a T-shirt of his. I had no idea where my clothes were in that room. I hadn't even seen the closet. I opened my eyes and saw sheer curtains with plantation blinds behind them. Light was trickling in from the big windows. I lay in bed thinking about the night before, and I was sure I was blushing.

I walked to the bathroom, which was gorgeous. I started hunting for ibuprofen. I had a bad wedding-champagne hangover. All my stuff had been neatly placed on the counter by Brooke. I washed my face, brushed my teeth, and put my hair up in a ponytail. I located my workout gear and put on a sports bra and a pair of workout leggings and T-shirt. A morning-afternoon run sounded like a good way to get all the champagne out. *Ugh. Headache.*

I wandered into the kitchen, and Bo was sitting at the kitchen bar with his laptop open. He was intently working on something, and it occurred to me that I might have married another workaholic. He was wearing a dark-gray V-neck T-shirt and black joggers. He looked so good. I started to blush again. I walked up, and he looked at me and smiled a knowing smile. "Hey, gorgeous."

I walked around him and moved my hands down around his

shoulders and onto his chest. I nestled my face in his neck. "Hi," I said. "What are you working on?"

"Anything to keep my mind off you, so you could sleep in. How did you sleep?" Bo asked.

"I slept sooo good. That mattress is amazing."

"Only the best for you, babe."

I smiled. "I feel so very spoiled, waking up in this house and seeing you first thing. Thank you. I know you have worked so hard to make this house, this week, and last night all so special." I had my face next to his as I stayed there. He smelled so good. *How does he smell so good all the time?* I stood up and started opening cabinets. "Where are the coffee mugs? I am in desperate need of coffee." *Ah, my beloved coffee espresso machine made it here.* I started talking to it. "Hello, old friend. Help a girl out and make it strong." I filled the bean hopper and turned around.

Bo was watching me. I looked at him, and my cheeks were instantly pink. I leaned against the counter and looked down, unable to meet his gaze. It had been a really long time since I had that kind of a night. He smiled that boyish smile, shut his computer, got up, and walked toward me until his body pressed against mine. He reached above my head for the coffee cups and handed me one while not taking his eyes off mine.

"Thank you, Mr. Channing. You are too kind." I laughed as I met his gaze.

He put his hands on my hips. "Last night, marrying you, being with you," he said, took a hand from my hip, and pushed a stray curl back behind my ear, "was the absolute best night of my life. You, El, are the best person I have ever known, and I cannot wait to live out this life with you." He tilted my face up to his and kissed me slowly.

We finished the kiss, and I said, "I really do love you so much, but right now, I desperately need some coffee." He laughed and went back to his computer. I got my coffee and went to sit by him.

"I don't think I knew you drank your coffee black," he said.

"I think you are going to discover so many fascinating things about me this week," I said flirtatiously.

He grinned. "I cannot wait."

We sat and chatted about morning routines, guests at the wedding, and what we would do for a whole week at the house alone. After I finished my coffee, I started looking for my blender to make my morning smoothie. "Do you want one?" I asked, as I poured my vegan protein mix in.

"I would rather have real food, El. Sorry."

I shrugged. "It's not for everyone," I said as I smiled at him, my handsome husband.

"I do love you, though."

"You mentioned that several times last night," I said as I laughed.

Chapter 62

AFTER BEING COMPLETE BUMS ALL afternoon, we decided to walk around the property. Bo told me all his ideas about what he wanted to do with the property. And he would absolutely do it, as he was very goal-oriented and organized. We talked about how we wanted to set up bank accounts. He said that he emailed me a document with his passwords and access to his bank accounts and business ledgers.

"Wow!" I teased. "You take this two becomes one thing real serious."

"I just want you to know that I trust you completely," Bo replied.

"Thank you." I said as I grabbed his hand and intertwined our fingers. "Let's definitely look at all that this week. We probably need to get it figured out before the kids come back and start asking for stuff. Also, Thanksgiving is in a few weeks. What are you thinking? Should we have it here?"

We decided to have Thanksgiving at my dad's ranch, but to do something with the kids over Christmas. Nobody needed anything, but a ski trip would be fun, and we both enjoyed skiing. Bo also wanted to celebrate with his parents and sisters. He told me that he used to avoid going home during the holidays because he always felt like the odd man out—no family but just him.

"Well," I said, "you sure got what you wished for and then some."

When we got back to the house, we worked out together in our home gym. It was amazing. A treadmill and a bike were there, along with every weight and band size hanging on the wall. *Bo really knows his stuff. He could be a personal trainer.* I was going to be so sore after doing a leg workout with him. I ran a few miles on my treadmill and then went to shower. Bo had a phone call to make in his office.

Bo had put this music system in our house so that we could play a song throughout the entire house or through the app in one room. I cranked up the volume and sang in the shower. I had told Bo before we got married that the shower was off limits. If I am in the shower, I am singing, praying, and thinking. It could be thirty minutes long. If he wanted anything from me, he just had to wait. I needed my space. I got dressed and went to see what he was doing.

Bo's office had a beautiful view of the front of the house where there were big oak trees. His desk faced the picture window. He was on a phone call, so I came up behind him and kissed his cheek. Then because he was not paying any attention to me, I came around and straddled him with my back against his desk. He hung up. I smiled. "Hi," I said. Our faces were inches apart.

He laughed. "Well, that is definitely a good way to get my attention."

"Who were you talking to?" I teased. He had made me pinky promise to make this time and this week be our time and week—no kid calls, no job calls, or nothing—unless it was an emergency.

"It was an emergency. The house we are building near Reimers Ranch, the guys somehow lost the keys. Probably accidentally thrown in the dumpster with the door hardware. It's funny because it happens about every third house I build. But the young guy I left in charge was a little concerned. I told him to just go buy a new door handle and keep the key in his pocket."

I laughed. *Poor kid.*

"And in case you don't know, you are more important than any lost key." He brushed his thumb over the scar above my eye. Then he brushed it across my lips. "You have the most beautiful lips I have ever seen. Have I told you that?"

"No, you haven't," I replied, feeling heat in my cheeks.

"I have thought it probably a million times since I first saw you. But it probably wasn't appropriate to say until right now."

How is he able to say simple things and leave me breathless? He is a charmer through and through.

"Also, you play your music louder than any teenager I have ever known."

I laughed and shrugged. "This is living with me. Take it or leave it."

"Oh, I will definitely be taking it." We started to kiss. He picked me up and carried me to the bedroom.

Chapter 63

NOVEMBER DAYS AND NIGHTS IN Texas did not disappoint. Outside, we ate our last dinner without the kids and then sat on the outdoor couch as the sun went down. We had been married for a week. *How is that possible? After spending all week with him, I cannot even picture my life without him.*

My back and head were against him, and my legs were up on the couch. His right arm was over my belly, and his left was playing with my hair. We were quiet as we watched the sky light up with stars. Both of us knew, but we weren't saying that the kids and dog would be back on the following day.

"What has been the most surprising thing you learned about me this first week of marriage?" I asked.

"Hmmm, good question." Bo thought for a minute. "I was thinking about this verse in the Bible where it states something like what you know in part, you will know in full."

"1 Corinthians 13:12, 'For now we see only a reflection as in a mirror; then we shall see face to face. Now I know in part; then I shall know fully, even as I am fully known,'" I recited. "It's one of my favorites."

"Perfect. I thought I knew you really well. I have known you for seven years, even though I was gone for three. But I was really only seeing obscurely in a mirror. I only knew you partly, but if you had asked, I would have said I knew you fully. But after a week of marriage, and I am guessing for the rest of our lives together, I will learn something new and fascinating about you every day."

"So what you are saying is that you have learned in the past week that you will need a lifetime to really know me?" I teased. "I think you are right. Dating and even being engaged and going through some hardship is just knowing half of what being married to that person is like. But you still haven't answered my question."

Bo paused and then said, "The most surprising and the thing that has caught me off guard about you is how intensely and passionately you love. I thought I knew that by watching you with your kids and singing your heart out to God. But that was nothing compared to how much you have full-on passionately loved me this week."

I took his hand that was on my belly and held it. "And I am surprised by my own heart and how ... overflowing my love for you is. It has grown each day. I ... I didn't think it was possible to love another person this much." Bo was getting choked up and I was wiping my eyes. He continued. "You know I wake up every day stunned that you are sleeping next to me. I have watched you sleep each morning for a minute. Seeing you sleep peacefully in my bed has moved me to tears each day. Those two things are what has surprised me about being married to you."

I sat up, moved to his lap, turned around, and hugged him hard. My face was in his neck, and his was in mine. "I get it," I mumbled into his shoulder. "Right now, I feel like my heart will break open because it is so full of love from you and for you." Tears started to come. They were joyful tears but also tears of sadness. Life was so fragile. "You cannot ever leave me, Bo. You cannot ever die without me." Bo didn't say anything. He just rubbed my back and held me tight.

Chapter 64

OUR WEEK AT HOME WAS the best. We lay around a ton. We spent a lot of time watching movies and catching up on each other's lives. We worked on the house. We did intense workouts. We worked on our budget, finances, calendars, schedules, grocery runs, and figuring out how to blend all of us together. We planned the rest of our lives together.

I guess that it would sound strange that we both enjoyed just playing house together. But we really did. We also planned our honeymoon. Bo suggested Paris or London, but I told him I was a homebody and a country girl. I liked staying relatively close to home. So we decided on Miami and a warm beach vacation in January, after the kids went back to school. The real world was coming back that night.

I was so very happy to see Tea, Whit, and my dog. Bo cooked an amazing dinner, and we heard all about their week at school. Tea was trying out for the school play.

"It is *Alice in Wonderland*, and I am trying out for The Queen of Hearts. I cannot wait to say, 'Off with her head,' to Jenny Jones, who will probably be Alice. Whit, will you please help me with my lines?"

Whit has never told Tea no. He was the best big brother. When I was pregnant with Tea and miserable, he would sit next to me and pat my arm. His red curls and blue eyes filled with concern for me. He was born with a loving and kind heart. He always shared his toys with and played with her, no matter what she wanted to do. They had a special bond, and Tea definitely took advantage of it.

Whit was invited to a music camp over the first weekend of Thanksgiving break. It was for kids aspiring to play in worship bands. I was so excited for him. He was fifteen, and he still hadn't complained that no one had taken him driving yet. Bo told him he would teach him how to drive. They really reminded me of each other. Both were kind and always willing to help others. Tea had been the squeaky wheel for far too long, and she always got the attention. Bo made sure to notice Whit and include him in everything he did.

Bo made an amazing dinner for us. We had a system down after a week of playing house. He would cook whatever meat he wanted and would make sure to roast me some veggies. Tea and Whit asked him if he was going to cook every night. Bo said, "That is my plan. And I will do the dishes every night too."

Tea announced, "That is the best thing I have heard all year."

I protested a little. "I can cook. I can make chicken enchiladas, gazpacho, and spaghetti. And, Bo, you shouldn't have to cook every night."

Bo looked at Whit, Tea, and me and said, "When I lived alone, it was depressing just cooking for and cleaning up after one person. I told myself if I ever had a family, I would cook and clean up every day. It makes me happy to do that for each of you."

I started to tear up. Tea got up from the table to hug Bo. "You are the perfect match for us because we never want mom to cook again. All the burnt dinners and ordering out is over. Hallelujah!" There was so much dramatic flair in that kid.

I rolled my eyes. "Rude!" And we all laughed.

While Bo and I were cleaning up, he said, "You make amazing kids."

"Aw, thank you. I am not sure I want to take any credit for the good because then I must take responsibility for the bad. And thank you for offering to help Whit do his driver's ed stuff. Should we give him my old Sequoia?"

"If you are OK with it. We need to get you a new car." He paused and then said, "You know, we never really talked about kids—about having kids."

I stared at him, thinking he had lost his mind. "What do you mean? I don't want any more kids. I thought you were happy with my kids." I felt my voice getting high-pitched.

"El, calm down. I was just saying that we never talked about it. You never asked if I wanted any. That's all."

I do not want to be pregnant again—ever. "Bo, I haven't had a real period in the two years since Tommy died."

"I figured you were on birth control, but you never said anything."

"OK, this is really a bizarre conversation to have after a week of …" Bo was smiling at, staring at, and mocking me. I lowered my voice. "Of lots of sex." We both started laughing.

He was right. We never talked about it. There was so much to talk about when blending our family, and with the attack and building the house, it just never came up.

I walked over to him and touched his arm. "I'm sorry. I just assumed you didn't want any. I was probably just too chicken to ask. Being pregnant with Tea finished me off. It was exhausting, and I got massive. She is why my belly is squishy and soft. The first three did not do it to me, just her."

"Your belly is not squishy." He rolled his eyes at me. "And I assumed you didn't want any more. But I had never asked you either. Truthfully, if you wanted another one, I would be 100 percent on board. But I am not going to ask you to do something you don't want to do or can't do." Bo went back to doing dishes.

Oh, man. He just wants his own kid, and he would be a phenomenal dad. I felt terrible.

"Bo, I am so sorry. I had no idea you would want a baby. But of course, you would. They are amazing and utterly exhausting. You would be such a fabulous dad." I hugged him tight from behind.

215

"Maybe you should have married someone younger of childbearing age with a tight belly," I joked but not completely.

Bo shrugged it off. "I am going to need to investigate this squishy belly you are telling me about." I laughed as he started to pull up my shirt.

"Um, you forget, we have two kids upstairs now."

"Right. Later then." And he winked at me.

Good grief. He is so handsome.

Chapter 65

WE STARTED GETTING INTO A family routine. I would get up early and go to my home office. My office brought me so much joy. Bo built beautiful bookcases from floor to ceiling and built a desk into them. I had so much joy putting all my beloved books on the shelves. I had one window, and I pushed my grandmother's chair up against it with a small side table. I sat in it, even with its broken springs and uneven legs. I covered myself in my favorite blanket while I read, journaled, and prayed each morning.

While I did that, Bo worked out and showered. Then we would meet in the kitchen. We would chat about the day and help the kids get their lunches together. Then he took them to school. It was so nice to have a partner. He was the absolute best partner a girl could have. I would work out and shower and then drive to the University for the day.

Most days, I could pick the kids up from school. But when I couldn't, Bo happily did it. We drove them to their extracurricular activities, and then he would make dinner. I had no idea how I managed life before him. Every night, I told him how grateful I was for him.

Early one morning, I woke up from a terrible dream, which was familiar. In the dream, Bo, my mom, and Tommy were all on top of a cliff. I kept trying to climb up and get to them, but it was too difficult. I kept falling. I was calling them to come and get me and not leave me all alone. I was begging and crying in the dream. It felt so real that when I woke up, I immediately sat upright in terror. When I realized it was just a dream, I rolled over, put my head on Bo's bare chest, and hugged him as hard as I could.

"You OK?" he asked.

"I had a terrible dream. I was all alone again, and you were not coming to get me," I said, almost whiny like a child.

"El," he said and rubbed my arm that was over his chest, "I am here. I am not leaving you. Wild dogs couldn't drag me away from you."

I lifted my head off his chest and looked at him. His blond, short, straight hair was sticking up and all messy. His jawline, lips, and nose were beautifully put together. His neck and chest were perfectly chiseled. He smelled so good like soap, outdoors, and a little leftover cologne. "I am so scared of feeling like that. Being alone. Like everyone is gone, and I am on my own again." I begged, "Please don't ever leave me."

"This dream really got to you. I am so sorry." He stroked my hair as I lay on his chest. I lay there quietly for a while, hearing his heartbeat and listening to him breathe.

I silently prayed and gave thanks for him. I thought back to when we had first met. It was the day when I was pulling the ball from underneath his truck. At that moment, I felt something like a pull toward him that I didn't understand. He said he knew, too, that we were it for each other, but the timing was all wrong, so we moved on. And then the tragedy of Tommy's death put me on a different path, and Bo came and found me.

Maybe Katie was right. Maybe there was a person that was specifically made for you—God's gift. But we messed it up by trying to find it in other people and not really believing that God cared enough to know who would fit us best. And boy did I mess it up. Getting pregnant at nineteen and then getting married right away. But God in His goodness blessed my marriage to Tommy, and we made it work. It was hard, but we did it, and we had four amazing children.

I started to see the sun come up. I didn't want to lose this moment of thankfulness for Bo and the deep appreciation for our separate paths that led to this moment. I started to kiss him on his chest and then his face and lips. "I need you. I need you to make love to me right now." And he did in his beautiful way.

Chapter 66

BO HAD BEEN DYING TO hunt out at the ranch. No kid was willing to wake up that early with him, so I went with him on Thanksgiving morning. It was chilly but not freezing. It was so peaceful. We just sat there in the dark and the quiet. I was snuggled up under several blankets, drinking my coffee and listening to the sounds of daybreak. I couldn't watch him kill a deer, so I was purposely not looking out the window. He leaned over and whispered to me, "Of all the hundreds of people I have been with in a cold deer blind, you are my favorite." I smiled at him. He was the cutest.

Once we were back inside the house, I made homemade pie crusts and got the apple and cherry filling ready. I could make really good pies. Katie's mom, Barbara, had shown me, and I had a knack for it. Maybe it was the soothing feeling of dough between my fingers and then rolling it out until it was perfect. It was a type of stress relief and a comfort.

Tea and Brooke were helping Bo with the turkey and sides. My dad was out taking care of the farm animals with Whit while Luke lay on the couch watching the Macy's parade.

"Mom," he said, "junior high kids are exhausting."

"One thousand percent. You are doing God's work sweetheart."

He threw a pillow at me. I wondered why boys always have

to throw things or put me in a headlock when I was just having a conversation. I thought I should study that on the following year.

On the drive up there, I had been telling Bo that I had a sabbatical coming up for work, starting in May. I really wanted to take time and think about what I wanted to do next. I had been talking with a criminal justice professor about my interest in victimology and the sociology of a criminal act, along with the fallout from it. I was looking for something even deeper and healing within the criminal justice system.

He directed me to a contact who ran the restorative justice program at a small Baptist university in town. I had met with her on the previous week. I explained to Bo that the restorative justice theory was born out of the failing of the criminal justice system to meet the needs of both victims and offenders. Practically, it involved work to heal victims and offered a path of redemption for offenders to rejoin a community. It simply sought to restore the victim, offender, and all who were involved back to wholeness. It really was a beautiful picture of forgiveness and healing for all, which was the story of Christ.

I was very excited about it. And I was reading all I could on restorative justice. Bo seemed cautious in his enthusiasm for my turn of interest. And I got it. He didn't want me to think about the attack too much. But no matter what he wanted, it was on my mind more often than not. I was viewing it as a third person and not a victim. I was analyzing and turning it around inside my head like a student who was studying it. Bo did not look like he believed me when I told him that.

Katie and her family came over for dessert and to watch some football. We bundled up and sat outside for some privacy. We had hardly gotten any time together since the wedding. I appreciated that she was letting Bo and I figure things out and spend time together.

"How are you?" she asked. "Because you look amazing."

"I am really, really good. I do miss you tons," I said.

"The bags under your eyes have disappeared like the stress in your life is manageable finally." Katie was looking at me through squinted eyes like she was making sure she couldn't see any residual stress in my face.

"Yep. I don't think I realized how much I was drowning until Bo came into my life and took so much of it away. I mean, money and parenting wise, his running kids around and cooking dinner has literally changed my life." I smiled.

"That is so amazing. I am happy for you. I think my stress about you is gone too. I always felt like if I didn't worry about you, who would?"

"That was the reality, unfortunately. But thank you. Thank you for hanging on long enough for Bo to work his way back into my life." I laughed.

"Well once he showed me the ring, I started letting it all go."

"Wait. When did you know?" I asked, incredulous.

"He showed me the ring in June at the rodeo. I mean, he showed me a picture of it. We were at the rodeo dance, and you were dancing with those old high school boys. I leaned over to him and said, 'You should probably put a ring on that finger to keep the riffraff out.' And he said, 'I am working on it.' And then showed me a picture."

Katie was laughing, and so was I. I could not believe those two.

Katie got serious and said, "Joey is in jail. We just found out Tuesday. She is in Abilene."

"Oh, Katie, I am so sorry. At least you know she is relatively safe right now."

Katie just shrugged, which was her way of saying the conversation was over. Joe Ellen, Joey, was Katie's younger sister. She had a drug addiction. It had been going on for years. Katie's parents had almost gone broke sending her to rehab since she had been seventeen years old. They finally had to put up some serious boundaries. Katie and John helped her parents financially, on the condition that they did not give Joey a cent and did not allow her into their home until she was clean and sober. It was so sad. Katie said that it would be easier if Joey would just die of an overdose and be put out of her misery.

Katie had told me to stop asking about Joey years earlier. She said that if there was any news, she would tell me. She blamed her parents for spoiling Joey. Barbara couldn't get pregnant for ten years after Katie. Joey was a sweet surprise. *Poor Momma Barbara.* I couldn't imagine what it was like to watch your child make bad decision after bad decision, year after year.

Katie could be stubborn and difficult sometimes, and anything to do with Joey brought it out. Katie's oldest, Kylie, looked so much like Joey, and I had always felt that Katie was hard on Kylie for that reason. I always had a soft spot for Kylie. I gave her extra hugs when she was around. Kylie would soon be seventeen, and I had felt Katie getting hyper anxious about it. But Katie shut down when I tried to bring it up.

Katie quickly changed the subject and asked, "How are you dealing with your trauma from the attack? Still seeing Peter?"

I sighed. "We haven't seen Peter in a month, since before the wedding. But I will start back after the holidays in January. I feel OK. I still struggle going out by myself, and Bo has made it way too easy for me not to go anywhere alone." I joked that he had locked me up in the castle on the hill to protect me, and I was not putting up a fight. "But when I drive into the city, and park in the dark garage to get to my office, I struggle."

"Does Bo know it is hard for you?" Katie asked.

"Not really. I don't want to worry him. He would probably insist on driving me to work," I said. "I mean, I would like to maintain a hint of independence."

"What does struggling in the parking garage look like?" Katie pushed.

"It never gets better. I keep telling myself that after parking and walking into the building and later walking out of the building over twenty times, I will calm down. But there is something about it that causes me to go on hyper alert. I have a rapid heart rate and breathing. I walk or run as fast as I can to the stairs. I can't take the elevator. It makes me feel trapped."

"Promise me you will go see Peter ASAP," Katie demanded.

"I will," I agreed and reassured her with a smile. "Oh, speaking of that, Bo is leaving for a couple of hunting trips. I will probably need to borrow you and the girls. He is going next week for five days and the last week in February for five days. If you can't, I can ask Luke. Or maybe we should just get two German shepherds if he is going to be traveling so much."

"We will be around to help, and a big fierce dog is not a terrible idea. German shepherd puppies are adorable." Katie swiftly changed gears. "So I am dying to know, how is married life?" She raised her eyebrows.

I knew exactly what she was alluding to. "It is not polite to speak of these things. Best to keep your comments to the weather or the roads," I said in my best English accent. We giggled. "Let me just say it is pretty amazing." I had an idea. "You and John should go on a second honeymoon and leave the kids with us. Y'all are reaching twenty years soon."

"Don't change the subject. Your cheeks are flaming pink. It must be pretty amazing," Katie joked.

"Stop!" I yelled as I threw a glove at her. Then we both started laughing. John poked his head out the door, which made us laugh harder. He rolled his eyes and went back inside.

Chapter 67

WHEN WE FINALLY WALKED BACK into the house, I went to find Momma Barbara and snuggle in beside her. Landry was already in her lap. Katie took up the other side.

"Well, what did I do to deserve all this?" Barbara asked, clearly enjoying the love.

"You are just the best, and we love you," I said.

Tea couldn't stand not to be included, so she came over and sat in my lap. Then Remy came and sat on Katie's lap. Barbara just laughed and said, "How I do love all my girls."

I could have just cried. *Thank you, Lord, for such a sweet woman. Even for her you have turned her mourning of her prodigal daughter into a plethora of daughters and granddaughters who love her.*

Later, I saw her in the hallway and gave her a hug. "I am so sorry about Joey." She knew we couldn't talk about it in front of Katie.

"Keep praying for her, Ellie. Don't give up on her," Barbara begged me. I knew she felt that Katie and John had washed their hands of Joey.

"I won't. I promise." I leaned back and looked her in the eyes. Then we hugged for a long time.

Later that night, Bo, my dad, and the boys went out to hunt wild hogs. So the girls and I cleaned up the kitchen, snuggled on my bed, and watched *Pride and Prejudice* with Kiera Knightly. It was one of Brooke and my all-time favorites. I couldn't concentrate on the movie. I kept thinking about Joey and how utterly heartbreaking it would be to know one of my daughters was out there in a very dangerous world and participating in a dangerous activity every day. Knowing Joey was in jail was a strange relief.

The next week, my dad came to stay with me while Bo was gone. He had some doctors' appointments and shopping he wanted to do. It was nice to spend time with him one-on-one. At night, we would sit by the fire, have a glass of wine, and talk about history, politics, and ranching. And I always asked him to tell me stories about my mom.

Then Bo came back. He was all jazzed about the moose he had shot. He had a blank wall in his office, which would be full of animals' heads. I collected books; he collected dead animals. We made it work.

Chapter 68

B O AND I DROPPED WHIT off at his hour music lesson and then grabbed some dinner for later. I wanted to run at the track at Tea's school while Bo picked up Whit. Tea was still at school for her dress rehearsal of *Alice in Wonderland*. I told Bo I would run for thirty minutes then go in and watch some of the dress rehearsal.

"Are you sure you feel comfortable running out here all by yourself?" Bo asked for what felt like the tenth time.

"Yes. The track is lit, and there is a basketball game going on, so there are plenty of people coming and going," I replied, trying to not snap at him. I just missed running outside. Katie ran with me on some Saturdays, but I just wanted to run outside when I wanted to. This seemed like a safe way to do it.

"OK." Bo backed off.

I jumped out of the truck and said, "I will meet you guys inside the auditorium in forty minutes." Bo waved as he drove off to get Whit.

I ran a warm-up lap and then stretched for a while. There were several people on the track: a couple and two young teens were walking, and a father and son were running together. It was all perfectly harmless.

I started to run. I didn't have my earbuds in because it was just too triggering. I ran the first lap and decided to pray for a person each lap. I started with my kids, and after four laps, that was one mile down. I was sweating. It was more humid than I had thought. I took off my sweatshirt. Then I prayed for Bo, my dad, Katie, and Barbara. During my cooldown lap, I prayed for Joey.

I slowed down as I finished and smelled impending rain. It felt very dark outside. The clouds were hiding the moonlight. My heart seemed to be beating faster than it should. I tried to shake out my arms and legs as I walked. I couldn't seem to catch my breath. I wasn't running that fast, but I was sweating more than normal.

I sat down on a bleacher and put my head on my knees. All of a sudden, I noticed how quiet it had gotten. I looked around. No one was on the track anymore but only me. My chest suddenly felt like someone was sitting on it. *What is happening?* I stood up to walk toward the school and to see if Bo was there. I couldn't breathe. I was looking all around for someone, but nobody was there. I could see that I was panicking. I tried to calm down, but all I did was start to hyperventilate. I walked to the back fence behind the bleachers and found myself crying and shaking. I slid down the fence and sat with my knees up. *Please, Jesus, what is wrong with me?* My head was on my knees, but my body was telling me to get up and run and that someone was after me. I argued with my body that I was fine and that nobody was around. I tried to get up and ended up leaning over and holding onto the fence. Then I vomited.

It occurred to me to get my cell phone. It was in my sweatshirt on the bleachers. Suddenly, I heard my name, but I was frozen to my spot by the fence. I saw Bo. He was running across the soccer field toward the bleachers. I saw him spot my sweatshirt and look around, calling my name. He finally saw me huddled by the back fence. "El, what is going on?" he yelled. "You scared me to death. I looked for you inside and outside. You weren't where you said you would be." He seemed just as panicked as I felt.

He got close to me and saw that I was shaking and that I had vomited. "El, what is … are you OK?" He came over and helped me up. We started walking back to the bleachers.

"I need my water. I don't know. I think it was a panic attack. It happened so fast. I don't know. I just got really, really scared, and I couldn't talk myself down." I was still shaking. I stopped walking and started to cry. I was so mad at myself. I pushed Bo's hand away from me.

I sat down on the bleachers and put my head in my hands. "Bo, I just don't know what happened. I was fine. Everything was fine. And then I lost … I don't know … I couldn't think straight. I couldn't breathe."

"El, it's OK. It was just too soon. You can try again another time."

I yelled, "It is not too soon. It's been three months. I just want everything to be normal. Why can't I just be normal and run whenever I want to?"

"Let's get you to the truck, and then I will go get Whit and Tea. Oh wait, I see them. They are coming. Let's just get home, and we can talk this through later."

I slouched in the truck. I was freezing and shivering, so Bo handed me his jacket. Whit and Tea hopped into the truck. Then Tea started in. "Mom, you said you would come in and watch me."

"I am sorry, Tea. I just, um, lost track of time."

"But you said you would. I am clearly not important to you, or you would have made time," Tea said, clearly pushing my buttons.

"You are important to me. I am sorry. But we will all come to watch you tomorrow night and the next day." I tried to placate her.

"You never have time for me or what I want you to do. You are always too busy with work or with everybody else." Tea was shouting at the top of her lungs.

I turned around and gave her the mom stare, but it was too dark for her to see it. "Teadora Parker, you need to stop right now before you say something you can't take back." I could feel my blood pressure rising, as if all the anger and fear from my panic attack were about to be unleashed. Bo kept glancing at me to make sure I was OK. Whit was silent as usual.

And true to form, Tea didn't stop. "You *never* do what you say. You care more about Bo than us. I asked you to do one thing."

I exploded. "Tea! What in the world is wrong with you? Just be quiet!

Tea started to cry, and I heard Whit talking to her. He was always better with her than I was. I hugged the car door and started to cry quietly into Bo's jacket.

Chapter 69

EVERYONE WAS COMPLETELY SILENT AS we drove up the hill to the house. Tea ran from the car into the house. Whit grabbed all her stuff plus his own because he was the best human there was. I walked in and went straight into the shower. I took a long one and then sat down in one of the armchairs in my bedroom. I pulled a blanket around me and just stared into a fireplace with no fire.

Bo walked in and sat in the opposite chair. "Whit and I ate and talked a little about what happened. I explained what a panic attack was, but I think he wants to make sure you are all right. Whit took dinner up to Tea."

I just nodded. Bo was probably realizing what a bad mother and messed-up person he had married and figuring out an exit strategy. "Do you want me to go talk to Tea?" Bo asked.

"No. I will go." I forced myself to get up and go upstairs. I got to the open loft with the big comfy couches and TV. I turned toward the kids' rooms. Tea was right. I hardly came up there. It probably looked like I cared more about Bo than her. The truth was that Bo was much more pleasant to deal with than her these days. I had only been in her room a handful of times. As I opened her door, I remembered why. Her room was a disaster. "Tea, can I come in?" I asked.

She was in her bed. She had showered, and she was reading. "Looks like you already are in."

Sheesh. "Tea, I am sorry about yelling at you tonight. I should not have told you to be quiet. It was unkind of me to yell at you. Please forgive me." I sat down on her bed. I debated whether or not to tell her about having a panic attack. I decided against it. I didn't want to make the conversation about me and my issues.

She rolled her eyes at me. "I love you. You are important. I am sure it feels like I don't give you the attention I used to give you, and I am not sure how to fix it. I don't know how to spread myself out for everyone, and I know I do not do it perfectly. Maybe we could have a special date night once a month. Brooke and I use to do that."

"I will think about it," she said as she dismissed me with a wave of her hand.

Good enough. I walked to Whit's room. He was so neat and tidy, even in his closet. I poked my head in. "Hey."

He looked up from the book he was reading. "Oh, hi, Mom." He smiled.

"Can I come in for a minute?"

"Sure."

"How are you?" I asked. I looked at him with his red curls, my freckles, and his blue eyes. He was getting so long and skinny. Luke had tried to show him how to bulk up with shakes and working out. Even Bo had made some gentle suggestions, but Whit was just not into it.

"I'm good, Mom. I am almost done with my driver's ed, so I can go get my permit. And school is good. I am working on a new set of songs for the youth worship band on Wednesday night. So yeah, everything is good."

I walked over and gave him a hug. He had been my hugger until recently. He was getting body conscious, and everything probably felt very awkward. "I am sorry about yelling at Tea. I feel really awful about it." I sat on his futon next to him.

"Mom, Tea was being rude. I am sorry you had a panic attack. Bo told me about them, and it sounded terrible."

"Yes, my body was just reacting to the stress I was feeling while trying to run by myself again. I wasn't ready. But I am going to try again soon."

"I can run with you. I like to run. I like it better than lifting weights."

Whit grinned at me. *What a handsome kid.*

"I would love for you to run with me. I will ask you the next time I feel like going. But no pressure. I know you are busy. And I just want to tell you how proud I am of you. You are an amazing human, and I can't wait to see how God will use your gifts and talents for His glory. Dad would be so proud of you too."

Chapter 70

I MADE MY WAY DOWNSTAIRS, AND Bo was cleaning up the kitchen. He looked up. "Better?" I shrugged and sat down on the bar stool at the kitchen island. "Do you want anything to eat? There is still the salad that you ordered." Bo gestured toward the fridge.

"No, not right now anyway. Bo, I am so sorry about tonight. I am sorry I scared you when I wasn't answering you. I am sorry that I yelled at Tea. I am sorry that you have to be in this messy family." I started to tear up.

Bo came around the counter to sit next to me. "El, I love you and Tea. It was a really strange feeling when you were arguing."

"That is called family tension. Welcome to a big family with lots of emotions." I tried to laugh.

Bo then asked, "Can we talk about you?"

"What about exactly?" I felt defensive, and I didn't know why. "I have an appointment with Peter lined up for next week, so I will talk with him about my panic attack."

"El, I just don't think you are ready to run by yourself. I mean, clearly you are not ready. Can you promise me you won't try again for a while?"

I felt myself getting offended. "I am not going to promise that. I will figure it out and try again. I just didn't know that I would panic. Now that I know, I can make a plan."

Bo kept protesting. "El, I don't think it is a good idea. I mean, I know you love to run outside. Maybe I can just sit in my truck and watch you on the track or follow you while you run."

I looked at him like he was out of his mind. "No. I need you to stop." And I got up and walked to our bedroom.

"El!" Bo said loudly. He followed me to the bedroom. I turned around to face him.

"I am not going to have you following me in your gigantic truck. I am going to figure this out."

Bo looked down at the floor like he was trying to measure his words. I was so angry that I couldn't run without having a breakdown. I was taking it out on him. I just didn't know who to be angry at.

Bo said, "El, I don't want to argue with you. I am trying really hard to understand why you want to torture yourself. Why do you want to do something that is traumatic? Why do you want to run alone outside ever again? Why do you want to study criminology and victimology and all the ologies?" I stifled a giggle. Bo smiled. "El, I love you more than I have ever loved anyone or anything in my entire life." He sat down on the bed. "The thought of you struggling, being scared, or being looked at by anyone makes me want to fiercely protect you. I know you can protect yourself. You proved that three months ago. I just don't want you to ever have to fight for your life again." His voice caught at the end of the sentence.

I walked over to where he was sitting and knelt down in front of him. I wanted to try to make him understand. I looked up at his furrowed brow. He was so handsome; it shocked me sometimes. "You cannot keep me locked up in a castle on a hill for the rest of my life. I must keep trying. And it may be a disaster like tonight. But I need my independence. I miss it. I want to go run or walk somewhere away from this house and not have a complete meltdown." I started to cry. "I want to understand myself—my PTSD—so he doesn't win. I want to learn and teach about restoring what was taken from me."

Bo reached for me and pulled me up to his lap. We sat like that for a few minutes and then Bo said, "I spent a lot of years wishing I could take you out, ask you questions, and listen to you talk. Then I walked away from you and created another life for myself. Then I came back and found you alone, hurting, and just as gorgeous, funny, and intelligent as before. Then I waited for you to say yes to me. Now I make love to you and share my life completely with you. I probably guard you and hold onto you a little too tightly. In fact, I know I do."

I sighed. I was not sure how to be independent enough, unafraid enough, and safe enough at the same time. Maybe if we had known each other when we were younger, we would already have our issues worked out. I asked Bo, "Do you think if we had met when we were younger, like mid-twenties, we would have seen something in each other, dated even, gotten married?"

Bo laughed out loud. "I would have thought you were hot, probably flirted with you, and asked you out until you said yes. Then I would have been solely focused on getting you in bed. So my answer is no. I was so immature, but thought I was mature. I was so lost to this world. Lord, when I think about what I put my parents through." Bo shook his head. "I am so glad we never met until I was in my mid-thirties and knew Jesus and His grace and forgiveness. And honestly, those three years in Florida were such an influential time in my life. I started reading books about God, which I know is shocking to you. But I had a lot of time on my hands."

I laughed and smiled at him. *Ah ha, he can read. He jokes he doesn't know how.*

He continued, "I got in a men's group at the church. Since no female could hold a candle to you, I was not dating. It was exactly the refining that I needed so that I could be here with you in this moment, finishing up our first argument." He gave me a big hug and stood up to let my dog inside.

I understood right then that marrying Tommy had never been a mistake. My marriage to Tommy helped make me into the person I was now. I was better at arguing, forgiving, asking for forgiveness, and understanding humanity's frailties. I was more humble and able to see things from an eternal perspective. I was so grateful for those twenty years with Tommy and grateful for the path that God brought me on so that I could be there in that moment with Bo.

I followed him onto the back porch. "It is hard to imagine what you were like in your twenties because you are such a kind, loving, and thoughtful person now." I put my arms around him and kissed him. "Thank you for coming back to Texas to check on me." His hands moved up my body and into my hair.

Chapter 71

I WAS COMING UP OUR DRIVEWAY after a long worship-band practice for the Christmas Eve services. The house looked so beautiful with its holiday lights along the roofline and porch and a big wreath on the front door. I smelled the fireplace being used and saw all the cars parked in the circular driveway.

Bo's family was there for Christmas, and Bo was so excited for them to come. They had arrived in the afternoon while I had been at practice. Two extra SUVs plus my dad's truck were in the driveway: Micah and Dinah's families plus Bo's parents. Bo said I didn't need to do anything. He had all the meals planned, and the sleeping arrangements were made. I had never seen him this energetic, giddy even.

I walked into organized chaos. Bo, his dad, his brothers-in-law, and my dad were in the kitchen talking while Bo made dinner. I gave each man a hug. Jeff, Micah's husband, was a fire fighter, and they lived in the same town they all grew up in. He was a big guy and a big hugger. "Bo, you gotta fatten her up. Is he treatin' you right? You know you can text me if you ever need reinforcements to keep him in line."

"Aw, thanks Jeff. I will keep that in mind. So far so good." I always felt so uncomfortable in large groups. I never knew what to say. I gave Matt, Dinah's husband, a side hug because he was a little more reserved. He was a junior high band director, and we could talk music pretty easily.

"How was practice? What are you singing tomorrow?" he asked me. I ran down the set with him and told him I was singing "O Holy Night,"[17] which was one of my absolute favorites. I had been known to sing it out of season often.

I asked where Luke was, and Bo said that he was upstairs with the kids creating an Xbox tournament of some kind. *Of course, he is.* He truly had a gift for kids and organizing games.

I walked into the living area where Bo's mom, Sarah, and his sisters were sitting. They each stood up to give me a hug. Bo's mom gave me an extra-long one. "It is so lovely to see you, Ellie. The house is decorated so pretty. Are you sure you are OK with us descending on you like this?"

"Absolutely! It really feels like Christmas now that y'all are here." Dinah had two girls who were thirteen and eleven while Micah had two boys who were nine and ten. They were just the perfect age for my kids.

Bo brought me a glass of wine, and I sat with these women, who were now my family, and talked. Micah was a writer and blogger while Dinah was a geography teacher at the high school in their town. It felt strange that they were a tad younger than me and that I had married their younger brother. Bo was thirty-eight, Micah was forty, and Dinah was forty-one. I wondered if Bo liked older women because he was around his sisters so much growing up. He liked that older female vibe.

When Bo yelled that dinner was ready, it was like a heard of elephants running down the stairs. Tea ran over to hug me, probably just to beat Luke to it. Luke picked her up and threw her over his shoulders just to hear her scream. Micah's and Dinah's kids ran over to me, hugged me, and called me Aunt Ellie. It was so sweet. All the younger kids were eating in the kitchen.

Brooke came quietly out of my office where she was sleeping that night. She got her quiet nature from me, but she also had intense shyness. When she was younger, she wouldn't talk to anyone but her family. In public and up to the age of six, she would lift my shirt and hide inside it. If going back into the womb was an option, she would have taken it. Going to a small college with a small studio art program had been good for her. She was thriving.

She sat next to me, and Bo sat on my other side. Luke was beside Matt, talking about middle schoolers. My dad was between Bo and David. We talked about anything and everything. It felt so good to be part of a big, loud family, which was such a contrast to my childhood. It was slightly intimidating. When I asked Brooke how she was handling the chaos, she whispered, "And when is everyone leaving?" We laughed.

Dinner was good. Bo made a roasted-vegetable risotto, with a salad, bread, and pulled pork. I put my hand on his leg, and he had his hand over mine through most of dinner. Brooke and I said the least, as bigger groups brought out my introverted side. Bo turned to me. He was smiling so big and enjoying every minute of the large family dinner. He quietly asked, "You OK?"

"Of course. Thank you for the yummy dinner and for taking care of everything tonight." I gave his leg a squeeze. After dinner, dessert, and a game of charades, I was done for the day. I gave Brooke a hug and thanked her for giving up her room to Bo's parents. They were all leaving late afternoon Christmas day to go home and celebrate with other family members.

I took a long shower and thought about how much fun we had had skiing for four days in Park City, Utah. We had rented a house right by the gondola that took us up the mountain to the slopes. Brooke and I skied the least. After all, there was shopping and coffee shops to visit. And since I was the oldest one skiing, I didn't want to hurt myself. My wrist still felt a little weak from the fracture.

And like everything else with my kids, it turned into a competition of who could go down the blackest slopes the fastest. Tea was really tearing it up; she was something fierce. I could not wait to see what God had planned for her. *Must be nice to be young and flexible.* She was at the point where she could ski circles around all of us except Luke. I prayed for a lot of protection over them out there on the black diamonds. We all came home exhausted but in one piece.

I went around and tucked everyone in, making sure nobody needed anything. It was like a giant sleepover, and Tea was in heaven. I only had let our kids have sleepovers at Katie and John's or relatives' houses. I had never been comfortable with sleepovers at friends' houses, especially ones I didn't know well. Tea was my only whiner about it. Whit and Brooke never complained, and Luke always said that he slept better in his bed anyway. *Same, Luke, same.*

Chapter 72

The next morning, the adults sat around the kitchen island, drank coffee, and talked. This was definitely more my speed. Micah was such a gifted writer. I loved to read, so we could talk books and writing all day. I started reading through her blog and instantly fell in love with her and her writing style. Dinah was very intelligent about other cultures and practices. I could pick her brain for days. Sarah had been an elementary school teacher a long time ago. I could picture her with little first graders, softly talking to them and giving them little hugs.

After the guys went out to the barn that Bo was slowly building, Micah and I chatted on the screened-in back porch. "I just want you to know how much we all adore you. You are the perfect wife for Bo. None of us have ever seen him this happy, even when he married the other one," Micah said.

"Oh, well thank you for saying that. At times, I feel like an intruder into your sweet family—an intruder with a ton of kids." I laughed at the image in my mind.

"Ellie, you are not an intruder; you are a huge blessing to our family. Bo has always wanted kids and a wife, and now he has it all!" Micah exclaimed.

Her words made me go back to that conversation we had had about kids a week after we were married. He had always wanted kids—his own kids. And that was perfectly normal. I just couldn't give him that. I was basically in menopause. And truthfully, even if I could have given him a child, I would rather not have. "Micah, he is the absolute kindest person I have ever known. All you girls did such a great job with him. He is so easy to be married to." We laughed. "Can you tell me more about the first wife? I am a little curious. He won't say much except that he blames himself for the reason it didn't work. He says he was selfish, but that is difficult for me to picture."

Micah smiled. "That sounds just like him, taking on all the blame. I mean, don't get me wrong, he wasn't living right. He was making a lot of money, turning over houses, and starting his own building company. And he has always been a saver but a fool for a pretty face."

Micah continued, "So the girl who shall remain nameless knew Bo less than a few months when Bo wanted to build her an expensive house. And of course, he wanted a family and a house so badly, he did it. So they got married without telling anyone. No one had even met her. And get this: When we finally met her, she was pregnant!"

"Oh, no!" I said. I was completely horrified that I didn't know about this. I felt my insecurity about the age of my uterus creeping in.

"Don't feel bad for him. It wasn't even his baby!" Micah exclaimed.

"What?" I was so confused.

"She had told him it was, which is why they got married so quickly. But after about six months into the marriage, they had a huge fight, and she told him it wasn't his."

Tears well up in my eyes. "This is the saddest story ever." *Poor Bo.*

"As you can imagine, afterward, things fell apart. But Bo was already halfway through building her dream house. Eventually, she went back to Dallas, and he finished the house, sold it, and gave her half of the profit, mainly to take care of the baby but also to finalize the divorce and be done."

I was literally stunned. How much pain he must have felt losing a marriage, baby, and home. "So awful," I whispered.

"But Ellie, God used it all for good. Bo was humiliated, devastated, and literally brought to his knees. He came and told us in person. It was the first time in a long time that he let us all pray for him and with him. He was undone by all of it.

"He left to go on a long hunting trip that involved cold weather and a tiny cabin. And when he came back, he was a changed man. Gone was the prideful and arrogant man. He was back to what he used to be: kind, thoughtful, and prayerful. We were so happy. He told me he encountered God in a powerful way out in the woods, and he was a changed man. So every year around the same time, he goes back out there."

"Wow! I mean, he told me a very shortened version of the story. I wonder why he hasn't told me all of it," I said, more to myself than Micah.

"Well, I think he will. I'm sure there are things about you that you haven't fully shared. It takes time to share the really hurtful and frankly embarrassing times." Micah patted my arm. "We are so thrilled that God brought you into his life. All your kids are just so sweet and gracious to us. Bo has a big family now, with a beautiful Jesus-loving wife. Like I said, we are thrilled!"

"Thank you for those sweet words. I have this nagging thought sometimes that he should have married a young twenty something who could give him his own children. I mean, you know, he would be such a fantastic dad." I tried to gauge Micah's reaction to see if Bo had said anything to her.

Micah thought for a second and said, "Nope. You are what he needs. At the dinner table last night, I watched him and you. He was so attentive to you, holding your hand, talking to you, looking at you, and you were reassuring and smiling. Nope. You are how his story begins and ends."

I felt slightly relieved. "Thank you, Micah, for telling me about that part of Bo's life. It is heartbreaking, but it helps me understand him better." I looked at my phone. "Oh, my goodness, I have to get ready. Tell everyone I will see them at the church for the Christmas Eve service."

Micah gave me a hug. "I cannot wait to hear you sing."

"I hope I don't disappoint, but really, it's all about Jesus anyway."

Chapter 73

I LAY DOWN IN BED AFTER grabbing a handful of almonds for dinner. My feet were killing me. I knew I should have worn more sensible shoes for standing and singing for three services, but fashion won, and my feet lost. My maroon stretch jeans, my black, sparkly shirt, and high-heeled boots looked amazing together. I had worn my hair up in a high, loose bun with big sparkly earrings. Tea and Brooke approved, so there was that.

Tea sang a little solo in the youth choir. She sang with such confidence and looked gorgeous in her emerald-green dress with her long dark hair. I couldn't stop telling her how amazing she did. I knew her loud inside voice could be used by God. I think I teared up each time I sang "O Holy Night." The words to that song were so powerful and relevant for any day of the week.

I started to hum the song as I thought about the words. For so long, the world had been in sin and in wrong thinking until God came, and our souls were finally stirred, and we recognized our worth through God's eyes. *Our souls are weary, so very weary Lord. But each day there are new mercies and new and glorious mornings.*

I thought about Bo and how he had hit rock bottom emotionally and spiritually with the loss of a child that he thought was his, his wife gone from his marriage, and a home he had built out of love and then sold. I was so grateful that God brought Bo to his knees and that God taught him his law of love and gospel of peace. The fact that Bo sold the house and gave her half the money spoke volumes about God moving in his heart. And it didn't surprise me at all.

I heard Bo come in, and he snuggled in beside me. "Hey," he said. "How are you?"

"I am good. It was a beautiful evening." I took his hand and held it.

He told me funny stories about that day in the barn. I laughed quietly and said, "Mmhmm."

Bo was lying on his back, and I lay on my side, getting as close as humanly possible. My hand was on his chest and his hand. I looked over at the clock. It was 12:30 a.m. It was our first Christmas together. "Merry Christmas, Bo. I love you."

Chapter 74

WE DECIDED TO JUST HAVE stockings for the kids and adults. We drew names for who we would give an actual gift to, and it had to be under ten dollars or homemade. Bo was so difficult to shop for; he had everything. He could go buy himself the world if he wanted to. I knew nothing about hunting. But I did find these rechargeable hand warmers, so he could put them in his pockets while he hunted like on the freezing-temperature duck-hunt adventure he had in February.

It was chaotic but fun, as all the cousins opened their stockings at the same time. We laughed a ton. Then came the adults. In my stocking, I had an Apple watch from Bo. He showed me how it had a 911 button that I could just press, and they would see my location. Plus, it had all the health-monitoring apps. It was going to take me a month to learn how to work it. I was not very intuitive with technology. He made sure to tell me that the main reason he bought it for me was because I was always losing my phone in the house. I would be able to find my own phone with the watch. I gave him a side eye. He insisted he didn't want to keep track of me 24/7. *Ha*.

I sat next to him in our big chair by the fireplace as we talked, laughed, and drank coffee with his family. Then we each took our turn giving our gift to the person we were assigned randomly. Brooke, of course, painted a picture for her person, Sarah. It was a beautiful painting. Whit wrote an original piano music score for Matt, who was thrilled. Tea sang a song for Luke about how he better sleep with one eye open because she would grow up and pay him back for all the big brother torture. It was hilarious. David had me, so he made a collage of pictures from when Bo was a baby, toddler, and kindergartner. I absolutely loved it. Luke had one of Dinah's boys and made him a board game. I had Micah, so I made her a devotional of my favorite Bible verses and what they meant to me. Bo had one of his nephews and made him a target to practice shooting at. My dad had Bo and made him a leather bullet-holder thingy.

It was such a fun Christmas morning. Bo went to make breakfast with Tea and the girls. I snagged my protein smoothie and went to get a workout before everyone started packing up to leave. I hoped I wasn't being rude, but then Jeff and Luke asked if they could get a workout in also. We three did a serious arm and back workout. I ran for three miles afterward. I was planning to attempt a 10K in the spring. I knew my running days were limited, according to my knees and my orthopedist. So I wanted to try one last 10k before I hung up my running shoes.

Later that afternoon, we waved goodbye to everyone. There were lots of hugs to go around and promises to see one another soon. Bo and I were maybe planning on going to visit over spring break so that Bo could show me all his childhood stomping grounds. We all went inside, and everyone took a nap—my beautiful, sleeping, family. I could not have been more grateful for each of them.

PART 8

PART 3

Chapter 75

Bo AND I HAD AN amazing time in Miami. We ate such good food and lay around on the beach or at the pool of the resort. We took long walks and talked. I asked him why he hadn't told me the full story about his ex-wife. He gave two reasons. One was that he was really embarrassed, and it was pride. But secondly, he didn't want me to hear about how much he wanted that baby because it might make me feel bad. Both sounded reasonable.

"The truth is, and I am embarrassed to say this, I wasn't planning on marrying her. She was just a diversion for the moment. That alone should give you a clue to how self-centered I used to be. We fought about ridiculous stuff all the time, mainly because we were investing only in physical intimacy and nothing else.

"Then within six weeks of our relationship, she told me she was pregnant. It never occurred to me to ask her if it was mine. I was so into the pregnancy. I didn't even know I would feel that way about a pregnancy. Thinking about my own baby gave me something else to think about besides myself. And it really was transformational to think about another life, both the mother's and baby's life.

"But like I said before, she was miserable in a small hill-country town. And I didn't want her to work. I just wanted her to take care of herself and my child. I realize now, thanks to Peter, that I was controlling disguised as overprotectiveness. And I was stifling her. And we fought.

"During one fight, she told me the baby wasn't mine. It was ugly. When I think about how I reacted, I shudder. She left. We were living in this little house we had on the property while I was building her house. I lost it. I just started breaking things." Bo shook his head and continued. "I went to see my parents and told them and my sisters everything. I cried. I knew my life was a mess. I had known the inside was a mess, but I could hide it. The outside was now out for everyone to see. A friend of my dad's had a cabin up in Montana and offered it to me. I went up there for five days and turned my cell phone off. No computer, nothing. I sat, thought, and started to read through the New Testament.

"You know how our pastor says when you start to read the Bible, it starts to read you? In God's grace-filled way, He exposed my sin to me. All of it. I ended up on the floor on my knees confessing all my brokenness and sin. And God was there. He had been with me all along. I just chose not to acknowledge Him, and I grieved that. I grieved that so hard.

"So you know the rest of the story. I made some commitments to God in that cabin: celibacy until marriage, which I might have reconsidered if I knew it was going to be eight years. But I really needed to practice self-discipline since I basically had none to speak of before that moment. I had in my mind the type of woman I wanted to marry, so I also decided not to date anyone unless I could see myself in a long-term relationship with her first. So that required getting to know her before any dating—a totally foreign concept.

"But all of that was so much easier said than done. My sin of compulsive habits and behaviors had built up over many years. I had some really hard days. I was listening to a sermon by Colin Smith, who said that when you find yourself in sin, ask yourself the question, 'How did I get here?' So I asked myself, *How did this habit of using women for my own selfish purposes gain so much power over my life?*

"The answer was that I had made an idol out of it. So simple. I went to it for comfort and for happiness. I basically worshipped my way into that lifestyle. The only way out of that mindset was to worship my way out. I had to practice gazing on the glory of God. And I did, and I broke free of it.

"Anyway, every year since, I go to Montana to that cabin and put all screens away. I read, pray, and listen for what God is telling me. And He always shows me where there is sin in my life, and I confess it and make a game plan."

"Wow," I said. "I love that you go back each year. So this is where you are going next week after duck hunting?"

"Yes. How do you feel about me after that story?" Bo asked quietly.

"Oh, Bo, I love the story because it is part of you and who you are right now in this moment. I am grateful that God loved you so much that He brought you to a place where you could acknowledge Him. I'm sure it was ugly but necessary. I love who you are and the person I have seen over the last four years. It reminds me of a verse in Ecclesiastes. It goes something like a person's wisdom brightens their face. Your face is bright with wisdom from all your experiences, even the really tough ones." Bo took my hand and kissed it. "It is hard to imagine you with other women," I said. I didn't even want to know how many women he had had sex with.

"Please don't imagine, please. I can say this, and it might sound like a line, but it isn't. Being with you and having sex with you has been completely different than any other relationship. First off because I waited and matured in eight years. What I came to realize is that I was having sex, but it was empty. Under God's covering, sex has a spiritual and emotional component that I have never experienced before. It's a whole new ball game with you. There is a connection that I have with you and that we have together that feels so strong and unbreakable. I have never experienced that before. Sex in the past always felt incredibly fragile—vulnerability wrapped up in massive insecurities and selfishness."

I stopped walking and looked at him. I stared into those kind brown eyes and smiled. "You are an absolute blessing to me, Boaz Channing. And I feel the same way with you. I love you more and more each day, which just seems impossible. I also completely understand the pain of having your life, what you thought it was going to look like, and then it being totally crushed. And I am so sorry about that." He squeezed my hand, and I saw a fleeting shadow of sadness across his face. *Lord, heal his heart completely.*

As we were walking back to the hotel, I started humming an old Crystal Lewis song. Crystal Lewis was the background music for high school. Katie and I would drive to neighboring towns with Crystal Lewis blaring as we tried to hit all her high notes. Something Bo had said brought it to my mind. Bo said that I had a song for every moment of the day. And I did. I think I started reaching for songs when I was little, to keep me company on the ranch. Now it was just a reflex that my mind did on its own.

"What song are you thinking about?" Bo asked.

"What a Fool I've Been"[18] by Crystal Lewis. Late nineties and early 2000. She is one of the vocalists I tried to imitate in high school." I started to sing what I remembered. It was all coming back to me as I hummed.

> I've lived dangerously
> Not noticing at all what I quickly could become
> so soon.
> He is always there.
> He's always been around.
> You will see Him when you change your view.
> What a fool I've been
> Just to think that I could live my life
> Like time was on my side.

This was my favorite verse. It was an amen verse.

I could not see through all the pain I caused.
I was lost for my sin blinded me.
We serve a great God,
For when we turn away,
He remains so faithfully close to you.

"Yep. That pretty much sums up my life. Amen," Bo said.

"It sums up every single person's life. We have all been fools and deceived into thinking we don't need God. We think we can be our own gods. Don't you think it's interesting that we both got married because of a pregnancy? I don't know if there is any type of life lesson in all our mess; just that God redeems. And that is enough, more than enough." I smiled widely at Bo.

"Smart and beautiful. How did I get so lucky?"

Chapter 76

I WOKE UP ON OUR LAST day in Miami feeling a little nauseous. I was struggling with the smell of coffee, so Bo went out and got me a soda. He stood there and watched me, in complete awe, drink it because he had never seen me drink a soda before.

"Better?" he asked.

"I think so. I must be coming down with a tummy bug. I'm sorry."

We packed and caught an Uber to the airport. I got motion sick on the plane and ordered another soda. Bo looked concerned. I told him that if he didn't want to get it, he should stay away from me. He looked at me and said sweetly, "I have tried, but I just can't. And anyway, I stayed away from you for three years. I haven't got any more staying away power left."

I smiled weakly at him, trying not to vomit on the plane. *Ugh.*

The next few days, I was off and on nauseous. I felt better when I lay down and closed my eyes. I didn't want to make a big deal of it. He was busy packing for his hunting trip and stay in Montana. Katie agreed it was probably a tummy bug. Then on the morning he was leaving, I started vomiting. As I lay down with my head pressed into the cold tile, he stood over me, debating what to do.

"Go," I said. "I will be fine. I absolutely want you to go." He looked stressed out. "It's better if you aren't here during the worst of it. You don't want to see things you can't un-see. Or hear things you can't un-hear." I was trying to make him laugh.

"I really need a husband handbook for this one," he said.

"The husband handbook says to do what your wife says. I want you to go do what you love. I want you to come back and have missed me really badly." He finally agreed to go after he got me back in bed with some crackers and soda.

I seemed to perk up by the third afternoon and felt like eating mac and cheese. So the kids and I made a big pot of it and watched a movie. Bo called, and I said I was eating dinner and felt better. He was not going to be able to contact me for a few days, which was fine. On Sunday, we went to church, and I was fine until I walked into my house and dry-heaved into the toilet. *What is happening?*

I got worse each morning. I had to call in reinforcements to help drive the kids in the mornings. I was fine by the afternoons but exhausted.

Katie walked in on her day off and threw a pregnancy test at me while I was lying on the bathroom tile.

"No!" I said.

"You know I am right. Pee right now." She was smiling while barking orders.

"No," I groaned. "It is not possible. I haven't had a period in almost two years." But I did have some spotting off and on during those two years. I refused to believe it was even possible.

"Have you been having sex?" she asked. I rolled my eyes at her. She laughed, opened the box, and pointed at the toilet. "Go!"

"It just isn't possible. It is not possible. It is impossible," I said as I peed. I curled up on one of our bedroom chairs, and she took the other chair as we waited. She went to get the results off the counter. She said that she hadn't looked, and she handed it to me.

"No!" I moaned. Then I threw the test hard across the room. I started to cry. I just kept saying, "No, it's not possible."

After about five minutes, Katie said, "Ellie, let me know when you are done with the tantrum." She was sitting there laughing at me—laughing at me!

"Be quiet," I said, then walked around the room while crying. Then I just got angry. "There is a big chance that I will lose this baby because I have very old eggs—very, very old. How cruel is this to Bo? Maybe I won't tell him. I have to tell him. He probably was up in his cabin praying for this. I'm going to kill him!" Katie was still sitting in my chair with her arms folded and still laughing at me. "Seriously, Katie, I am having a crisis, and you are not helping," I yelled at her.

"OK then, sit down." Katie pointed to the chair opposite her. I sat. "By some miracle—and yes it could very well be a miracle—you are pregnant. You need to calm down, put on your big-girl panties, and start making plans. You need to get a high-risk pregnancy OB. You need to get on folic acid immediately. I need you to get on the scale so we can determine if you are losing weight. And then you are going to put on the biggest smile you have and tell your husband you are pregnant tomorrow night when he gets in. I will take the kids for the weekend."

I laughed. It was so ridiculous. And Bo was going to lose his mind with joy. I was scared I would lose the baby. I didn't even know how far along I was. *Six weeks? Two months?* I didn't want to hurt Bo by telling him and then losing the baby. And it would probably be my fault—my bad egg.

I told Katie the whole story about Bo, his first wife, and how horribly it ended. Katie listened open mouthed. "He is going to be thrilled."

"I know." I went and picked up the pregnancy test and threw it at Katie. We laughed, and then I cried. I was too old to be pregnant.

Chapter 77

I PLANTED MYSELF IN FRONT OF the fireplace with my favorite blanket, the Sprite I had been sipping on all day, and a book. But I kept rereading the same page. I was waiting for Bo to call and tell me that he was boarding the flight home. He would get in late that night, but I knew I wouldn't be able to sleep until I told him. My phone rang, and it was Bo.

"Hey beautiful. I am at the front gate. I caught an earlier flight. I didn't want to scare you when I opened the garage. I will see you in a minute."

I had no idea why, but the surprise of him being so close made me cry. I was a jumble of emotions. I was happy for him and panicked for me. Plus, I had all the anxiety about possibly losing the baby and how sad he would be. I couldn't wait to see his face, but I was also really nervous because when I told him, it was going to be real. We were going to have a baby in less than nine months. My life as I knew it—as I liked it—was over. The tears came. I felt as though I was the most selfish human on the planet because I didn't want to be pregnant.

I got up to grab some tissues but decided I should just get the whole box. It might be one of those nights. As I was walking back into the kitchen for the box, Bo walked in. He tossed his stuff on the floor, grabbed me, and twirled me around. "I missed you so much."

I laughed because he was such a goof. He put me down. Then he looked at me, and his smile faded. "What is wrong?"

And I started to cry. "No, nothing is wrong. I mean, I know it looks like something is wrong. I am happy."

Bo looked at me with a frown. "I'm thoroughly confused. What is going on?"

"I'm going to tell you; I just need a minute. I didn't expect you home so early, so I am a little thrown off." I took a deep breath. "After I tell you this, please do not ask if I am joking because I would never ever joke about this." Bo's eyes were so big that it made me laugh. He probably thought I had been drinking. I took another deep breath. "I'm pregnant." *There. I got it out.* I was just watching him. We were still standing in the kitchen, and he hadn't shaved in a week. He looked so much older with a beard. I liked it.

Every emotion was flashing across his face. "Wait. What?"

"I kept vomiting in the mornings and feeling terrible. I took a pregnancy test—well actually, Katie made me take one."

His eyes got bigger, and his face lit up. He took a step toward me, not saying anything. Then he took a few steps backward and leaned on the counter. He was in complete and total shock. He turned away from me. I walked over to him and put my hand on his back. "Bo, are you OK?" *He better not pass out,* I thought. He wiped away a tear. *Oh, wow.* I cried sympathetic tears and wrapped my arms around him from behind.

He turned around, placed a hand on my belly, and said as he wiped away tears with his other hand, "I can't believe it. I just can't believe it."

"Bo, let's go sit down. And trust me; I can't believe it either." We sat down facing each other on the couch.

"How far along are you?" He was smiling so big that I was annoyed.

"I don't know. We have a doctor's appointment next week. Maybe two or three months. I have never been sick like this before, so it is all new to me. And I haven't had a period in forever. Katie says that I was under so much stress when Tommy died that I had lost so much weight and stopped having periods. I thought I was done with them, but I must have dropped an egg. It is a miracle. I mean, what are the odds after two years of nothing that I would be capable of getting pregnant?"

Bo leaned back and took my hand. He had regained his composure. "It is a miracle. I can't believe it. Wait, why were you crying?"

"I am having mixed emotions about being pregnant." I teared up again. "I am scared that I could miscarry because I am too old to be having babies. I am worried how you will take it if that happens. I am not looking forward to being pregnant or up at all hours for the next four years of my life. It's a lot for me lot to take in."

"I hear you," Bo said. But I didn't think that he did. He literally could not stop smiling. "While at the cabin, I confessed my sin of wanting to control your every move out of fear of the unknown. It is something I think I will always struggle with; honestly, I have always struggled with it. I left feeling so much freer. I couldn't wait to just be with you and the kids. I got lucky and on an earlier flight. And then I walked in, and you told me this." He was beyond happy. I knew that he would be. He couldn't stop hugging me the rest of the evening. Suddenly, I was exhausted. While Bo finished unpacking and got his laundry started, I went to bed.

He came in and lay down with me. "I am not sure I can go to sleep right now, but can I just lie with you?"

"Sure," I mumbled.

"El, I can appreciate this isn't what you saw happening this year—or ever—for us. And I know this puts a lot of strain on your body. I am sorry. If I could take it away, you know I would."

"I do know," I said quietly.

"Whatever you need, El, I am here." Then he laughed, which made me laugh for no reason. "Thank you, babe, for taking one for the team—team Channing. Channing, party of three." We kept giggling. "Also, I am buying you a new car."

"OK." I felt resigned to the pregnancy. "Can we keep this to ourselves until we know it is going to stick? Only Katie, you, and I know. I don't want to tell anyone until after we get our first major sonogram so we know the baby is OK."

"I would like to tell my parents so they can pray for us and the baby," Bo added.

"OK. We do need some prayer." Despite what Bo said, he fell asleep with his arms around me. *OK, Lord. I guess we are doing this—again. Help.*

Chapter 78

THE NEXT MORNING, I WAS vomiting and dry heaving into the toilet. I would walk from our bedroom to the kitchen, put my head on the cool quartz countertop in the kitchen, take a sip of Sprite, and a bite of cracker. Then I would go back to the bathroom.

Bo was clueless as to what to do. I told him to stay out of my way. And when I lay down midmorning to take a nap on the couch, I yelled towards the kitchen where he was eating breakfast. "How could you do this to me?" I heard my phone ring, but it was next to Bo on the counter.

"It's Katie. Do you want me to answer it?" Bo asked after looking at the caller ID.

"Fine." I was mad at her too. Bo put it on speakerphone so that I could hear them happily talk about me. *Awesome.*

Then Bo said, "She is mad at me. I don't really know what to do. I have never seen her this miserable."

Do they think I can't hear them?

Then Katie said, "Bo, she is doing great. The fact that she is puking so much means the hormones needed to keep the baby growing are in a high amount."

"Really? So the sicker she is, the better off the baby is? That is a bad trade off."

I put my pillow over my head. I could not listen to another word. I could hear Katie laughing through my pillow.

Bo tapped my shoulder. "Hey, do you want to talk to Katie?"

"No," I managed to croak out.

Katie laughed. "She is mad at me too. In fact, did she tell you she threw the positive test at me?"

"No. Well she hasn't thrown anything at me yet, but I will be watching for it." They laughed.

They were just being mean. "I hate you both," I said. And they both cracked up. I got up, walked to the master bathroom, and slammed the door. I could not believe them. I could not believe I was pregnant again. I sat against the wall with my head on my knees and close to the toilet. At least I had a clean bathroom to live in for the next few weeks. Bo had insisted on getting a cleaning crew to help with the house. They were amazing, and they did a fantastic job. I was grateful for that.

Bo walked in. He sat next to me and then pulled me into his lap. I cried. I hated being so overly emotional. *Thank you, hormones.* He sat with me and rubbed my back. "I'm so glad you designed an extra-large toilet room. It's like you planned this," I said, laughing a little.

He laughed a little too. Then he said, "You are doing amazing. You are going to get through this, El. You are the toughest woman I know.

Chapter 79

W E MADE IT TO TUESDAY when we went in for our appointment with the high-risk OB. Her name was Dr. Warner. She was calm and reassuring. She said I was definitely not the oldest pregnant mother she had seen. She prescribed some medication to help with the nausea. She spent some time chatting with us and then asked if she could take a look. It was mostly so that she could try to figure out a due date. I was going to warn Bo about the vaginal ultrasound, but then I remembered that he had been through this before.

I was actually getting excited about seeing the little peapod. Bo took my hand. We looked at the monitor. As things came into focus, I thought I saw two peapods. *But what do I know? Except that I have done this four times.* She looked at us and smiled. *Oh, no.*

"Congratulations! Twins." She paused to let that sink in.

I inhaled sharply and sighed an, "Oh, Lord." And then I went into shock. I kept saying twins. That's all my brain could do. I didn't even know what Bo's reaction was. I turned my head to look at him. He was all smiles.

"Due date is late August, early September."

No wonder I had been so much sicker than before—twins. I would never sleep again. I got dressed, and we met her back in her office. She wanted me to come in every two weeks for an ultrasound and blood work. I was to call her immediately if I started spotting or cramping.

"And Ellie, we need to discuss weight gain. Your current weight is borderline underweight." I glanced at Bo. He was listening intently to Dr. Warner. She showed us a chart. "This is where I need you to be at minimum in two weeks. The meds should help. Here are some listed food options to help you put on the weight." My eyes filled with tears. I had just gotten back into shape after healing my wounds from the attack. Any control, real or imagined, that I had over my life was about to be over. I still lived in that precarious place of if I could control my food intake, I felt like my life was under control. I had been functioning this way for so long that I didn't know how to let go.

Dr. Warner looked at me and saw my reaction. "Ellie, I will put you in the hospital if you are not able to keep up. Your babies need all the nutrition they can get. It is for less than nine months. You want these babies to be healthy, right?"

"Yes." I sniffed and wiped a tear away. Bo took my hand. Everything felt completely out of my control. I did not like it.

"They will be born before their due date, so you have got to get them the nutrients they need. I will set you up for a 3-D ultrasound in about ten weeks. We will do an amnio also. You can do this, Ellie. You have a team surrounding you. You have a husband who loves and supports you. Our goal is to keep you healthy so that you end up with two beautiful, healthy babies."

Bo and I walked out of the office in a daze. We got in the truck. He started it and turned to me. "El, I am speechless." He looked upward. "Twins," he said softly. "What are the odds?" He took my hand and pressed it to his heart, and he prayed right there. It was a prayer of thanksgiving, protection, and health. He got choked up. He took a deep breath, smiled at me, and drove home. We rode in silence, contemplating the wonder of it all. I hadn't spoken since Dr. Warner had told us we were having twins. I had no words.

Halfway home, he looked at me with concern. "You feeling OK?"

"I'm just overwhelmed. It is a lot to sort through. How I need to change how I eat—at least the portion size. How I need to add more fat to my diet. I still want to work out, but how do I do that safely?"

We swung by the pharmacy and got my prescriptions. I took it right away. We decided to call Bo's parents. Sarah answered.

"Hey, Mom, can you get Dad and talk to us on speakerphone?"

"Of course. You guys OK?"

"Yes, Mom, we are great."

Bo told them our news. He could not stop smiling. I really would have been thrilled for him if it wasn't for my body being used for the insanity. His parents were over the moon.

"Twins! What an amazing gift from God. Ellie, how are you feeling?"

"Honestly, a little scared, a little nauseous, and I could use a nap."

Sarah said, "Honey, you are going to get through this. You will be lifted up in prayer every single day until those babies are here. You just eat and take naps. Bo can handle everything."

David said, "Bo, I will be praying for you, son, that you stay healthy and are able to be a rock for Ellie."

"Thank you, Mom and Dad. And will you please keep this news to yourselves until Ellie gets through the next two months? She wants to be sure that the babies are OK before we tell anyone?"

"We will," they said in unison. They were the best.

Bo reached for my hand in the car. I looked at him and said, "I am going to be as big as a house. I cannot believe you did this to me."

Bo laughed. "Me? Hey, if I remember my biology class, you are the one who dropped two eggs."

I laughed but then said, "Bo, what if I can't hold onto them? This uterus has been through a lot."

"I know you are worried about miscarriage, but here is the truth: God gives, and God takes away. Blessed be the name of the Lord. He is still good if these babies make it all the way or if they don't. And if they don't, we will see them in heaven. We get to meet them either way."

I loved him so much for saying that. "I just don't want to fail you or them."

He looked at me and said, "No matter what, you won't have failed. Will you promise to let me help you? Let me know everything you are feeling. We can do this, but you have to let me in all the way. Sometimes I see you just muscle through on your own. I want us to be a team, all the way. OK?"

"OK," I said. But I probably would have agreed to anything at that point.

We went inside the house. I ate a big spoonful of peanut butter and took a nap.

Chapter 80

I WAS SNUGGLING WITH TEA ON the couch in front of a nice fire. "Mom," Tea said, "I was really worried about you. You were throwing up so much. I think I was scared that you would die like Daddy. Like fast."

"Oh, Tea." I leaned down to kiss the top of her silky dark hair. "I am so sorry I scared you. I scared myself. I haven't been that sick in a long time."

"Promise me you will get your flu shot next year." Tea pointed her finger at me.

"I promise." I had gotten my flu shot, but we were telling her and everyone that it was the flu. I felt so bad for telling half-truths. I looked at Bo, who was in the kitchen. He smiled at me and winked.

"Mom, I need to go to the store and get Valentines to give my friends tomorrow." Tea jumped up. "Can you take me after dinner?"

"I think I can." I looked at Bo, and he looked worried. *Good grief.* I had to be able to drive places. I was really much better except right when I woke up in the mornings. I would take my anti-nausea medicine with some type of bubbly drink and crackers. I had to work really hard to keep it down so that it could do its magic. Bo had been taking the kids to school. I would go back into work the following week. My TAs had been thrilled to take over the lectures, but I missed my students.

I told Tea to go get Whit so that we could eat. I walked over to

Bo, who was making vegetable soup and sourdough bread. He had done a lot of research that week on safe workouts for me and healthy food for pregnant moms. I had my very own personal chef and a very hot personal trainer. I hugged him from behind and put my hands in his front pockets. He laughed.

"I promise I will be careful driving to Target, but I need to do normal things," I said.

"I know you do. I will just follow your every movement on my Life360 app, so it's fine," he teased. I giggled.

"And then when I get into the store, you can track my every move and even my heart rate thanks to my Apple watch." I placated him.

Bo turned to me, wrapped me in a hug, and said, "Thank you for putting up with my stalker-like tendencies. You are the best." I rolled my eyes and laughed.

As Whit was coming down the stairs, I asked him, "Do you need any Valentine's Day cards or candy to give to anyone?"

He smiled shyly and said, "No."

"What about Lucy from church?" Tea sang in her most annoying little sister voice.

"She doesn't go to my school," Whit answered.

Tea shrugged. "I still think you should get her something. Don't you, Mom?"

Whit looked horrified. I answered, "No, they are only sitting together at church and youth night, so they aren't quite at the level of Valentine yet."

Whit sat down with a look of relief and said, "I printed out my certificate for the first part of driver's ed, so I am ready to go get my permit." He looked at Bo.

"OK, great. We will get you an appointment. You are on your way to newfound freedom." Bo smiled.

Then Tea said, "Once he gets a car, he will never be home, and it will just be me and you two." Tea sighed. Bo and I looked at each other and tried not to smile.

Chapter 81

THE NEXT MORNING, I WAS working in my home office when Bo called me to come out front. It was chilly outside, so I walked onto the front porch with a blanket over my shoulders. Parked in our circular drive was a brand-new white Chevy Suburban with Bo leaning against it. He yelled, "Happy Valentine's Day!"

"Bo! Oh, my goodness. I cannot believe you!" I yelled back.

"Come down and sit in your new truck!"

I walked down the stairs and around to the driver's side. As I got in, I saw a white box with a red ribbon. I looked at Bo, who was standing with the passenger door open. I opened it. There was a white-gold necklace with two hearts interlocking and two diamonds. I looked up at him and saw him grinning from ear to ear. He loved to surprise me. He climbed in and put the necklace on me. I started to get weepy, which was a direct result of double the amount of hormones running through my body.

"It's so beautiful." I got choked up. I still couldn't wrap my head around having twins and the fact that there were two babies inside me. I shook my head in disbelief.

"I read that by day fifty, they have fully formed hearts. Their hearts are beating right now." He took his thumb and brushed my tears away. He tipped my chin and kissed me.

Chapter 82

TWO WEEKS LATER, I STARTED to notice that I had a little belly and that I could not button my jeans. I bought five pairs of my favorite yoga pants and made sure I had enough bulky sweaters to get me through five more weeks until my big ultrasound and amnio. I was hoping everyone either wouldn't really notice or would just think that married life agreed with me as I got slightly chubby.

Katie and John came over three weeks later to drop off the girls for spring break. They were going on their twenty-year anniversary trip. I couldn't wait to have some time with Kylie, Remy, and Landry. As the girls ran up the stairs to put their stuff away, Katie and John cornered Bo and me. "You guys sure you are up to this?" asked John.

"Absolutely! I am looking forward to hanging out with my favorite girls. Plus, they entertain Tea, and it is a good cover for why we are going nowhere for spring break," I replied.

Katie gave me a big hug. "How are you feeling today?"

"Like I drank too much beer." I showed them my belly pouching out over my yoga pants.

"I do not think you are going to be able to hide that much longer. Are you fifteen weeks?" asked Katie.

"Yep. So far, so good. And the morning sickness has calmed down. It is still there but not as bad. It just comes in small waves instead of a tsunami."

John gave me and Bo a hug. "We are praying for you both every day."

"Thank you, John. It means more than you know." Bo gave Katie a squeeze, and they were off.

"Bye, girls!" Katie yelled up the stairs. Kylie and Remy yelled goodbye, but Landry came bounding down the stairs and hugged her parents. We all waved to them as they drove off.

"Auntie Ellie, can we bake cookies?"

"Let's! But can Uncle Bo help too because I still am not sure where everything is in my kitchen?" Landry approved, and we went into the kitchen in search of cookie ingredients.

After two-dozen cookies and a new movie on Disney Plus, everyone went to bed. Kylie and Landry slept in Brooke's room while Tea and Remy shared her room.

Bo and I took all the kids out hiking the next day. It was beautiful weather. We packed a lunch, and the girls hiked and played all over Pedernales Falls State Park. I sat and watched Bo jumping around and playing with the girls. I thought about how almost a year earlier, we had gone to a wedding, danced, and talked about us. *Now look at us! Married and pregnant. I could not have even imagined this a year ago.* God always had a hope and a future for us, and it was always more than we could have ever dreamt of.

I stared at Bo and his five-foot ten-inch frame. He was all muscle. His blond hair was under a ball cap. He had a perfect jawline, big brown eyes, and a big smile that lit up his whole face. I hoped that those babies looked just like him. I couldn't even picture my life without him. How incredibly blessed I was. He loved me, my kids, and Katie's kids so well. He was going to be a phenomenal dad. I couldn't wait to see him hold the babies. I thanked God for getting us to fifteen weeks. I prayed that all our children would live to glorify His name.

I was thinking about a Bible verse I read in Ecclesiastes 6. It said that the Lord blesses us, but only by His grace could we actually enjoy the blessings. *Thank You, Lord,* I prayed, *for Your grace to enjoy all that You have given me.*

Chapter 83

Bo AND I WERE LOUNGING by our pool, watching the sunset. Katie had taken the kids for the evening. The next day, we would have the 3-D ultrasound and amnio. While we were excited to find out the gender, we were also nervous about the amnio and the health of the babies. Dr. Warner had been really positive about how the babies were doing. She also had said that I looked healthy but that my weight could be better. But she would take it.

It had been hard keeping my anxiety in check since I had found out I was pregnant. Every twinge or muscle twitch would terrify me if I let it. If I didn't take each thought captive, I would catastrophize, thinking of everything that could go wrong with these babies. I found that getting on my knees every morning and acknowledging that God alone held my next breath in His hands and these babies' next heartbeats was calming.

Bo was talking to his parents. They were praying for us and the babies regarding whatever the ultrasound and amnio would reveal. And we were going to tell the kids that weekend. I could barely wear my yoga pants, and bulky sweaters were getting a little warm in April.

When he got off the phone, he looked at me with that expression that he reserved for only me. "You look so beautiful in the sunset's light. How is your body holding up today?"

He was sweet to me. He was all about team Channing, party of three. He paid so much attention to me, listening to my fears and reassuring me of every anxiety I felt. It filled my heart to know that he thought about me during the day and how I was doing as much as I thought about him. It occurred to me that what most people wanted was for someone to think about them and wonder how they were doing. And I had that someone right beside me.

"Thank you for the complement. And my body feels OK. I am hitting that stage where I look down at my body and wonder what in the world is happening to it. It isn't mine anymore. They have taken up residence and have no intention of leaving."

"Well," said Bo as he put a hand on my hip, "can I just say I am enjoying your body and the new curves."

"At least three out of four of us are enjoying it. That is something."

Bo laughed. I loved it when I made him laugh. He had the warmest, most genuine laugh.

"I can't wait to see them in 3-D tomorrow," he said. He was so excited. "What is that face?"

"This world can be cruel with health issues for tiny babies who haven't even been born." I sighed.

He leaned back and said, "I didn't want to tell you this any sooner because I wanted to make sure I wasn't speaking this too soon to you. But while I was at the cabin in February, one thing I was praying about was letting go of wanting a child of my own. I left the cabin knowing that I was healed from that regret. And then I walked in the door, and you told me you were pregnant. The unexplainable and unexpected goodness of God just made me weep that night. And I have felt His assurance that these babies are going to be OK and that they will make it. Maybe that is just plain human hope, but it feels like more than that." Bo's eyes filled with tears. "God is as good as His word. He took what was broken in me and a loss that felt unfixable and gave me a triple portion. He gave me you and two babies. And I fully comprehend that I couldn't earn that or even deserve that, but He gave this all to me anyway."

Now I was tearing up. We both sniffled and then laughed.

Chapter 84

WE WERE IN THE SONOGRAM room looking up at the big screen. We had had the amnio earlier. And there they were: two beautiful babies. We both wanted to know the gender of the babies as soon as the sonographer could tell. After a bunch of measuring and looking at all the organs, the sonographer asked if we were ready.

"Yes!" we said in unison.

"Baby A right here is a girl. And Baby B is a boy. One of each. And they both look healthy."

"Oh, my goodness, they are perfect. Bo, can you believe it is one of each?" I looked over at Bo. He was trying not to lose it in front of the sweet sonographer. He couldn't talk, and I was overflowing with joy. They were OK. The babies were going to be OK. I held his hand and squeezed it hard.

He whispered, "They made it. We made it. Thank you, God."

The sonographer smiled and said, "Amen." She printed out some pictures for us.

I stopped at the restroom, and Bo went outside to call his parents. By the time I walked out, he was sitting on a bench with the phone to his ear and tears running down his face. His parents were praising God for His faithfulness, and they could not wait to tell his sisters.

We stopped by the grocery store for a weekend's worth of groceries, as everyone was coming over for dinner that night. Brooke was probably already at the house with Luke, and Katie's family was coming at around six. I would probably have to tell Brooke as soon as I hugged her. She would definitely notice my belly.

By the time we had gotten to the store, both sisters had called Bo. They were so excited and happy for us. Micah and Dinah both said they would come to help. And Sarah was planning on moving in for a month or two or however long we needed her. I felt so very grateful. Maybe, just maybe, I would get a little sleep after all.

Chapter 85

I T WAS MAY, AND I was in week twenty-two. I looked almost nine months pregnant. It was ridiculous. I was at my office, packing up. I was going on sabbatical, and the timing was perfect. I had a full year to focus on research and writing at home. God's timing was always perfect. I was going to work within a restorative justice program to explore how sociology could work within and add to it. As I taped the last box of books and pictures shut, I got a text from Katie. All it said was "911," which was our code for "drop everything and call me now."

I called her immediately. She answered before the first ring. "Ellie." She was sobbing. "Ellie, it's Joey. She is dead."

Oh, no. Oh, Jesus, I prayed, *please cover her right now with your peace.* I sat down. "Oh, Katie. Oh, Joey. I am so sorry—so, so sorry."

Katie took a breath. "The police found her this morning in Galveston, dead from an overdose." She started to cry again. "My poor parents. I just … I am so mad at Joey for doing this to them. To us. But I am grateful she is out of pain."

"She just got a little lost. We all get a little lost sometimes."

"I am almost home. I have to go in and tell the kids. John is on his way. You are coming over, right?" Katie was half-talking and half-crying.

"I will be over soon with food. I love you, Katie." I called Bo. He had been bringing boxes down to my car all morning.

"Bo."

"El, what is it? Are you OK?"

"Yes, it's Katie. Her sister Joey died of an overdose this morning."

"Oh, no. That is terrible. I will be right up for the last box, and then we can get you to her."

"Thank you." He knew what I wanted to do before I asked—not all the time, but he was getting pretty good at it.

We pulled up to Katie's house an hour later. Bo was going to get food for everyone. Katie literally had no food in her house except coffee and Goldfish crackers most days. She and John worked so much, and the kids ate everything as soon as she bought it. She could not keep her pantry stocked no matter how hard she tried.

When I walked in, there was Kylie, eyes red. "Oh, sweetheart," I said and wrapped her in a big hug.

"Auntie Ellie, Mom is so upset. I haven't seen her like this ever."

"I know Kylie; I know." I rubbed her back and stroked her hair.

"And I know I remind her of Aunt Joey because we look similar. I don't know if I should just hide my face or what." Kylie sobbed.

"Kylie, you have a beautiful face. Do not ever hide it. Maybe sometimes it reminds your mom of Joey, but there is no reason to be worried about your face hurting your mom. She is going to hurt even if you didn't look like your aunt. Death of a loved one just hurts. And listen Kylie." I took her hands and made sure she was looking at me. "Tea looks so much like her dad, and I delight in that. That is the legacy of family, and it is a beautiful thing."

"OK," Kylie said with her head buried in my shoulder. "You know, Auntie Ellie, it is really hard to hug you with two babies in the way." I laughed, and she giggled.

John walked in with Remy and Landry. They both ran to me and joined the hug. They didn't know how to respond to their mother crying in her room. Katie was such a doer and a force that they were not used to seeing her so vulnerable.

"How is she?" I asked John.

"A mess. One minute, she is yelling about the hurt Joey put them through, and the next, she is holding a picture of Joey at her medical school graduation and crying."

I nodded. It sounded about right. I told John that Bo was on the way with food and then walked up the stairs to Katie. When I got to her room, I found her in the closet, sitting on the floor. She looked up at me and said, "No one knocks anymore, I guess."

"Oh, Katie, how are you holding up?" Katie had her head buried in her knees. "Katie, if I get down on this floor with you, you may have to send Bo to get me up." I slid down the wall and plopped down beside her.

She started to cry. I leaned into her, and she leaned into me and went into that heart-wrenching mode of loud sobbing. She was grieving for a life that never had the chance to get started.

Joey was so smart. Her PSAT scores were insanely high. She was being recruited for colleges by her sophomore year. She was also a really good basketball player. She was tall and lanky like her dad. And then in her senior year during the first game of the season, she fractured a vertebra in her back. And while rehabbing, some worthless doctor gave her addictive pain killers, and she lost her way.

Later that evening, we were all in Katie's living room. Tea was hanging out with Remy. Landry was sitting next to me on the couch. Kylie was on my other side. Katie was on the phone with her parents. Bo and John were talking quietly in the kitchen.

Landry asked, "Do you think Joey is in heaven and sees Uncle Tommy?"

"I have heard," I said, "that the instant you die you are in heaven and that everyone who knew you and had gone into heaven before you comes to greet you. I like to imagine that Tommy was there. He had known Joey since she was nine years old. She was the flower girl at our wedding," I continued.

"When she was fifteen, she went to beach camp with her church—the same one your mom and I grew up in. And they had youth camp for a week at Galveston Island—the same place where she died. And guess what? She got baptized in the ocean. I was very pregnant with Brooke, and your mom and I drove down for the day to see her get baptized. Joey was so excited to see us and to be baptized. We have it on a video somewhere. And I think there is some symbolism in the fact that she confessed her faith in Jesus in the ocean and that is the same place where she went to heaven."

I looked around. They had come into the living room, and they were listening. Katie came and sat down next to Kylie. "I remember. It was a beautiful day at the beach," Katie said through tears.

We all told stories about Joey. I had met her when she was two years old. It was almost like she was my little sister too. She always tagged along and wanted to be included in everything we did. Sweet Joey had auburn hair like Katie's. She had blue eyes, and her lips were forever in a pout when she didn't get her way.

As we were leaving that night, Katie said, "My parents want a going home ceremony next week. It could be several weeks until the autopsy is done. Mom wants to know if you will sing."

"Absolutely. And I will call her tomorrow. I love you, Katie." We hugged for a while.

"Thank you for being here," she said, as if I would be anywhere else.

Chapter 86

I MADE MY WAY CAREFULLY DOWN the stairs after tucking in Tea. I looked down, and Bo was sitting on the couch watching me. "I am a little front heavy, so just going slow," I said.

"I don't know how you do it, El—five months pregnant with twins, spending the whole evening with Katie, and you still manage to look beautiful."

"It's probably the dim lighting," I joked. "Thank you." I sat down next to him. I was in a cute teal halter top with pregnant jeans and chunky sandals.

Bo smiled and said in his slow East Texas drawl, "You don't even look pregnant from behind except that you walk like you are a little off-balance."

"Ha, ha, ha," I retorted.

"But your arms are super toned thanks to my personal workouts." He smiled as his hand went from my shoulder to my cheek. I was grateful that he still found me attractive. Not all men would be happy that their thin and toned bride from a few months earlier was now forty pounds heavier. Being pregnant felt like the least sexy thing on the planet.

"El, I don't think it is a good idea to drive all that way to sing at Joey's service. Dr. Warner doesn't want you going more than an hour away," Bo reminded me.

"Well, I am going. This is important, I am feeling great, and the babies look good," I said decisively.

"I think you should call Dr. Warner and just ask her if you should drive over three hours away and then stand on your feet that long singing and helping afterward. I know you; you will help until you are about to fall over," Bo argued.

"I am not going to call her. I will just go the day before the service to get everything organized and to be there for that family— my family. I will do the service and then go back to Katie's parents' house to help with the food. And I will come home the next day."

"El, do you hear yourself? You cannot be in the middle of nowhere Texas for three days. What if something happens? There is no good hospital anywhere around there." Bo was getting a little intense.

"You could come with me. Luke could watch the kids. Katie is a doctor."

"She is a dermatologist," Bo insisted.

"She is the best doctor I know. She has photographic memory. She has memorized everything medical, including everything about my pregnancy."

"El, I don't want you risking your health and the twins."

I stood up with my hands balled into fists. I felt like I was a melting down toddler. "Bo, they have always been there for me. I am going to be there for them. End of discussion." I walked toward the bedroom.

I shut the door behind me without looking back at Bo. I paced my room. I was livid. He could not tell me what to do. *What is it with men?* He was completely incapable of looking at this from the perspective of the empathy and devotion I had for Katie's family. He just focused on the physical, what he could see, and not what I felt. I had gone from Tommy, who did not give me the attention I needed, which resulted in me doing whatever I wanted, to being married to Bo, who was so attentive that we had to talk through every decision. *Ugh.* I sat down on the bed and sighed.

I remembered something our pastor said one Sunday. "Do you

want to be right, or do you want to be married? You cannot make peace by standing on your rights. Jesus left his rightful position to come make peace with the world." I knew I was clinging to my rights too tightly. I sighed again. I should not have walked away. Being a peacemaker meant moving toward the conflict. If I wanted to be married—and I did—I needed to finish the conversation instead of shutting it down.

I opened the bedroom door. Bo was a few feet from it and about to walk in. I looked up at his big brown eyes, which were right below that wrinkle he got when he was worried. He rubbed the back of his neck, which I noticed he did when he was a little uncomfortable. I wondered if I was that easy to read.

"El, I am sorry if I upset you. I wasn't trying to."

"I am so sorry for walking out on you—on us. I am going to pull the pregnant-and-tired card along with the emotionally spent card."

Bo smiled. "Well played. I should not have brought it up tonight. I need to work on my timing."

I leaned into him for a hug. He could still get his arms around all of us. "I can't wrap my head around the fact that Joey isn't out there in the world anymore. The hope we all held onto was that one day she would turn it around. But it never happened. It makes me think of that Bible verse I think is Isaiah 57. It says something like the righteous person is taken away from the evil yet to come. Maybe God knew she wasn't going to turn it around, and in His mercy, He wanted to spare her from any more evil. In His mercy, He took her."

"I find a lot of peace with that thought," Bo replied. "And in the psalms, David asks God to help him understand that our days are numbered; we are transient people, who are only here for a short time. Life is too short to be upset with each other. Can we pray about you going at least?"

"Yes."

"Come on. Let's get you three to bed."

"Whenever you say 'you three' it feels like I am a three-headed monster."

He laughed. I loved the sound of his laughter.

Chapter 87

WE CALLED DR WARNER TOGETHER on speakerphone, which slightly annoyed me. *Does Bo not trust me to call on my own?* Come to think of it, he probably didn't because I probably wouldn't call. I already felt like these babies were taking over my life. I couldn't even make a phone call on my own. Dr. Warner was OK with me going as long as I monitored my blood pressure, sat down most of the time, kept my stress level low, stayed hydrated, and ate.

Katie was leaving that day to drive up to be with her parents. Bo, the kids, and I would drive up Friday. The service was on Saturday, and then we would come home on Sunday.

Friday morning, Bo found me in my closet having a meltdown because I had nothing to wear. Literally nothing fit me. It was like my belly grew overnight. I didn't have anything to wear to the funeral or anywhere. The floor was strewn with clothes that didn't fit anymore. I glared at Bo and threatened, "Don't even look at me. In fact, don't ever touch me again."

He just leaned against the wall with his arms folded across his chest and that slow smile of his. He wore faded blue jeans and a white T-shirt. *Ugh. Why is he so handsome? So not fair.*

"El—"

"I hate being pregnant. I hate it. I hate that I hate it because really, I am just a terrible person. I am vain. I liked my body the way it was. Now it's like I am a water buffalo." I started to cry.

287

"Water buffalo is a little harsh, El. Come here." He started to walk toward me.

"I said don't touch me ever again!"

He started laughing. He knew I wasn't serious. "For the record, that is not what you were saying last night."

I balled up a sweater and threw it at him. He ducked. I started to laugh. "Well, today is a new day, so don't take one step closer to me." He laughed as he dodged all the outfits I threw at him.

I went to lie face down on the bed as I mourned the loss of my body. He leaned down to me and said, "I 100 percent love your body. I love how it was before you were pregnant, and I love it now. I love how your body is strong as it holds those two babies in it. I love the curves you have now. Even your cheeks are a little fuller. I know you want your old body back. I promise that once these babies are born, I will help you do whatever you want to do. If you want to run a marathon, I will get you there. If you want to do an Ironman, I will hire someone to get you there." He kissed my head and walked into his office to get some work done. I told him that I loved him a bunch because I did. I couldn't help myself.

On our way out of town, we stopped at Target so that I could get myself some bigger clothes. *Joy.* It was also so that Bo could grab a ton of groceries to bring to my dad's house. There was no way for my dad to prep for the onslaught that was about to arrive. Luke and Brooke were coming too.

By the time we got to the register, each kid had a new outfit, a few odds and ends, and a bunch of groceries. I had a theory that Target lighting made people spend more money than they intended to. Everything looked so shiny that they had to buy it. Bo swallowed hard when he looked at the total. I pretended not to notice.

Chapter 88

WE ROAD TESTED THE NEW Suburban with two kids, two full-grown adult kids, all our stuff, Bingo, Bo, and myself plus two. Dinah called me while we were driving. We caught up on family news.

"Why are my sisters calling you now and not me?" Bo asked teasingly.

"Because they know you and are worried about me," I teased back. "And anyway, I'm doing all the hard work carrying your babies around." Bo smiled.

Next, I was on the phone with Katie, as we were planning the service with her parents on speakerphone. Katie and I were going to sing a few songs we used to sing to Joey when she was little. We were singing oldies but good ones. The songs brought back a memory of Barbara picking Katie and me up after Wednesday night youth group. She had little three-year-old Joey in her car seat. Katie and I would be singing, and Joey would try to join in. I closed my eyes wanting to hold onto that mental picture of Joey alive and without poison running through her body.

Bo touched my hand. "You OK?"

I opened my eyes. A few tears escaped. "I was just remembering Joey as a baby." I sighed. This was going to be a hard few days.

Then Luke, Tea, and I ran through a few songs in the car. We were going to end with me singing "I Still Believe"[19]. We picked it because we wanted people to know that even after all the heartache of loving an addict, we still believed in a good God. I had been practicing it, and I had a hard time singing the last few words. I got so choked up at the end. Luke wanted to hear it a cappella, which was good practice anyway because it was just going to be a piano playing a few chords.

I sang it, but I couldn't finish the end—twice.

> I believe in love.
> I believe in peace.
> I believe someday,
> You'll return for me.
> I believe in things
> I cannot see.
> And when my heart says no,
> I still believe.

"Maybe," suggested Tea, "you could have people join in the last chorus, and then they can't tell if you can't get it out."

"Good idea," I replied as I turned around and smiled at her in the very back seat.

"Or we could all get on stage with you and sing the last chorus together," added Luke.

"I like both ideas. Let's ask Katie tomorrow. We need to be at the church by noon to practice."

We were almost there, and Bo and I were having a discussion. I wanted him to drop me off at Katie's on the way to my dad's ranch. I just wanted to see Barbara and Brad and hug them. Katie could drive me over to the ranch later. Bo was not a fan of that idea. I rubbed my temples, trying not to get frustrated. I didn't want to have the same argument we seemed to always have, especially in front of the kids.

"Bo, can we compromise? Drop me off, drive the kids to my dad's, unload, and then come and get me. Please?" He thought about it and agreed. I rolled out of the suburban and walked into their home.

"Hello?" I said loudly as I walked through the side door. I went into the kitchen, and I saw Brad first. I hugged him for a long time.

"Thank you for coming, Ellie," he said gruffly.

I couldn't seem to let go of him. "Oh, Brad, I am so very sorry." When he let go, we both wiped our eyes.

He looked down at my belly and said, "There was a rumor that you were pregnant with twins, but I wasn't going to believe it until I saw it."

I rolled my eyes. "I know. Can you believe it? Because I still can't."

Barbara and Katie walked in. I hugged Katie first. "How are you doing?" I looked at her face, and her eyes and nose were red. *Poor thing.*

"I am an emotional train wreck. Just trying to get it all out before tomorrow." She got a tissue to wipe her eyes.

I looked at Barbara. She did not look well at all. I said nothing and hugged her. "I just can't believe it. I can't believe she is gone," Barbara said over and over. I remembered feeling that way about Tommy. It was like you had to keep saying it to yourself to convince yourself that it was true. We all sat, chatted, and ran through the service.

Barbara took my hand. "You know, you have always been like a third daughter to me. It means the world to me that both of you are singing tomorrow. Joey always loved listening to you both. I remember how you would take her back to her room and sing to her so that she would go to sleep. And you always could do it."

"Yes, I remember," I said. I remembered carrying her to her room. She was always sticky and sweaty, with dried tears from not wanting to take a nap. I would stay with her and sing until she fell asleep. "I used to sing 'I Believe in Jesus.'" I started to sing it.

I believe in Jesus.
I believe He is the Son of God.
I believe He died and rose again.
I believe He came for us all.
And I believe that He's here now,
Standing in our midst,
Here with the power to heal now
And the grace to forgive.

Katie joined in and then Barbara and Brad. We were smiling through tears. I heard Bo drive up, and I hugged each of them and told them I would see them on the following day.

Chapter 89

"YOU HAVE BEEN EXTRA QUIET tonight. You doing OK?" Bo asked as I lay down in bed.

I sighed. "I just feel heavy with grief." I scooted over and lay next to him, with his arm under my head. "Right now, it feels like I am cursed like death follows me around. My mom, then Tommy, and now Joey. I sometimes get scared that I am the carrier of death. It's me and my presence in people's lives that cause them to die. I know it doesn't make sense and isn't true. Just some moments, it sure feels true." I turned and buried my head in his shoulder

"El, I am sorry. Death follows all of us around, waiting for its turn. None of us gets out of here alive." Bo rubbed my back until I fell asleep.

My eyes popped open, and I rolled over. It was 4:00 a.m. I was pretty sure I was not going back to sleep. I quietly got up, walked to the living room, and grabbed a blanket. I opened the front door and went to sit on the porch in a rocking chair. I just sat and rocked, letting my mind rest. And I started to sing softly. I sang the song I used to sing to Joey again and again. It was such a simple and beautiful song.

At some point, Bo came out and sat beside me. I kept singing for a while. I finally stopped. I could see the sun peeking over the horizon. All the birds began to sing. I decided it was my turn to listen to them. I looked at Bo, but his eyes were closed. I loved it when I could just stare at him and contemplate the wonder of it all. *How am I his wife? How am I carrying his two babies?* How impossibly amazing it all was. I reached for his hand.

He then said, "I'm just going to keep asking if you are doing OK. I don't know that I have ever seen you this melancholy."

"I once heard Amy Grant say something like, 'I process my faith and life through song.' And I just woke up needing to process. This life can be so overwhelming sometimes." I went and sat on his lap, all bundled up in a blanket. It felt safe. He was someone I always felt safe with. He put his hands on my belly, and the twins started to move around. We just sat together and watched the sunrise as Bo gently rocked all four of us.

Chapter 90

I WAS UP ON THE STAGE of the church that I had grown up in. As a child, it had seemed so big, but as an adult, it seemed so small and worn. I was working with the pianist on the songs. Ben was an old friend from High School. Ben, Katie, and I were all in choir together at school and church. Katie and Ben didn't want to change the key of "I Still Believe." They both believed I could do it. Ben said he would slow it down. It was going to be such a quieter, higher note song than I was used to.

Ben tried to encourage me. "Ellie, you just sang it almost perfectly. You are doing it just like you always do. You always doubted yourself when we were teenagers too. You never knew how intimidating you were to all the guys."

Katie laughed. I smiled. "I must not have been that intimidating as you did ask me to the prom."

"I did, as a friend. We were both pretty quiet, but Katie kept it lively, as always." We were all laughing and then telling do-you-remember? stories.

I walked over to Bo. I was not feeling very confident. I told Bo that this might be where I fell flat in front of everyone. He took my hand and prayed over me.

The church was full of flowers from all over town. The parish hall was full of food for after the service. There was nothing like a small-town community where people come together during another family's devastation.

The pictures of Joey up at the front were mesmerizing. I couldn't take my eyes off them. It felt like she was still here if I kept looking at the pictures. So much potential was gone. There was only one picture of Joey with Kylie as a toddler. The girls never knew her because Katie would not let her around them unless she was clean. And Joey rarely was clean. I wondered if Katie regretted her decision.

Bo was sitting in a chair, keeping tabs on me. He made me sit down every thirty minutes, and Katie backed him up. I was outnumbered and annoyed.

People started coming thirty minutes before we were to begin. Everyone was commenting on my belly. Unfortunately, everyone knew how old I was—43—and I was getting looks. *Sheesh, small towns.* I was going to be part of the dinnertime conversation all around town tonight.

Bo and my kids were sitting a row behind Barbara, Brad, Katie, and her family. I prayed that my kids' memories were not being triggered by being at another funeral. It had almost been three years since Tommy had died. I wondered how often they thought of him; I sure did. Mostly at night or early in the morning, my mind would instinctively continue to draw on our relationship and share the joy of our children with him. I think sharing your life with someone for twenty years makes it impossible to completely move on, as many probably believed that I had.

Katie and I got up after the minister gave the welcome. Katie took the microphone. She told of the times we sang to Joey and how she was our best audience as we tried out new songs and new notes. She talked about how I sang to Joey as a toddler, as I was the only one who could get her to nap. "So as we put her down for her final rest here on Earth, we have a song or two, which are her favorites, to carry her to heaven." Ben started playing, and we sang Joey's favorite songs.

Then three different people came up to tell stories about Joey.

I was sitting by Bo and holding his hand. I cried and laughed at some of the stories about Joey. Then Brad and Katie got up to talk about Joey.

Katie said, "I know that my sister wasn't perfect. Yet there is a sanctity of each life on this earth. And while the last part of her life did not look like many of our lives, she kept getting up each day, just as each of us here keep getting up each day by the grace of God. She was a beautiful human being, gifted in really special ways. She was trying to get through life like all of us, in our imperfect earthly bodies. She made some mistakes. I find solace that in the eyes of Christ, she is covered and clean because she knew Him as her Savior, though she lost her way for a while."

Katie was struggling to get through it. I walked up to the piano. "And it has been hard for our family to watch Joey struggle with the torture of drug addiction. But even through it all, I still believe that God is good. And in His goodness, he took her to be with Him."

My music started. *Oh Lord*, I prayed, *please help me do this well.* I took my time and focused on making my voice match the notes. I sang,

> When I can't feel your love for me,
> The pain in my soul it won't let me sleep.
> I imagine you here, and it dries up my tears.
> Even though I can't see, I still believe
> Just when I think, my faith is gone
> I hear your sweet voice crying out, "Hold on."
> It's amazing how we were always meant to be,
> And now I can breathe again.

I made it through the toughest notes on the bridge, and then Katie came up and joined me near the end. The rest of the congregation stood and sang the chorus.

I believe in love.
I believe in peace.
I believe someday you'll return for me.
I believe in things, that I cannot see.
So when my heart says no,
I'll still believe.

I was so glad she was up there because the tears I had kept at bay came, and I couldn't get any words out. I knew I had hit almost all the notes perfectly up until then. I felt like I had just gotten done with a workout as I had gone up and down the scales. It was probably because the twins were squeezing my lungs.

It was a holy moment as all the people in the congregation confessed their belief in a good God. I thought about how the words of the song explained my spiritual life to a tee. They explained to my soul why I kept going through all the pain and heartache of this life because I believed in something bigger than the brokenness of the world.

Katie and I hugged. I went to sit down while the minister closed the service. As I walked toward Bo, it hit me. My mom's funeral service had been in this same church. I could see myself as a five-year-old sitting in the front row, with blond pigtails, a black-and-white dress, and black patent-leather shoes. Granny Elouise was sitting next to me and holding my hand.

I suddenly did not feel well. I had been involved in too many funerals in my life. I remembered something I read by Nancy Gutherie: "Suffering is a mystery. Our task is not to decipher exactly how all of life's pieces fit and what they all mean, but to remain faithful and obedient to God." I slid in next to Bo. Bo took my hand. I was a little shaken. I don't know if it was nerves, a lack of food, the Holy Spirit, or remembering my mom all at the same time.

"You nailed it, Mom," Luke leaned over and said. Brooke smiled at me. Tea came and sat next to me and hugged me. Whit gave me a big grin. Those four plus Bo were really the only audience I cared about.

Bo whispered, "It was beautiful. I have never heard you sing like that. Are you OK? You are shaking a little."

I nodded. I hated death. I hated how it stole from people—how it stole from me and my kids. Now it stole from Katie and her family. *Why am I capable of getting through most days, and then bam, it hits me so hard? I don't have a mom. I lost the father of my children and my first love. There is never any resolution that a book or a well-timed word can provide.* The tears were falling fast. I leaned into Bo and silently cried at the pain this world could mete out. The promise of heaven was the only solace and remedy for certain death for each of us; the promise was eternal life through Christ's righteousness. Each day, we were one day closer to heaven.

After the service was over, we stood in the foyer of the church and talked with old family and high school friends and Joey's former teachers and coaches. It felt like I had introduced Bo to the entire town. After I finished talking to my high school history teacher, I felt completely wiped out. My back and feet hurt. I was starving because there was nothing but southern-style fat and sugar in the parish hall to eat. I could feel tears pricking my eyes. Bo was right. Being here for Katie took a lot out of me.

I scanned the foyer and walked inside the sanctuary. Bo was talking to my dad and a few of his ranching friends. I made eye contact, and he came right over. Before he could say anything, I said, "I'm done."

He looked concerned. "You are pale. Sit here, and I will pull the Suburban around." Bo walked across the street to the parking lot. He helped me into the seat and went around to the driver's side. Before he could get his seatbelt buckled, I was in tears.

"I'm hungry," I whined. "And nobody in this backwater town knows how to bring a protein-packed meal." I was hangry.

He pulled into the Taco Shack's parking lot and got me two black-bean and cheese tacos and an ice water. I loved him more in

Rose Wilson

that moment than I thought possible. And then I realized again what God had been showing me over and over: I needed someone to help me. I had slowly been in burnout mode when God had brought Bo back into my life. His protective attributes that I stubbornly fought against might be what I actually needed. This life was just too much. It was too much emotionally and physically to do it alone. As much as I wanted to go over to Barbara's house and sit with her, I couldn't. I physically had nothing left. I lay down at my dad's house and fell asleep.

Chapter 91

WHEN I WOKE UP, THE house was quiet. I found everyone outside with iced tea on the front porch. I went to sit next to Bo.

"You feeling better, Mom?" asked Tea.

"A little. That was really a hard few hours. Thank you for asking, sweet girl."

After sitting for a while and chatting with everyone, I decided I wanted to go see my mom—her gravestone. I asked Bo if he wanted to come with me.

We drove out to the cemetery in silence. We got there, and Bo looked at me for a minute. "I'm worried about you."

"I think the funeral just reminded me of my mom's funeral and Tommy's, and all the heartache and emotional baggage I carry from them caught up with me. Some days, it is just difficult to make sense of a good and perfect God, death, and sorrow. Some days I just feel covered by it like I can't move through the day well. Sorrow weighs so much."

Bo squeezed my hand and then came around to help me out of the Suburban. I showed him my mother's family plot: the Heaths. Then we went to her grave in the Whitmore plot. There was a blank stone next to her, waiting for my dad. Granny Elouise Whitmore and her husband Devon were next to it.

"Elouise Ruby Whitmore Parker Channing. That is quite a name. It's almost bigger than you," Bo joked.

"It's a mouthful," I agreed. I showed Bo the big oak I used to climb as a child.

I knelt at the foot of my mother's grave and felt the overwhelming sadness of my motherlessness. I looked at Bo. "I wish so badly that I had a mom. Each time I am pregnant, it hits me hard." Bo got down beside me. We sat quietly as the sun was setting.

As I looked at Bo, love for him washed over me. *He gets me. He doesn't judge me. He sits with me.* He had watched the sunrise with me that morning and the sunset at my mother's grave. He was right next to me when I needed him.

I took his hand. "Bo, I love you so much. You are exactly what I need in my life. Thank you for being my partner through the hard stuff and the fun stuff of this life. I cannot get over the fact that I get to be with you for the rest of my life and that you chose me."

Bo teared up. "El." He swallowed hard. "I could say all the same to you and more. You are sacrificing your body to carry two of my babies. That, in and of itself, leaves me indebted for a lifetime." I smiled at him. Bo moved closer to me, and we were knee to knee. He pushed rebel curls back behind my ear. He brushed my cheek with his thumb. "You are the most amazing woman and human I have ever known. I love you. If I could make all your pain go away, I would do it in a heartbeat."

"I know you would. Thank you for caring for me and working to protect me, even though I give you some pushback," I said, laughing a little.

"I wouldn't have it any other way."

I kissed him. Then I turned toward my mom's headstone. "See, Mom, I told you he was a good one."

As we sat to watch the sun finish setting Bo said, "We haven't really talked about baby names. I really like the name Heath for baby B."

"Mmmhmm. It does sound nice. I like it," I said. Then I told him what I had been thinking about. "I was thinking of Josephine for Baby A. Call her Joey. Thoughts?" I also loved Jo March from *Little Women*, so there was that.

"Heath and Joey Channing. Sounds like double-trouble. I like it." Bo laughed.

"What about middle names? I could pick Joey's, and you Heath's?"

"I have been thinking about that too," Bo said. "How do you feel about Heath Thomas Channing? The reason, before you ask, is this: I want your children to feel part of our babies' lives. Bringing their dad's name in makes a connection for them. Those four amazing kids of yours have blessed my life so much in the last year. I want to honor Tommy for the good he poured into them as their father."

I was shocked. "I don't know what to say. It is a beautiful sentiment. I think they would love that since none of them carry his name." I started to get teary eyed. "OK, my turn. It is kind of similar to what you were thinking. The word *zaya* in Hebrew means hope. After Tommy died, I needed God to renew my hope in Him and His plan every morning. And Bo, He did. He kept hope alive in me. And there were really dark and low moments for me. But the next morning, I would have hope stirring in me. I probably never told you this, but the night before you showed up at church, I was in a really dark place. Life was overwhelming me, and I was dropping so many balls. Everything felt insurmountable. I was sitting in the kitchen, with my head on my knees, just begging God for help. It didn't really occur to me until later the next day after Katie said something about God sending you to help me, that I made the connection."

"Wow," said Bo. "I love it. Josephine Zaya Channing and little Joey.

"Let's keep their names to ourselves until they are born. What do you think?" I asked.

"Definitely."

Chapter 92

I FLOATED THROUGH THE NEXT FEW months in our pool willing Heath and Joey to stay in as long as possible. However, the stretch marks along my side were growing every day. I showed Bo and pouted about them. He just said, "Battle scars, babe. They will remind me what you did for us." Then he kissed my hand.

Lord, how is he able to make me feel beautiful when I look like I swallowed a beach ball? Two beach balls.

By the end of July, I was ginormous. It was too embarrassing to go anywhere. I stopped singing at church and talked to Peter online once a week. He introduced me to the book "The Body Keeps the Score" by Dr. Bessel van der Kolk.

> The emotions and physical sensations that were imprinted during the trauma are experienced not as memories but as disruptive physical reactions in the present.

Basically, trauma lodged itself in our bodies. It explained why the smell of rain, unexpected darkness, and loud sounds started my heart racing. I was pretty much a mess when the power went out in a thunderstorm.

Katie would come and float with me in the pool, always bringing her stethoscope so that she and I could listen to the twins. It was good of her to do that because it helped me remember what I was doing and who I was doing it for. And I was entertained by all our new farm animals.

That summer Bo, Tea, and Whit worked on the barn and bought some cows, goats, chickens, and a potbellied pig. The pig was Tea's. She treated him like a little baby. She named him Duncan and carried him everywhere. But since we weren't going anywhere that summer, the animals completely entertained the kids. And Bingo was living her best life herding the goats.

Bo had stopped taking new construction jobs so that he could finish the jobs he had and spend the next year taking care of me and the twins. His mom and sisters were ready to come help. Since we had made it through most of July, Sarah would stay with us once we brought the babies home. Everyone would be there for Thanksgiving and Christmas. All of this meant that we wouldn't really be alone with the twins until they were about four months old. I was so grateful for that plan. Sarah and David were called Lolly and Pops, which were the cutest grandparents' names ever.

Dr. Warner was impressed I hadn't gone into labor yet. She believed they were measuring at just under four pounds. So she was pushing me to lay low and let them gain as much weight as possible. Bo and I were working hard every night to convince them it wasn't time yet. We were praying our brains out, and God had been so faithful in keeping them inside. But I was struggling to imagine what two more weeks would do to my belly. My vanity was taking a big hit this time around. Some moments, I would think that God was punishing me.

I was almost eight months pregnant and was glaring at Bo. I was hot. I was huge. I had to pee every thirty minutes. I could barely breathe or eat. Katie had come by, and I could hear Bo warn her before she walked outside to the pool. "She is very unhappy with me today."

"As she should be," Katie replied as she walked out all skinny in her bathing suit.

"You can't come anymore. I can't stand seeing you all skinny in a normal bathing suit," I yelled at her. I heard Bo laughing. *Ugh.*

Later that evening, I watched trash TV while hiding under my bedcovers. No one needed to look at me like this.

Bo lay down beside me and tried to snuggle with me. I was too hot to be handled. I fell asleep and had this strange dream. I was pushing a big rock but not a rock up a hill. I was trying to hold it so that it wouldn't roll down. My legs felt weak like they did in dreams. They couldn't hold me up. It felt like I was walking in water. I jumped to the side, and I watched the rock roll down the hill. I woke up with a yell. I sat up. I was wet. *Did I pee on myself? No. It's water. My water broke!* "Bo!" I yelled.

"El, why do you keep yelling?" he asked groggily. As he moved, he felt the water. "Whoa!" He was up.

"I am calling Dr. Warner." She called me right back. She would meet us at the hospital. It was 4:00 a.m. I felt a small contraction. *Yep, their birthday will be August 1.*

Bo got showered and then grabbed our bags. The car seats were already in the car. I called Katie to come over while Bo called his parents. All of a sudden, I was overcome with joy and was smiling and laughing. I grabbed Bo's arm. "They are coming today. I did it. I wasn't sure I was going to make it. We did it!"

Chapter 93

B O WAS HOLDING MY HAND. I felt the pressure of the knife and the pulling and pushing of Dr. Warner to get them out. "Baby A!" said Dr. Warner, and she held her up. "Baby B!"

Bo was super emotional. He couldn't stop smiling while wiping away tears. "I can't believe it; I'm a dad. A boy and a girl. God is so good." Bo went with the babies to the NICU, and Dr. Warner tied my tubes because I was so done. I was not taking any chances. They finished sewing me up and wheeled me to recovery.

The pediatrician, Dr. Laura Mann, met me there. "Ellie, they look really good. Great job, Momma. And your husband cannot stop the waterworks. What a sweetheart you have. They will all three meet you in your room."

Katie found me in recovery. "Ellie, you did it!" And she gave me a very gentle big hug. "I saw them in the nursery. They are both so gorgeous. But of course, they are. Everyone knew you two would have beautiful babies."

When we got permission to move me to my room, Katie walked beside me while holding my hand. Bo was in the room holding Joey. She was wrapped in pink. He handed her to Katie and looked at me. I nodded.

"Katie, we are pleased to introduce you to Josephine Zaya Channing. Joey for short."

Katie's reaction was priceless. Her mouth was open. "No way."

She looked at both of us. We nodded. "No way," she whispered. Tears started to fall onto Joey as she held her. "I need to sit down," she said as she found the rocker. Bo picked up Heath and brought him to me. He looked like Bo. He had beautiful dark eyes and blond hair. Katie was right; Bo could make a gorgeous baby. Katie finally brought Joey over to me, and I saw her. She was beautiful. She had the same big brown eyes as her brother.

Throughout the day, the room became full of Bo's family members and mine. It was such a joyful day. My kids absolutely loved the names. Katie's crew came by as well and held the babies. Landry sat next to me on my bed and held Joey. She was all smiles because she would now get to boss someone around. Bo's parents were overjoyed with the babies. Those two babies brought so many so much happiness. What a gift they are already were to the world.

Bo walked over with Joey, as I fed Heath. He sat on the bed with me, and he could not stop smiling. The evening summer sunlight was pouring through the windows. Everything looked hazy and warm.

"El, you are the most beautiful and strongest woman I have ever known. You did it. You brought two healthy babies into my life." He started to tear up again. "Marrying you was the happiest day of my life. The second happiest was today. The third happiest was when I saw you after three years, and you said yes when I asked you out to lunch."

"Same," I said.

Epilogue

I WALKED INTO THE KITCHEN WITH another bag full of trash from outside. Whit walked in behind me and took my bag out through the garage to the trash cans. We had been cleaning up after celebrating all weekend. It was August 1, and the twins were three years old. I was exhausted. I collapsed onto one of the kitchen stools at the counter-height bar. Bo's back was to me as he cleaned the kitchen up.

Whit walked back in. He was getting a degree in music at the state university down the road. We saw him almost every weekend. The twins adored him. He kissed my cheek and hugged Bo, as he got ready to head back to his dorm.

Luke came inside with his girlfriend, Lacy. She was an elementary teacher at the school he taught and coached at. She was just darling, and after hanging out with us, she surprisingly kept coming back. "Bye, Mom. Bye Bo. Thanks for dinner!" He and Lacy were holding hands. "Where are the birthday twins?"

"Katie is giving them a bath." I nodded down the hall. The twins had overtaken the guest room or what used to be the guest room.

"Mom, I will see you in two weeks for our beach trip," Luke said as he gave me a hug from behind. We still went every August to honor Tommy's legacy and remember him together.

"Bye, Mr. and Mrs. Channing. It has been such a fun weekend

meeting everyone," Lacy said, and she and Luke walked toward the garage.

"Thank you for putting up with all of us, Lacy. I think what you experienced this weekend is called baptism by fire. We are a lot, and we are loud." Barbara, Brad, Katie's family, and Bo's entire family were there. Lacy laughed and waved.

I turned to Bo. "I really like her."

"Me too. She is one of the good ones," Bo answered.

I looked at my phone as it buzzed. It was Brooke. She was spending the summer in Europe, studying art history. She would graduate from college that December. Bo and I were praying that she would find a job and get off the family payroll soon.

"Brooke says hi and belated happy birthday to the twins," I told Bo.

Bo came and sat down next to me. I turned to look at him and smiled. He took my hand.

"I feel like we haven't had a minute to check in since Thursday when my parents' and sister's families got here. How are you? You sang beautifully at church this morning. And you are always the most beautiful woman in every room. No one would ever know you had six babies," Bo teased.

"Please stop reminding me how many children I have," I teased back. He kissed my hand and intertwined his fingers with mine.

"Have I told you that I love you recently? Because I do." He smiled that forever charming smile at me. "And I was thinking we should celebrate making it three years." He brought me a glass of wine, and we toasted.

"Yes, and amen!" I said.

Bo touched the scar on my eyebrow and slowly brought his thumb down my cheek to my lips. He could still give me butterflies. He looked at me so intentionally that I felt seen by him. Truly, he was the love of my life.

He leaned forward and kissed me, and I kissed him back. *Maybe we will celebrate later.*

310

Katie walked in, holding each twin's hand. "Here we are. Clean as a whistle."

I put my arms out, and Heath ran to me. Joey ran to Bo. "Oh, my goodness, let me smell you." I tickled little Heath with my nose, and giggles from both ensued. I picked up Heath. "Oh, wow. Now that you are three, I can barely pick you up. You are sooo big!"

"Daddy is stwong like me." Heath said and went to Bo, who then had one in each arm. They could be triplets. The twins had towheads and big brown eyes like Bo did. They really had been the sweetest babies. The first few months were rough, but we made it with a lot of help from everyone. Bo was so hands on that he even read books and wanted to potty train them on his own. He changed every dirty diaper, so I guessed he was motivated. He amazed me every day. He told me that I got to do all the kid stuff with the four and that now it was his turn with the two.

I said good night, and Bo took them off to their room to put them to bed. Joey was already half asleep on his shoulder. They had had a busy and overstimulating weekend, with gifts, family, and swimming.

Katie sat down next to me. She had been so amazing with the twins. She came over on her day off and took them to get ice cream, go to the park, or to her house to spend the night just to give Bo and me a break. They adored her. I gave her a side hug. "Thanks for celebrating with us. Where is the rest of your crew?"

"I think they are all out front stargazing with John's new telescope."

"Oh, right. Can you believe we have gotten to three years with twins, and everyone is still in one piece?" I laughed.

"It takes a village," Katie quipped with a smile.

"One thousand percent. I would have drowned a thousand times over if it wasn't for you and Bo's family. Thank you for all you do for us."

"You know I love every second. They are the sweetest little munchkins. Are you ready for threenagers?"

"Ha, ha, ha. I'm ready, but Bo has no idea what is about to happen." We giggled. Knowing Bo, he would tackle it like a construction project, read up about it online, and build a game plan.

Before we walked outside, I sneaked down the hallway to peek into the twin's room. They were in their beds, and Bo was kneeling beside Heath's bed praying with him. Joey was already asleep and hugging her birthday "unitorn." She couldn't say hard Cs yet. Heath had his birthday dinosaur. I watched Bo pray with and for Heath. I could not love that man more.

I walked onto the front porch and saw Tea taking her turn with the telescope while John directed her gaze. Tea had grown into a beautiful young lady. She was sixteen and very into musical theater. She was a main character in the summer musical at the park that year. She was the mayor's daughter, Zaneeta, in *The Music Man* three nights a week in July. I couldn't be prouder of her.

Kylie was sitting on the porch steps and looking up at the stars. She was at the small Baptist university where I taught. We had coffee or lunch once a week. I moved permanently two years ago to the smaller university where the pressure to publish and research was not a huge part of my job. The focus was on teaching and interacting with the students, which I loved. And it left me more time to be at home with the twins. The twins went to preschool on Tuesday, Wednesday, and Thursday, and they were home with me on Monday and Friday. If I had to work those days, Bo, Kylie, or Katie watched them. I loved my village. God had blessed Bo with more work than he wanted, which allowed him to pick the jobs. He was so good at what he did, and I was thankful.

Remy, at fifteen, looked so much like Katie at that age. And Landry, at twelve, was going to be taller than both her sisters. I loved those girls like my own. What a gift it was that Katie and I shared our families with each other. *Every good gift comes from God. Thank you, God.*

Everyone left, and Bo and I were sitting on the front porch like we had so many times. "Remember when I made you promise me that we would sit out here as often as possible?" Bo asked.

"Yes, on our wedding night," I said as we rocked in our big white chairs. We looked at each other and smiled. "I do love being married to you, Bo Channing. Best decision I ever made."

"Come on. Let's dance," Bo said. So I stood up barefoot and on my tiptoes and put my arms around his neck. He held me tight. He smelled so good like sunscreen and light cologne. He nestled his face into my neck.

"El, I love you. Thank you for saying yes to me. Thank you for those two babies. Thank you for always moving toward the light of Jesus, even when it isn't easy, every single day."

Dear reader,

As you can tell, I love a good love story. And the truth is most of us are all desperately looking for a person to fill the ache in our soul that wants to be intimately known. However, there is no person on earth that can love us unconditionally and perfectly but the Lord our God.

God wants to know us, wants to spend time with us, will walk beside us and hold us up in the dark places this life can bring. Our God is totally invested in our complete healing from the hurts of this world, and will cover us with the cup of His hand. You can trust Him to love you perfectly.

He is waiting for you, wants to spend time with you, and wants to walk with you through this world. Consider walking with Him toward the light and away from the dark. You only have to ask Him.

1. Shawn McDonald, "Rise," *Closer* (Brentwood: Sparrow Records, 2011).

2. Nancy Guthrie, *Holding on to Hope: A pathway through Suffering to the Heart of God* (Carol Stream: Tyndale, 2002), 49.

3. David Leonard, Jason Ingram, and Leslie Jordan, "Great Are You Lord," *Great Are You Lord* EP (Franklin: Essential Records, 2016).

4. Phil Wickham, "House of the Lord," *Hymn of Heaven* (Nashville: Columbia Records, 2021).

5. Bethel Music,kalley "Spirit Move," *Have It All (Live)* (Redding: Bethel Music, 2016).

6. Ashley Gorely, Ben Johnson, David Fanning, and Matt Thomas, "Take My Name," *For You* (Nashville: Stoney Creek Records, 2021).

7. Ronnie Dunn, "Neon Moon," *Brand New Man* (New York City: Arista Records, 1992).

8. Mark Narmore, "Moon Over Georgia," *Extra Mile* (Nashville: Columbia Records, 1991).

9. Alex Nifong and Elvina M Hall, "Jesus Paid It All," *Worship Circle Hymns* (Woodland Park: Worship Circle Records, 2019).

10. Church of the City and Jon Reddick, "You Keep Hope Alive," *Church of the City* (Nashville: Church of the City, 2020).

11. Phil Vasser and Rory Michael Bourke, "Bye-Bye," *I'm Alright* (Nashville: Curb Records, 1998).

12. Taylor Swift, Max Martin, and Shellback, "Bad Blood" (Taylor's Version), *1989* (Taylor's Version) (New York City: Republic, 2023).

13. Derek Webb, "We Delight," *In the Company of Angels—A Call to Worship* (Franklin: Essential Records, 2001).

14. Elyssa Smith, "Surrounded Fight My Battles," *Surrounded* (Nashville: Rocketown Records, 2017).

15. Andres Figueroa, Hank Bentley, Mariah McManus, and Mia Fieldes, "Tremble," *Glory and Wonder* (Franklin: Provident Label Group, 2016).

16. Matt Stell, Allison Veltz, and Ash Bowers, "Prayed for You," *Everywhere but On* (New York City: Arista, 2018).

17. Carrie Underwood, "O Holy Night," *My Gift*, (Los Angeles: Capitol Records, 2020).

18. Brian Ray, J-Raw, and T-Bone, "What a Fool I've Been," *Fearless* (Nashville: Metro One Music, 2000).

19. Kirk Franklin, "I Still Believe," *Fearless* (Nashville: Metro One Music, 2000).

Printed in the United States
by Baker & Taylor Publisher Services